Also by Ray Hobbs and published by Wingspan Press

An Act of Kindness - 2014

Following On - 2016

A Year From Now - 2017

A Rural Diversion - 2019

A Chance Sighting - 2020

Roses and Red Herrings - 2020

Happy Even After - 2020

The Right Direction - 2020

An Ideal World - 2020

Mischief and Masquerade - 2021

Big Ideas - 2021

Published Elsewhere

Second Wind (Spiderwize) - 2011

Lovingly Restored (New Generation Publishing) - 2018

First Appearances

Ray Hobbs

Wingspan Press

This book is a work of fiction. Names, characters, settings and incidents are either the product of the author's imagination or used fictitiously. Any resemblance to actual events, settings or persons, living or dead, is entirely coincidental.

Published in the United States and the United Kingdom
by WingSpan Press, Livermore, CA

The WingSpan name, logo and colophon are the trademarks
of WingSpan Publishing.

ISBN 978-1-63683-014-8 (pbk.)
ISBN 978-1-63683-988-2 (ebook)

First edition 2021

Printed in the United States of America

www.wingspanpress.com

1 2 3 4 5 6 7 8 9 10

This book is dedicated to those who believe, to paraphrase Virgil's famous avowal, that love transcends all obstacles, real or imagined.

RH

Things are not always what they seem; the first appearance deceives many; the intelligence of a few perceives what has been carefully hidden.

Plato, ca 385 BC

I am indebted to my brother Chris, who acted, as ever, both as a soundboard and as a ready source of ideas from planning to final draft, whilst helping to fuel my enthusiasm throughout.

Author's Note

As usual, I find it advisable to provide a guide to the jargon, or navalese, that might otherwise impede the reader's understanding and enjoyment of the story.

The **sloop** was a convoy escort vessel, smaller than the destroyer. It was superseded by the frigate, possibly because 'frigate' sounds more threatening.

The **red ensign**, a rectangle of red with the Union Flag in the left upper quadrant, is the flag of the Merchant Navy. The **white ensign**, its Royal Navy equivalent, bears the cross of St George on a white background, with the Union Flag in its left upper quadrant. It is generally agreed that the Union Flag is known as the Union Jack only when it is flown from the jackstaff of a ship.

The **gunlayer** was the rating who actually aimed the gun and therefore enjoyed some standing among his shipmates. Other members of the gun crew were responsible for reading and reporting the range of the target and loading the gun. Each was indispensable, but someone has to take the credit. The term originated, as many did, in Nelson's time.

The **gunlayer-armourer** operated and serviced small-calibre guns and their mountings. The **quarters armourer** was his grown-up equivalent, being responsible for large-calibre guns (4 inches and above) and their mountings. Deafness was an occupational impairment that affected gunnery specialists, partly because of the effect of repeated gunfire at close quarters, but due in some way, it has been alleged, to the shouts and screams of gunnery instructors at *HMS Excellent*, Portsmouth. *Excellent* was decommissioned in 1985, and the inhabitants of Portsmouth were once again able to hear themselves think.

A **midshipman** was and is a trainee officer. At one time, midshipmen joined the service at fourteen and were often treated with disdain by commissioned officers and ratings alike, who addressed and referred to them as 'snotties'. Since then, education legislation has made the minimum age for entry seventeen-and-a-half. As for the rest, we live in more enlightened times. At least, we hope so.

In World War II service parlance, a **bottle** was simply a reprimand, although no one seems to know why.

A drop of 'roughers' is a spell of rough weather. Whilst uncomfortable, it deterred U-boats from coming too near the surface, and it rendered certain unpopular duties impossible, e.g. scrubbing and swabbing the upper deck.

The word **pusser** has three meanings. One refers to the Senior Service and the authority it wields; another describes the attitude of a senior rating or officer who is inflexibly strict or 'anchor-faced'. It is also used to denote ownership or issue by the service, e.g. 'pusser's rum' or 'pusser's bedding'. The word was originally a reference to the long-obsolete office of paymaster, or 'purser'.

Grog was the over-proof rum issued daily to the Lower Deck until 1970, when Prime Minister Harold Wilson decreed that alcohol and technology were best kept as strangers. It took its familiar service name from Admiral Edward Vernon, known as 'Old Grog', because he had his coats made from grogram (silk and wool mixture) cloth. Vernon made his mark in naval history when he instigated the practice of diluting rum with water, thus rendering it incapable of being bottled and saved for binge drinking. Prior to 1970, a sailor's paybook was stamped immediately on issue with the initials 'G', 'T' or 'UA', signifying 'Grog', 'Temperance' or 'Under-Age'. The service has always maintained its priorities.

The **Middle Watch** is from midnight to 0400 and is marginally less unpopular than the **Morning Watch** (0400-0800).

Springs are the lines that prevent fore and aft movement when a ship is tied up alongside. They also reduce tension in the mooring lines and are used in 'springing off', or holding the ship by its stern spring so that the bows move outward, ready to 'slip' and leave the mooring. Clever stuff.

A **flag officer** is any officer holding a rank higher than that of captain. He is so called because the ship carrying him flies a flag or pennant commensurate with his rank. When junior officers and ratings join the ship, the flag serves as a warning to them to keep their heads down.

Saluting the quarterdeck is one of the Navy's oldest traditions. It began in the 16th century as an act of religious observance, when a crucifix could be found on that part of the ship, but the more modern practice of saluting when coming on board is seen as an acknowledgement of the authority represented by the colours (the white ensign) flown above the quarterdeck. It takes little effort and is a pleasing reminder that a gesture of respect need never become out of date.

A sailor's **oppo** was his friend. It originated from 'opposite number', meaning the rating who did the same job in the opposite watch.

Since time immemorial, sailors have referred to their gabardine raincoat as their **'Burberry'**, even though, as far as I know, the service garment has never borne the label of the celebrated manufacturer. It is simply gentle irony, familiar slang, or 'Jackspeak'. In the irreverent recitation 'The Gospel According to Jack', the victim suffers unspeakable abuse at the hands of his attackers, but their worst crime by far is that they 'pinched his Burberry' before leaving him for dead.

The **OOD** is the Officer of the Day, the duty officer when a ship is tied up alongside.

An **OD** was an ordinary seaman, a new recruit not yet passed out as an **able seaman** (originally 'able-bodied seaman') or **AB**. Otherwise, the term OD was used derisively to describe a rating deemed clueless or naïve.

Going **Ashore** sounds self-explanatory, but the term is also used when naval personnel leave a shore establishment and enter civilian society.

Adrift can mean literally 'drifting at sea', but it is more often used to mean 'late'.

The **'chippy'** was the ship's carpenter. His duties were assumed in the late 20th century by the Shipwright Artificer. Nowadays, we have to accept that plastics are the new timber.

To **secure**, is to stand down from a particular task or watch.

New recruits have been known to remain for hours at their allotted station, waiting dutifully to be dismissed, until eventually acquainted with the meaning of the order 'secure'.

A **pipe** is simply a message transmitted via the Tannoy, or loudspeaker system. At one time, it was often, but not always, preceded by an alert sounded on a boatswain's call, hence the term 'pipe'.

A sailor's '**party**' was his girlfriend, although Wrens have also been known to use the word in referring to boyfriends. However, in these enlightened and inclusive times, the word has all but disappeared from the naval lexicon, giving way in some cases to 'partner'.

HMS King Alfred was a converted sports complex in Hove, Sussex, used in World War II as the initial-training establishment for temporary officers. It served an unexpected but essential purpose at a difficult time.

A **bulkhead** is simply a wall. Perversely, the **deckhead** is the ceiling, the **deck** being the floor.

A **scuttle** is to the Royal Navy what a porthole, or port, is to outsiders. A hinged **deadlight** is used to cover it in order to darken ship.

The **Master-at-Arms**, 'Jaunty' or 'Crusher' was, at the time of the story, the most senior rating in the Regulating Branch. He was, in effect, the ship's feared and respected chief policeman.

A '**set**' is a beard and moustache, a full 'set' of whiskers. No officer or rating may grow one without the other.

I apologise for the intrusion and leave you, hopefully, to enjoy the story.

RH

1

September 1941

Portsmouth Dockyard

The new uniform with its two gold, wavy rings felt strange to Ivor, and not simply because of the suddenness of his promotion. He had spent his leave in civilian clothing, an unusual luxury in wartime, and one only ever extended to survivors. Now, only his lieutenant's rings marked him out as different from the youngsters, self-conscious in their new uniforms and fresh from the training establishment in Hove, although a closer look would have dispelled any suggestion of inexperience. Ivor was just twenty-three, but his dark hair was already beginning to show flecks of grey, and the wrinkles at the corners of his eyes might have been the legacy of hours spent watchkeeping at sea or of experiences he preferred to leave at the back of his mind.

He looked around for someone who might be able to help him, and noticed a civilian wearing a bowler hat and carrying a clipboard. The hat alone suggested authority; the clipboard promised order.

'Excuse me,' he called, raising his voice to compete with the sounds of hammering, sawing, the men shouting above the noise, and the general dockyard din.

'Yes?'

'Can you tell me, please, where I might find Lieutenant Commander Newell?'

'Lieutenant Commander Newell? He should be in one of them.' The man waved his clipboard vaguely in the direction of several timber huts.

'Which one?'

'Search me. You'll find their names on the doors.'

'Thank you.' Ivor picked his way through the impedimenta of industry that occupied the dockside. There were boxes and crates that had once housed valves, pipe fittings, gauges, sprinkler heads, steam traps, switches, junction boxes, conduit fittings and trunking, and all around them, the spaghetti-like profusion of cables and hoses.

The label on the door of the fourth hut read: *Lt. Cdr E. F. Newell, R.N., H.M.S. Maynard.* There had obviously been a mix-up over the name of the ship, but Ivor knocked and waited.

'Come.'

He pushed open the door, removing his cap as he did so. The officer seated behind the desk was dark-haired with greying temples, lean and possibly in his forties, which made him old for a lieutenant commander.

'Lieutenant Ivor Loveday, sir, reporting for duty aboard *HMS Hosta* as First Lieutenant.' As he spoke, the words sounded impossibly pompous, but he gave it no further thought, being more concerned with the name of the ship on the door. 'Perhaps there's been a mistake,' he suggested.

'No, there's no mistake. How do you do, Loveday?' Newell offered his hand. 'Would you care for a cigarette?' He opened a silver cigarette case and offered it to Ivor, who took one.

'Thank you, sir.'

'Unless I'm mistaken, you're a day early. I wasn't expecting you until tomorrow.' He re-examined the document in front of him. 'Yes,' he confirmed, 'the twelfth.'

Ivor took the proffered light and explained. 'I was bored, sir. I thought I'd make an early start in my new appointment.' He imagined Lieutenant Commander Newell would explain the discrepancy in his own time.

Newell waved him to one of two wooden chairs. 'You were on survivors' leave and you were bored? Either you had an ulterior motive or you're a force to be reckoned with, Number One.'

The form of address sounded strange. *Taunton*'s first lieutenant had been a remote authority figure, unlikeable and unworthy of respect. Ivor hoped he would perform better in the role. 'It was neither, really, sir.' He realised he had to tell the story sooner or later. 'My home was destroyed in the Blitz last March, and both my parents were killed. I have a brother in Ireland and another serving in the RAF. There wasn't much for me to do on leave.' He kept to himself the compulsive need he'd felt for the company of other naval personnel, those who understood something of the ordeal of having their ship sunk beneath them, even if they'd never experienced it themselves.

'I'm sorry, Number One. I didn't know that. All I've been told is that you were serving in *HMS Taunton* when she was torpedoed. A wretched business. Only twenty-four survivors, I'm told.'

'Yes, sir. There are only twenty-one now.' Unbidden, Ivor's thoughts returned to that night in the Atlantic, the frenzied shouts from below decks, the more orderly commands from the bridge, the frantic fumbling to release the boats and Carley floats before the ship slid beneath the waves, and the biting cold of the wind through sea-drenched clothing. It was better not to dwell on it. 'A wretched business,' he agreed.

His captain consulted the same document. 'You have the reputation of being an excellent gunnery officer. I must say,' he said, putting the document down, 'in the time you've had, you've done well to achieve excellence in any discipline. What was the date of your commission?'

'The fifteenth of July, nineteen thirty-nine, sir.'

'Right. You served at Tyne Division RNVR from nineteen thirty-five, I see.' Looking up again, he said, 'I detect an accent. Is it Tyneside?'

'Not really, sir. It's probably a mixture. I've lived in various parts of the country, and I tend to absorb elements of dialect.'

Newell consulted the document again. 'I see that you'd been promoted to leading seaman before you received your commission.'

'That's correct, sir.' Ivor waited for the customary swipe at the Wavy Navy, not that he cared at all, but he was pleased, nevertheless, when none appeared to be forthcoming.

'Where are you staying?'

'In barracks, sir.'

'Good. We'll have a look around *Hosta* and then I think we'll go to the wardroom for lunch. Before that, though, I'll tell you what's in store for us.'

Ivor's curiosity had been aroused when he first received orders to join the twenty-five-year-old escort ship, and now he was even more intrigued. 'I'm rather curious, sir,' he said.

'You might well be.' Newell accepted a cigarette from Ivor and proceeded. 'As you probably know, *Hosta* is a sloop of twelve-hundred-and-fifty tons, about the same size as *Taunton* and also, like her, a relic of the last war. She was slow, coal-burning, and she mounted two four-inch guns.'

'I believe she served as a decoy for U-boats.'

'A Q-ship, that's correct, Number One, and now that her single engine has been overhauled and she's been refitted with oil-fired boilers and two quick-firing, four-inch Mark Nine guns, she will be a Q-ship again, not a great deal faster than she was, but a damned sight easier to refuel, safer and cleaner for the absence of coal dust, and with her firepower intact. When she flies the white ensign, she will be either *HMS Hosta* or the oceanographic survey ship *HMS Maynard*.' Pausing in his description for a moment, he said, 'I imagine that goes some way towards answering your question.'

'Yes, thank you, sir.'

'Under the red ensign, however, she will be, among others, the *Motor Vessel Snowdonia*.'

Ivor was still puzzled, at least to some extent. 'What's the reason for her second identity, sir, *HMS Maynard*?'

'That will be her name when she's tied up alongside and under the scrutiny of prying eyes, as she might well be at this very moment. She'll only ever be a merchant ship when she's at sea, and *HMS Hosta* when she's in action against U-boats.'

'I see, sir.' It was perfectly simple. The ship's true identity had to be concealed in harbour as well as at sea.

'Good. You'll have control of two guns without the aid of direction equipment. It's as primitive as that. Now, as your reputation goes before you, what's your formula for excellent gunnery?'

'Care of the guns, discipline, drill, pride and a sense of belonging, sir. I take what I learned at *HMS Excellent* and add the human touch that was never allowed through the main gate.'

Newell allowed himself a half-smile. The harsh ethos of the gunnery school on Whale Island was a by-word throughout the service. He asked, 'Where does the pride begin?'

'That's the human element, sir. I encourage healthy competition between the gun's crews, and good relations between crew members. I exercise the crews individually at first, only directing them by Tannoy when I consider them competent.'

'Why?'

'So that the rest of the ship's company don't hear me pointing out their shortcomings, sir. It's enough that I do it. Gunnery ratings don't need to hear my strictures repeated mischievously on the messdeck.' He hesitated when he saw Newell smile again. 'I hope I don't sound as if I know all the answers, sir, but it worked for me in *Taunton*.'

'I'm delighted to hear it, Number One. You'll have other duties, of course, as First Lieutenant. How confident do you feel about those?'

'I've performed most of those duties, sir.'

'As a sub?' He was openly sceptical.

'Yes, sir. I served under a particularly lazy first lieutenant, who farmed out his duties whenever he could get away with it. I learned a great deal from him.'

'Did you really?'

'Yes, sir. As well as learning the tasks he preferred to shirk, I learned from him how *not* to lead men. He was a misanthrope and a bully, and I don't intend to be either.'

'I see.' Newell sat back and surveyed his new second-in-command. 'You know, Number One,' he said, 'I'm not at all sure what to make of you. You're surprisingly, if not alarmingly, self-assured for a newly-promoted officer pitched into an appointment as first lieutenant.'

'It's the nature of the beast, sir. I see no point in worrying about something that's yet to happen. For all I know, it may never happen, so worrying about it would be a waste of time and effort.'

'I suppose that's logical enough.' Newell offered him another cigarette.

'Thank you, sir. I just think that an hour's preparation is better than a sleepless night.' He accepted a light and continued. 'If I sound smug, I don't mean to, and I can only apologise for it, but it's the way I live. You see, I grew up, as many did, during the Depression, and I saw what worry could do to people, how it could dominate every moment of their lives and age them prematurely. I'm not criticising them – goodness knows, they had plenty to worry about – but I had no intention of going the same way.'

Newell had been listening, occasionally nodding agreement or acknowledgement, and now he had a question to ask.

'Did you go through school with the same carefree attitude, Number One?'

'Yes, I did, sir. I'm sorry to say that it was largely misconstrued.'

'I had a feeling it might have been.'

'The general feeling was that I was lazy, sir. My headmaster's comment on my leaving report read, "Does the barest minimum in order to survive. Success in any field other than that of sheer indolence is unlikely." ' Ivor shook his head at the foolishness of the notion. 'Nothing could be further from the truth, sir. He simply confused pragmatism with laziness. If I saw a good reason for doing something, I made the effort.'

Newell looked at him sharply. 'I hope you're not going to cherry-pick your duties as First Lieutenant.'

'Absolutely not, sir.' Ivor was careful to sound suitably shocked at the suggestion. 'This whole thing is worth a hundred percent effort.'

'Which whole thing would that be, Number One?' Newell was still apparently trying to come to terms with Ivor's unusual approach to responsibility.

'The war, sir.'

'Oh, that whole thing. Yes, quite.'

'Yes, sir. You need only look at my record at Tyne Division and *HMS Excellent*. I was awarded top marks in Watchkeeping, Ocean Navigation and Gunnery, although, as far as recent service aboard *HMS Taunton* is concerned, I'm afraid it's likely to be a while before Lieutenant Commander Nesbitt is sufficiently recovered to put pen to paper.'

'What were his injuries?'

'Exposure and hypothermia rather than actual injuries, sir. When I telephoned the hospital, their comments were guarded, but I gained the impression that he was making a slow recovery.'

'You enquired after your captain?' Newell was clearly impressed.

'He inspired loyalty, sir, but I also telephoned to enquire about my gunnery ratings, at least, those who'd survived the sinking. I'm afraid I made rather a nuisance of myself.'

'I can't believe that, Number One.' Leaving irony aside for the moment, Newell rose to his feet and said, 'Let me give you a conducted tour of the ship.'

Ivor followed his captain out of the hut, negotiating once more the obstacles of dockyard activity, until they came to a ship that must have measured, according to Ivor's estimate, some 250 or more feet overall.

'She looks very much like a merchant ship, sir,' he observed.

'That's the general idea, Number One. Just keep your fingers crossed that the enemy agree with your description.'

'Quite, sir. I was only thinking that she had a head start in that respect.'

'They were built as Q-ships, so it's only to be expected.'

'I see, sir. I didn't realise she was purpose-built rather than converted.' He followed Newell on to the gang plank, saluting as he stepped aboard.

'There's no need to salute the quarter deck until the ship's commissioned, Number One,' said Newell.

'Of course, sir. I was just showing respect.'

Newell stopped to say, 'You have a sense of history, then.' Possibly seeking a connection, he asked, 'What did you do before the war?'

'I was a newspaper reporter, sir.'

'A journalist, eh?'

'That's a very grand title, sir. I was just a reporter on a local paper. I covered council meetings, weddings, funerals, retirement presentations, school prize-givings and what cricket matches there were to be reported on.' He shrugged. 'It was all basic stuff, but I was happy enough doing it.'

'You didn't find it frustrating, then?'

'Not in the least. People shared their lives with me, and that was fascinating in itself, but there was also the knowledge that Friday was a special day for many, because it was the day the *Observer* was delivered.'

'Really?' The concept was evidently one that Newell had not so far encountered.

'Some of the older people, and particularly those less able than others to get out and about, live their lives vicariously through the pages of *The Tynemouth Observer*, sir.'

Newell shook his head in perplexity. 'You're an unusual fellow, Number One. Come and look at your charges.' He led the way to 'A' gun, which stood on the fo'c'sle beneath a tarpaulin shroud. Lifting the shroud, he said, 'Not very impressive at this stage, is it? Of course, by the time the ship is re-commissioned, this gun will be gleaming.'

Ivor inspected the gun, noting its neglected and rusted mechanism. 'That will be an improvement, sir.' He would have preferred to see its elevation and training gear thick with grease and ready to move smoothly and precisely in the gunlayer's hands, because the ship and the lives of its crew might soon depend on it, but he kept the thought to himself. If he were a reliable judge, his captain must already have formed the opinion that he was too big for his seaboots, although he wouldn't be the first to think that.

'My background is less interesting than yours,' said Newell unexpectedly. 'I joined the service in nineteen-oh-eight as a fourteen-year-old midshipman, I was commissioned in nineteen-fifteen and made redundant in nineteen thirty-three.'

'I'm sorry to hear that, sir.'

'Thank you, Number One, but I wasn't alone. Redundancies were distressingly common during the inter-war years.'

Now that Newell had chosen to speak about himself, Ivor was curious to know more. 'If you don't mind my asking, sir, how did you spend the period between your redundancy and your recall to the service?'

'I instructed Merchant Navy officer cadets in seamanship and navigation.'

Ivor could only try to imagine the differences in attitude and regime between the two services. 'That must have been quite an adjustment for you, sir.'

'It was a humanising experience, Number One.' With an odd smile, he added, 'I wasn't always as approachable as I am now.'

'I'm sure I have much to be thankful for, sir.'

2

November

With the commissioning ceremony out of the way, *HMS Maynard* put to sea on a westerly course that would eventually bring her to the Lizard, where she could change course and head into the Irish Sea. The bridge's other occupants were the Captain, Ivor, the signalman, the two lookouts and a sub-lieutenant, a hesitant youth of twenty-one, who viewed Ivor with wary respect and the Captain with something bordering on dread.

Ivor asked him, 'When did you last take a fix, sub?'

The sub-lieutenant started guiltily. 'I'm just about to, sir.'

'Better get on with it before the Captain asks you where we are,' he advised, catching a glance from Newell as he spoke.

'Of course, sir. Aye, aye, sir.' Like a frightened mole, the sub-lieutenant burrowed beneath the bridge counter and emerged with a sextant.

'Take it easy, sub,' said Ivor. 'Accuracy before speed.'

'Aye, aye, sir.' The Navigating Officer proceeded to fix the position, reading the angle between the horizon and the sun, and then making the requisite calculations. Eventually, he wrote the position on his notepad and showed Ivor, who nodded approvingly.

After about two minutes, the Captain turned to ask, 'What's our position, sub?'

'Sixty-two degrees North, seventy degrees, two minutes West, sir. Portland Bill is on our starboard beam, sir.' He gave a sigh of relief and a grateful nod in Ivor's direction.

'Thank you, sub.' The Captain swept the horizon before saying,

'Will you take over, Number One? I'm going below. Call me if you need me.'

'Aye, aye, sir.' Ivor took the Captain's place at the front of the bridge. It was a pleasant day and quite warm for early November. Visibility was excellent. 'Sub,' he said, 'keep an eye on the ship dead ahead, will you?' It was unfortunate that seeing the youthful sub-lieutenants on board had whisked him back to that night in August, when the torpedo exploded and he'd seen fellow officers and ratings drown. He told himself that he couldn't be everyone's protector, but that was common sense, and emotion was a stranger to logic.

'Aye, aye, sir.' The eager sub-lieutenant lifted his night glasses to observe the ship more closely.

'You're Cartwright, aren't you?'

'Yes, sir.' Remembering his manners, Cartwright said, 'Thank you for prompting me about our position, Number One. I don't know what I'd have done if the Captain had asked me earlier.'

'You'd have caught the rough edge of his tongue, sub.'

The starboard lookout interrupted them. 'The ship dead ahead is a fishing vessel, sir. It's heading towards us.'

Guiltily, Cartwright lifted his binoculars again.

'It's all right, sub,' said Ivor. 'I distracted you.' Leaning towards the voice pipe, he called, 'Bridge, wheelhouse.'

'Wheelhouse, sir. Cox'n at the wheel.'

'Steer starboard ten, Cox'n.'

'Starboard ten, sir. Ten of starboard wheel on, sir.'

'Very good.'

The fishing vessel was responding to *Maynard*'s landward change of course by making its own alteration to seaward. As the two ships passed, the fishermen gave a friendly wave, which Ivor returned. 'Midships, Cox'n.'

'Midships, sir. Wheel's amidships, sir.'

'Steady.'

'Steady on due west, sir.'

'Very good, Cox'n.'

'Why have we altered course, Number One?' The voice from behind Ivor was the Captain's. 'Oh, I see, a fishing vessel. Carry on, Number One.'

'Aye, aye, sir.'

When the Captain had disappeared down the ladder, Cartwright voiced his fears to Ivor. 'There's so much to remember, Number One. I'm afraid I'm bound to forget something.' He sounded like a frightened schoolboy, which was what he had been only three years earlier.

'Set yourself a routine,' Ivor advised him, 'write it down and use it as your daily programme. Include routine fixes, plot any hazards on your chart, and basically, think ahead.' Revising his mantra for Cartwright's benefit, he said, 'Remember that an hour's preparation is better than a bottle from the Captain, or even worse, a court martial.'

'Thanks, Number One. I'll remember that.'

'Good. It's time for another fix, isn't it?'

'So soon?'

'You can't get enough practice with the sextant, sub. It should become second nature to you.'

'Right. I mean Aye, aye, sir.' Cartwright took out the sextant again.

After a while, the Captain returned to the bridge. Taking Ivor on one side, he said, 'If you don't know where we are by this time, Number One, there's no hope for us.' He nodded towards Cartwright, who was returning the sextant to its box. 'That must be the third fix he's taken in the past hour.'

'I'm just trying to bolster his confidence, sir. Until a few months ago, he was working in an insurance office. It's a big adjustment for him to make, but he'll be all right once he gets organised.'

'I know.' With the characteristic half-smile that had become familiar, Newell said, 'You're not doing too badly yourself, Number One.'

'Thank you, sir.'

'That's all right, but don't let it go to your head.' Raising his voice, he asked, 'What's our position, sub?'

More confidently than before, Cartwright told him.

'Good,' said Newell. 'You're on the ball, sub. Keep it up.'

The other sub-lieutenants were an unknown quantity, at

least as far as Ivor was concerned. Moore had been consistently seasick since Portsmouth Point, a misfortune that provided some entertainment for his fellow sub-lieutenant Anderson.

That evening, Ivor went to the wardroom to enquire after Moore's health.

'He's in the heads, Number One,' reported Anderson gleefully. 'He keeps calling out to someone called Hughie.'

'When he comes out, give him a tot of neat rum and tell him he must drink it.'

'Aye, aye, sir, but isn't rum only for the Lower Deck?'

'Yes, Anderson, but I think they can spare a tot for medicinal use.' He turned to leave, but stopped in the doorway to say, 'We'll soon be entering the Irish Sea, and the weather forecast is far from good. Maybe you'll need a tot then.'

'Oh, I doubt it, Number One.'

'You'd better hope you're right. If you're seasick, your life won't be worth living, and particularly after the way you've treated Moore.'

At 2355, Ivor went up to the bridge to relieve the Captain.

'Hello, Number One. How are the subs taking this drop of roughers?'

'Cartwright's fine, sir, Moore's lauding the health-giving property of pusser's grog, and Anderson is face-down over the big white telephone, rueing the day he brought his mother and the midwife together in the same room.'

'Oh dear.' The Captain was smiling as he left the bridge.

Ivor wriggled inside his duffel coat to warm himself and peered through the squalling rain.

After a while, a cough from behind alerted him to the presence of another person on the bridge. He turned and recognised Leading Steward Denison.

'Hello, Denison. Come to join in the fun?'

With the reserved and deferential air of a family retainer,

the steward said, 'I thought you'd like some kye, sir.' Denison handed him an enamel mug containing the Navy's favourite source of foul-weather comfort, a drink made by cutting hard, dark chocolate into flakes, dissolving them in boiling water and adding condensed milk.

'Thank you, Denison. That's most thoughtful of you.'

'Not at all, sir. Would you care for a sandwich? It's corned beef, sir.'

'I feel like a spoilt child. Yes, please.'

Denison felt in his duffel coat pocket and took out a sandwich wrapped in a linen napkin.

'Thank you again, Denison. By the way, shouldn't you be tucked up in your hammock at this time of night?'

Almost as a rebuke, the leading steward said, 'The welfare of my gentlemen is my primary concern, sir.'

'Your dedication does you credit.'

'Thank you, sir. Goodnight.'

'Goodnight, Denison, and thank you.'

'The pleasure is entirely mine, sir.' He disappeared down the bridge ladder, leaving Ivor to keep watch, braced now by the doorstep sandwich and glutinous beverage, which was already warming his hands through his gloves.

Partly from the Captain's address to the ship's company and partly from his own enquiries, Ivor had learnt a great deal about the ship and her history. In her previous commission, she had two U-boat sinkings to her credit as well as one so badly damaged as to be of no further use to the *Kaisliche Marine*. The new *Hosta* had the same firepower as before, as well as a twin two-pounder pom-pom as secondary armament, and twin Vickers machine guns for use against U-boat gun crews. In addition, she carried torpedoes and depth-charges, and was protected by anti-torpedo nets. One feature that remained unchanged, however, was the planks of spruce that had been packed into every available compartment to make the ship buoyant in the event of a torpedo finding its way through the nets.

He stood on the bridge, leaning against the coaming and feeling the vibration of the ship's single engine as it pushed her through the turbulent waters of the Irish Sea, and he felt a surge of affection for his new mistress. The Captain had imagined it was ignorance of protocol that had led him to salute the quarter deck prior to commissioning, but it was a gesture of genuine respect for a ship brought out of well-earned retirement to serve her country again.

He thought about those things and many more as he kept the Middle Watch.

At 0355, the Captain arrived to relieve him, but Ivor remained on the bridge for the moment.

He asked, 'Did you have anything to do with Q-ships in the last war, sir?'

'No, I spent the war with the Harwich Force under Admiral Tyrwhitt. Why do you ask?'

'It's just that I'm a newcomer to Q-ships, sir, and I've been wondering quite how we're going to set about decoying U-boats. It's a closed book, as far as I'm concerned.'

'Then let me open it for you.' The Captain rubbed the last vestige of sleep from his eyes and explained. 'We will sail astern of the convoy, giving the impression of being a straggler. Now, torpedoes are expensive, and there's a limit to the number a U-boat can carry, so a captain will not normally waste one on a straggler. Instead, he'll surface in order to demand the ship's papers – that's for intelligence purposes – and to order the victim to refrain from using his radio. Then, unless he's a complete scoundrel, he will allow the ship's company to take to the boats before he sinks their ship by gunfire. Most U-boats carry the eighty-eight millimetre gun. I imagine you're familiar with it.'

'Yes, sir. It's a projectile and cartridge type, which makes reloading slightly slower than it is with our quick-firing pieces. Having said that, the U-boat crews are extremely well-trained, so we have to be quicker and more accurate.'

The Captain looked at him wryly, 'That's why they appointed you,' he said.

'When will we begin working-up exercises, sir?'

'Just as soon as we've taken on stores in Liverpool.'

—⧓—

Apart from giving engine room and wheelhouse orders, Newell was silent as he concentrated on negotiating the entrance to Canning Dock and thence Salthouse Dock. Having done that, he asked, 'Can you see Berth Six, Number One?'

'Yes, sir.'

'Very well, I'll let you put the baby to bed, bows facing to seaward, if you please.'

'Thank you, sir.' Ivor was a little surprised to be entrusted with such a task, but he was careful to show no sign of it. Taking over the con, he said, 'Stop engine.'

The Cox'n answered, 'Stop engine, sir. Engine stopped.'

'Dead slow astern and hard-a-port.'

'Dead slow astern and hard-a-port, sir. Dead slow astern. Wheel's hard-a-port, sir.'

Ivor waited as the ship swung almost two-hundred-and-seventy degrees. 'Stop engine. Midships.'

'Stop engine. Midships, sir. Engine stopped. Wheel's amidships, sir.'

'Dead slow astern. Starboard five.'

The Cox'n repeated the order and reported accordingly.

Ivor watched, and adjusted his course. 'Midships.'

'Midships, sir. Wheel's amidships, sir.'

'Port Five.'

Again the Cox'n reported back.

'Midships. Stop engine. Dead slow ahead.'

The ship slid into her berth with the gentlest of touches against the hemp rubbing strake of the dockside.

'Stop engine.'

'Nicely done, Number One,' said Newell.

'Thank you, sir. Finished with engine, thank you, Cox'n.'

'Finished with engine, sir.'

To the deck parties, he said, 'Make fast forrard, make fast aft. Secure springs.'

'Welcome to Liverpool, Number One. Is this your first visit?'

'Yes, sir.'

'Mine too, but it makes a change from the North Sea.'

Ivor had become used to the Captain's dry humour, and he'd come to expect it. Anything else that happened now would be a complete surprise.

3

Leaving the ship in the care of Anderson, who was Officer of the Day, the Captain set out for Western Approaches Headquarters, to report to the Flag Officer in Charge. Ivor went ashore that afternoon simply for a look around. Liverpool had been extensively damaged during the Blitz, but there was still a number of imposing buildings on the waterfront, and he spent some time admiring them.

A glance at his watch reminded him that two hours was probably long enough for an inexperienced sub-lieutenant such as Anderson to be left alone, so he returned to the ship.

He reached the head of the gangplank and saluted the quarterdeck, expecting to be challenged. However, having saluted him, the quartermaster stood woodenly to attention.

'Aren't you going to challenge me, Quartermaster?'

'Challenge you, sir?'

'Yes, I'm waiting for you to ask me to identify myself.'

The quartermaster, an ordinary seaman with little experience, was nonplussed. 'But I know who you are, sir. You're the First Lieutenant, sir.'

'How can you be sure of that, Harrison? For all you know, I might be my identical German cousin Albrecht the Ale Cart, first among Hitler's drinking oppos and last to be thrown out of the *Hund und Ente*. Ask me for my identification.'

'Aye, aye, sir. Sorry, sir. May I see your identity card, sir?'

'By all means.' Ivor took out his Naval Identity Card to show him. 'Don't forget to tick my name off, Harrison.'

'Aye, aye, sir.' The quartermaster obliged before asking, 'Sir?'

'Yes?'

'What was the name of that German pub, sir?'

'The *Hund und Ente*? The Dog and Duck. Are you thinking of giving it a try one day?'

'No, sir.' Harrison was trying not to laugh. 'I just want to tell my oppos what you said.'

'Just as long as you remember everything else I've told you, Harrison. Carry on.'

'Aye, aye, sir.'

Ivor looked around for Anderson, but there was no sign. However, as he made his way below, he heard unusual noises coming from the forrard seamen's messdeck and sounding suspiciously like female voices.

A seaman saw Ivor through the doorway and hissed the warning, 'It's the "Jimmy"!'

'Quite right, Allen,' said Ivor, surveying the gathering, which included three Wrens. They appeared to be enjoying tea, bread, margarine and plum jam. Everyone came to attention, including Leading Seaman Beaumont, who said, 'May I speak to you, please, sir?'

'Of course, Beaumont.' Ivor stepped outside the mess and waited for an explanation.

'I was down here when some of the lads brought the Wrens on board, sir. It was about an hour ago. The girls had been looking at the ship from the dockside, and the lads asked them if they'd like to come on board. Well, sir, I suppose I could have sent them packing, as we're engaged in work of a sensitive kind, but I thought if I did that, it might excite the girls' curiosity even more, so I let them stay, sir. They're probably excited enough to have been on board a ship.' He added, 'The lads know they're in for a bottle for this, 'cause I've warned them.'

'Thank you for telling me that, Beaumont. You did absolutely the right thing.' He thought quickly. 'Where was the senior rating of the watch when this happened?'

'I don't know, sir.'

'Was the OOD around?'

'Mr Anderson, sir? No, sir.' As an afterthought, he said, 'It's a bit like the *Marie Celeste* this afternoon, sir.'

'I'm inclined to agree, Beaumont.' He stepped inside the mess deck again. 'At ease, everyone. Have you enjoyed your tea, girls?'

There was a trio of 'Yes, thank you, sir,' and then one of them, a pretty girl with light, reddish hair that hung in ringlets despite the pins that attempted to confine it, said, 'We don't get jam as good as this in our mess, sir.' Her accent came unmistakably from the north-east.

'Don't you? That's too bad.' He seized on one of the more guilty-looking ratings and said, 'Jackson, go to the galley and bring back a tin of plum jam.'

'Aye, aye, sir.' Jackson departed, no doubt relieved to be away, albeit temporarily, from the scene of his crime.

'Now, girls, I hate to break up the party, but I'm sure these men won't want you to be here when the Captain returns.' A look around the mess at the nervous expressions of its occupants confirmed his surmise.

Able Seaman Jackson appeared breathlessly at his side with a four-pound tin of Mrs Ellison's Home-Made Plum Jam (HM Forces only).

'Thank you, Jackson.' Ivor took the jam from him and handed it to the Wren who had expressed her fondness for it. 'Put this under your Burberry and take it back to your mess,' he told her. 'It's a souvenir from *HMS Maynard*.'

'Thank you, sir.'

'You're welcome.' He thought her hair was the colour he'd heard people call strawberry blonde, and she was very pretty. 'Right, lads,' he said, 'escort your guests to the gangway and then come back here.'

The Wrens bade him a cheery farewell, and the girl with the Geordie accent made a point of saying, 'Thank you for the jam, sir. It's very kind of you.'

He couldn't resist saying, 'You're welcome, pet. Hurry along now.'

The girl gave him a strange look before departing with the others.

When the shamefaced ratings returned, he looked at each of them without speaking. Finally, he said, 'You know it was wrong of you to invite anyone on board without permission.'

'One of them said, 'We're sorry, sir. We didn't think.'

'So I gather. It would have been wrong in any ship, but the fact that this ship is about to engage in service of a special nature made it a particularly irresponsible thing to do.' Their faces showed genuine contrition, so he ended with, 'It must never happen again. Do you hear me?'

There was a chorus of, 'Yes, sir.'

'Good, because if it did, I should not be so lenient.' Confident that he'd made his point, he said, 'In future, you can leave it to the Captain to issue the invitations. Carry on.'

His next call was at the Chiefs' and Petty Officers' Mess, where Petty Officer Thompson was surprised to see him.

'PO Thompson, where were you an hour ago, when the starboard watch invited a party of Wrens on board?'

'I didn't know nothin' about that, sir.' The PO's eyes were filled with alarm.

'No, you were nowhere to be seen. As Senior Rate of the Watch, you should have been making regular checks on the gangway. Instead, you allowed an inexperienced quartermaster to proceed in partial ignorance of his duties, and a party of Wrens to treat the forrard mess as if it were Fortnum and Mason's Restaurant.' He was gratified by the continued look of apprehension on the PO's face. 'Those seamen are new to the job and they can be excused on this occasion, but you have no excuse.'

'No, sir.'

'You're a disgrace, Thompson, and you'll have to work very hard to change my opinion of you. Now, find the Officer of the Day and ask him to report to me in my cabin.'

'Aye, aye, sir.' Thompson went in search of the missing officer, and Ivor headed for his cabin.

A few minutes later, Sub-Lieutenant Anderson stood outside the curtain. He cleared his throat and said, 'You sent for me, Number One.'

'Yes, Anderson.' Ivor pushed the curtain aside to allow him inside. 'What's been happening while I've been ashore?'

Anderson immediately looked more relaxed, no doubt thinking that it was a routine summons. 'Nothing, sir. Everything was under control.'

'Under whose control, Anderson? Where were you when the starboard watch invited female company on to the messdeck?'

'Sir?' Suddenly, Anderson's bland features gave way to guilt.

'I came on board to find three Wrens being entertained by a party of seamen. I'll ask you again. Where were you?'

'I was probably on the bridge, Number One.'

'On the bridge,' echoed Ivor. 'In case you haven't noticed, we're tied up alongside. What reason had you to be on the bridge, unless you were preening yourself?' In the short time Ivor had known Anderson, he had been aware of his unrealistically superior self-image. 'Which is the most important part of the ship when she's alongside?'

'I don't know... I mean, the gangway, sir.'

'Oh, you remembered. Yes, the gangway, which was left to a clueless OD, who didn't even know he was supposed to challenge visitors and returning members of the ship's company.'

'I didn't realise, sir....'

'I should add to the clueless OD a bone-idle petty officer and an Officer of the Day who was physically and mentally absent, if not incompetent. The quartermaster didn't know his job because the Duty PO hadn't bothered to tell him, and the PO got away with it because you were on the bridge re-enacting the Battle of the River Plate.'

For the first time, Anderson was speechless.

'I'll leave it to the Captain to decide what to do with you. Meanwhile, you might bone up on the duties of a Duty Officer in case you're ever entrusted with the task again. Dismiss.'

'Out of the whole boiling lot, the one member of the ship's company who showed initiative, common sense and a responsible attitude was Leading Seaman Beaumont, sir.'

'Thank goodness for Beaumont, then.'

'I explained the situation to the seamen involved. They were just thoughtless, sir.'

Newell asked, 'What about Thompson?'

'I gave him a roasting, sir. He'll be as good as gold from now on.'

'And Anderson?'

'The same, sir, although I said I'd report the incident to you.'

'Thank you, Number One. You dealt with it wisely. I take your point about the seamen involved. They were allowed one mistake, and your soft-pedal reprimand was entirely appropriate.' He opened his briefcase and took out a document.

'Thank you, sir. There is one other thing.'

'What's that?'

'One of the Wrens was particularly impressed with our jam, which is apparently superior to theirs. I took the liberty of giving them a tin of plum jam. I thought a cosy memory of *HMS Maynard* might camouflage any interesting impressions they might have gained from their visit.'

'Good thinking, Number One.' Newell picked up the document he'd taken from his briefcase, 'Now, let me fill you in on the meeting I had this afternoon.'

The next day, Ivor went to Western Approaches Wireless Station to pick up the amendments to the confidential books. He could do so confidently in the knowledge that the ship was in the safe hands of Lieutenant Commander Newell. Sub-Lieutenant Anderson had received a second reprimand, this time from Newell, and he was feeling considerably more humble than he'd been for some time.

Having made his number with the Duty Officer at the Wireless Station, Ivor placed the amendments in his captain's briefcase, loaned to him for the purpose, and was on his way to the exit when he recognised a face from the previous day's tea party in the forrard mess. It was the girl with the strawberry blonde ringlets and blue eyes, who'd been so taken with the jam. In fact, they recognised each other almost simultaneously, and Ivor was about to speak to her, when something caused her to trip and sprawl headlong.

He crouched to help her up, holding her until he was sure she was all right. 'Gan canny, pet,' he cautioned, picking up her hat and handing it to her. 'Have you hurt yourself?'

'No, I'm all right, thank you, sir.' In her confusion, she replaced her hat and saluted him. It seemed that her only injury was embarrassment.

'Are you sure?'

'Yes, thank you, sir.' She stood for a moment, undecided, and then asked, 'I hope you don't mind me asking, sir, but are you a Geordie?'

'No,' he admitted. 'At least, only by adoption, and I don't suppose that counts.'

'It depends,' she said a little unsurely, but with a hint of mischief, 'whether we like you or not.'

'I lived on Tyneside for five years,' he told her.

'Whereabouts, sir?'

'Tynemouth.'

'Oh, that's posher 'n where I come from, sir.'

He was about to say something conciliatory, when a woman's voice asked, 'Is there a problem, sir?'

The girl stiffened, evidently recognising the voice, and Ivor looked over her shoulder to see that the question had come from a youthful Wren third officer.

'There's no problem now, third officer, but there might be.' He pointed to the shoulder bag that had caused the girl to trip. 'Some blockhead left her handbag loafing outside that door. It might be a good idea to reunite it with its careless owner before it breaks someone's neck.' He looked meaningfully at her until, suitably shamefaced, she picked up the bag and slung it over her shoulder. When she'd gone, Ivor said, 'Now we know who the blockhead was.'

'Yes, *her*.' A measure of feeling went into the second of those two words.

Ivor asked, 'What's your name?'

'Nine four—'

'No, just your first name.'

'Grace. Why do you want to know that, sir?'

'Because I want you to meet me when you're next off watch.'

She stared at him with wide-open eyes. 'Do you mean you want me to go ashore with you, sir?'

'Yes. When do you get an evening off?'

'Tonight, sir, but we're not supposed to go out with officers.'

'I can keep a secret if you can.'

She looked guiltily around her. 'All right, because you're nice,' she said, 'but we'll have to be careful.'

'Do you know a restaurant called *The Grapevine*?' He'd noticed it the previous afternoon.

'Yes, it's very posh.'

'I've been chucked out of posher places, Grace. Meet me there – I'll be in good time, so you won't be kept hanging around – and my name's Ivor. Can you be there for seven?'

'Yes, sir, I come off watch at eighteen hundred.'

'Good, I'll see you then. Goodbye, Grace.'

'Goodbye, sir... Ivor.' Still confused, she remembered at the last minute to salute him.

He returned her salute and walked to the exit. As he did so, he saw the Wren officer whose shoulder bag had caused Grace to trip. She was quite fetching in a china doll way, and he noticed that she'd attracted the attention of two sub-lieutenants, a development that seemed to give her some satisfaction, although he suspected that her sights were usually set somewhat higher. He walked past her, returning her salute and theirs, but otherwise ignoring her.

4

Ivor was enjoying a pink gin and a cigarette, and listening to the band, which comprised piano, bass, saxophone and drums. They were playing soft background music when he saw Grace in the doorway. He stood up to greet her as the waiter helped her off with her coat.

'Grace, you look lovely.'

She looked down at her sage green dress and said, 'Thanks, but it's nothing special. I haven't got many civvy clothes here. It's not as if I get much call to wear them.'

'Come and sit down.' He guided her to the chair that the waiter had drawn out for her. 'You wear clothes well,' he said.

'What do you mean?'

'You look good in them. You can buy fashion,' he told her, but you can't buy style. That comes naturally, and you have plenty.'

'If you say so.'

'What would you like to drink?'

'I don't know. What's that you're drinking?'

'Pink gin.'

'What goes into that?'

'They put a dash of Angostura bitters into the glass, swirl it round, and then pour the gin into it. Would you like to try one?'

'Yes, please.'

Ivor turned to the waiter. 'Another pink gin for the lady, please.'

'Certainly, sir. With water or tonic, sir?'

'Tonic, I think.' It would be a good idea to dilute it for her.

'I don't think I've ever been called a lady.' Looking around her, she said, 'And I'm not used to being in places like this, either.'

'Don't worry, the natives are friendly.' He'd already seen her grimace as she reacted to the smoke from his cigarette, and he stubbed it out, resolved to make the rest of the evening a smoke-free occasion. It was even possible that he might give up altogether, in which case, Grace was already an improving influence on him.

Leaning forward confidentially, she asked, 'Did you give those sailors a bottle for inviting us on the ship yesterday?'

'I gave them more than a bottle. I had them flogged and keelhauled. It's the only way with their sort.' Close up, he noticed that her make-up was discreet, but the effect was most engaging.

'Be serious, Ivor. I was concerned for them after they'd been so nice to us. I didn't like the idea of them getting wrong 'cause of us.'

'I just told them to behave themselves and not invite visitors on board without permission.'

She asked innocently. 'Was it wrong of us to accept their invitation?'

'No, because you didn't know either. Don't worry about it.'

She looked visibly more relaxed, and then said, 'They got a shock when you came on board. Why did one of them call you "Jimmy"? Is that one of your names?'

'He didn't call me that. That's what I am, "The Jimmy", otherwise "Jimmy-the-One", the First Lieutenant.'

She absorbed that information and asked, 'Is that high-up?'

'High-up? I'm the lynch pin of the ship. Even the captain has to ask my permission before he can go to the heads.'

'You're havin' me on again.'

'Only in a nice way. I'm actually second-in-command. What did you do before you joined the Wrens, Grace?'

'I was a secretary. I kept quiet about my civilian job when I joined. I wanted to do something more... to do with the war.'

'Something more military?'

'Yes, so I went into signals. I'm a coder, so we'd better say no more about that.'

'Quite right. Tell me about your family.'

She thought. 'There's not a lot to tell, really. My brother's a draughtsman, but he's away in the army, my dad's a fitter in the shipyard, but he's spent as much time out of work as he has actually workin'. My mam's a sales assistant at Binns' department store. It's her wage that's kept us going most of the time.'

He nodded sympathetically, interrupted when the waiter arrived at the table with the menu.

'I'm afraid the veal is off, sir.'

'Don't worry. What's not on the menu?'

The waiter leaned forward conspiratorially to say, 'Game pie, sir, a real treat.'

Ivor looked across at Grace, who said simply, 'I'll be guided by you.'

'Right, we'll have the game pie. What do you recommend as a first course?'

'We have an excellent Ardennes pate, sir. Our chef excels in them.'

'Is he from the Ardennes?'

'I fear not, sir.'

'It's just as well. Given the situation over there, he'd only be distracted. We'll have the pate.'

'And to drink with it, sir?'

Ivor looked at Grace, who deferred, as usual, to him.

'What do you recommend?'

'While stocks last, sir, we have a rather nice red Bordeaux.'

'In that case, we'd better grab a bottle before it disappears.'

'Very good, sir.' The waiter left them.

Grace asked, 'What's pate, sir— I mean, Ivor.' She blushed a little. 'It's hard to break the habit.'

'Posh potted meat. It has lots of good things in it as well.'

She looked uncomfortable. Presently, she said, 'This can't be much fun for you, Ivor. I mean, I haven't a clue about these things.'

'Grace, listen. Give me your hand.' When she looked at him strangely, he explained, 'I can't talk to you about important things when there's daylight between us.'

'Okay.' She let him take her hand, which felt soft and inviting, so he stroked it with his thumb.

'I asked you out for the pleasure of your company, not because I thought you were an expert on French *cuisine*. Now, give it a fair try, and you'll enjoy it.'

'All right.' She looked at him squarely. 'In that case, it's your turn to tell me about your family.'

He waited until the waiter had brought the wine, noted his approval and poured it for them. 'Very well,' he said. 'Being Welsh, my mother insisted on calling me "Ivor". She intended it to be spelt with an "f", the Welsh way, but my father registered the birth, and he could only spell in English.' He reconsidered that for a moment. 'Well, Yorkshire, anyway.'

'It must be like the League of Nations at your house.'

'No, it's more like a pile of rubble. It was bombed last March.'

'Oh, no. Was there anybody at home?'

'Both of my parents. My older brother's based in Northern Ireland, and the younger one's in the RAF.'

'Oh, me an' me big mouth. I'm sorry, Ivor.'

'That's all right.' Her guilt made him feel guilty as well. 'You weren't to know.'

Possibly to bury her gaffe, she asked, 'What's your brother doing in Ireland?'

'Working for the Ministry of Pensions.' He shrugged dismissively. 'He wouldn't have been much use to the war effort, anyway. I can't imagine he's all that useful to the Ministry of Pensions, but that's a matter for them to live with.'

She was still burdened with embarrassment. 'I'm sorry I blundered in with that remark,' she said.

'You mustn't be. It was a shock, but it could have been a lot worse.'

'How could it have been worse?'

'I never had a close relationship with my mother and father, and neither did my younger brother Huw. They were completely wrapped up in their firstborn.'

'What's he called?'

'Eric. He's the only one that didn't get a Welsh name.'

'It sounds as if he got everything else.'

'Almost everything, but Huw and I are capable of making our own way in life.' He decided to share a memory with her. 'I was given a week's leave in March of this year,' he said, 'and my mother had asked me to call at the jeweller's next to Newcastle Central Station. You probably know it.'

'Aye, but I'm not what you'd call a regular customer.'

'Neither am I. Anyway, she'd left two rings with them and she wanted me to collect them. One was in for repair and the other for engraving. The setting of her engagement ring needed some work, and she'd inherited a man's signet ring that she wanted engraved with my father's initials. She said that if I paid the jeweller, she'd reimburse me when I got home.' He could see that Grace was gripped by the story so far. 'I took a taxi to our home in Tynemouth, but it went no further than the end of the road where we lived. It was closed to traffic, because, where our house and several others had stood, there was a pile of smoking wreckage. The warden told me that there were no survivors.'

'Oh, Ivor, that's awful.' Then, still keen to know more, she asked, 'What happened to the rings?'

'Under the terms of the will, Eric inherited the estate, but Huw and I were each allowed to choose a keepsake, so we kept the rings. It was just as well we had them, because most of the contents were burned with the house. Anyway, Huw was particularly keen on the signet ring, so he took that, and I kept the engagement ring. That way, my mother kept her word and reimbursed me for the jeweller's bill as well as leaving us with our keepsakes.'

'That's quite a story.' She digested it before saying, as if she'd just realised it, 'You know, another difference between you and me is that I say, "me dad" and "me mam", and you talk about your "mother" and "father".'

'I'm only posh when I'm trying to impress a new girlfriend,' he assured her.

'Oh, is that what I am?'

'I hope so.' He noticed that the waiter was coming, so he released her hand.

'For you, miss, and you, sir.' The waiter put down their first course and left them.

'You know,' said Ivor, 'he reminds me of Leading Steward Denison, who looks after us on board ship. He's a regular Jeeves, more like a butler than a steward.' He noticed that Grace was looking at her pate, perhaps wondering what to do with it, so he demonstrated by taking a piece of toast and loading it with pate.

'You must live like kings on that ship,' she observed, doing the same with hers.

'Not on an open bridge in a force ten,' he told her.

'I don't suppose so, but what do I know about anythin'? Hey, this is really nice.'

'What did I tell you? You must learn to trust me.'

Grace continued to enjoy her first course. After a while, she said, 'What's the game in game pie?'

'It'll be a mixture, maybe of pheasant, partridge, and possibly pigeon to eke it out. 'At all events, they only use the breasts. The rest isn't worth the effort. You see, from breaking out of the egg to falling from the sky, the game bird devotes its life to developing its breast, and all for our benefit.'

She was studying him warily.

'What's the matter?'

'I'm just waiting for you to make a joke about breasts,' she said.

'Who, me? Joke about them? Let me tell you, there are some things in life I take very seriously.' He put on a thoughtful look and said, 'Not many, I'll admit, but food is one of them.'

'Of course. I've spent too much time working with sailors. All they ever talk about is... you know.'

'I know, Grace.' He was sensitive to her embarrassment.

Reverting more comfortably to a previous topic, she asked, 'How did you come to move to Tynemouth?'

'It was my father's work. He was manager at the Labour Exchange.'

'The dole office? I bet he was never out of work.'

'No, he wasn't.'

'What did you do before the war, Ivor?'

'I was a reporter on the local paper.'

'Oh, aye?' New interest dawned. 'What paper was that?'

'*The Tynemouth Observer*.'

'A posh paper.'

'Not very. It comes a long way behind *The Times* and *The Daily Telegraph* in the posh stakes.'

'That's just being silly. What shorthand do you use?'

'Pitman.'

'Same here. We could have a competition some time, you and me.'

'Why not?' The quartet, who had so far played unintrusive background music, began to play 'A Nightingale Sang in Berkeley Square.' He asked, 'Would you like to dance?'

'Wey aye. I love dancin'.'

'It was high time they played some proper dance music.'

'I like this one an' all.'

He led her to the dance floor, and they joined the couples already there, but his mind was only partly on the music. Apart from the time he'd helped her up after her fall, it was physically the closest they'd been, and he was delightfully conscious of her scent, a fact she was quick to realise.

'It's not my perfume,' she said. 'I cannot afford that kind of thing. A girl in my cabin let me have a little dab.'

'It smells wonderful on you.'

'Haddaway.'

'No, I mean it.'

'You're just full of it, Ivor.'

'Now you've cut me to the quick.' He danced on in silence. He'd been conscious from the start that she was a good dancer; in fact, they moved so well together, enjoying the popular song, that it was a shame when the music reached its end and they had to return to their table.

'You dance well,' he said,

'You're not bad yourself.'

'We should work at it. There could be a future for us as the Fred Astaire and Ginger Rogers of Tyneside.'

'Just as long as you don't call me "Ginger". I hate that.'

'I wouldn't dream of it. In any case, you're not ginger, you're strawberry blonde, although with your fondness for plum jam, maybe I should think of a new name. How about "Mirabelle plum blonde"?'

'Do you ever take anything seriously, Ivor?'

'Apart from pheasant, partridge and pigeon? Not if I can help it.' He refilled her glass.

'This wine's really nice. I like it a lot better than the pink gin, really.'

'Leave the gin, then.'

'Don't you mind?'

'Certainly not. I don't want to have to carry you back to the Wrens' quarters.'

'It wouldn't be very clever,' she admitted, 'and you are clever, aren't you? You must be clever to be an officer.'

'Not in the least. Listen, when we lived in Yorkshire, I went to an ancient grammar school there, although goodness knows how I passed the scholarship. Anyway, the motto on the school gates read: "*Digni Et Vos Este Favore*".'

' "Be also worthy of favour," ' she translated.

'Who's a clever girl? That's right. It was a sixteenth century pun, you see. The school was founded by the Reverend Doctor Favour, a fierce man who took life very seriously.'

'But you never did?'

'Hardly ever, and that's why I left school at sixteen with the worst kind of report. I gained a School Certificate, though, but only two distinctions. The rest were passes. I was hardly worthy of anything, so what could I do but join the local paper?'

'What were your distinctions?'

'English Language and Literature. I imagine you did better than that.'

She wrinkled her nose modestly. 'I matriculated,' she said, 'but my family couldn't afford for me to go any further.'

'You're now about to graduate on to the game pie,' he told her, as the waiter approached their table.

'I'm looking forward to this.'

'Quite right.'

The waiter put two helpings of game pie on the table. 'I'll be back with the vegetables in a moment, sir,' he promised.

Grace inhaled the aroma that rose from the pie, and said, 'It smells lovely.'

'In that case, will you come ashore with me again?'

His question seemed to surprise her. 'All right. I don't see why not.'

'I just noticed that you say "don't", and not "divven't".'

'I know I'm not high society,' she chided, 'but I'm not an ignoramus either.'

'Of course you're not. I'm sorry.'

'That's all right.'

Satisfied that he was forgiven, he took out his diary and said, 'If you give me your surname and official number, I'll drop you a line at the Wrens' quarters when we're in Liverpool again.'

'Are you going to sea already?'

'I don't know yet.'

'I'm sorry. I shouldn't have asked you that.'

'No, you shouldn't. What's your name and number?'

'Headley – that's with an "a" – nine four eight three six two seven.'

He made a note and put his diary away as the waiter arrived with the vegetables.

'Will there be anything else, sir?'

'No, thank you. Everything looks truly magnificent.'

'Thank you, sir.'

When the waiter had gone, Grace asked, 'What's your surname, Ivor?'

'Loveday. Help yourself to vegetables.'

'Thank you.' She took potatoes, carrots and cauliflower.

'Dig in, Grace. It's all paid for.'

'I've got quite enough, thank you. Is that really your name? You're not just havin' me on?'

'Ivor Reginald Loveday,' he confirmed.

'What a smashin' name. "Loveday".' She appeared to weigh the name on her tongue.

'In medieval times,' he told her, ' "Love Day" was the feast when people were expected to reconcile their differences. I imagine quite a few babies were started as a consequence, and what better memorial could there be than to name them after the day they were conceived?'

'It always comes down to that with fellas, doesn't it? By the way, this pie's beautiful, an' the gravy's lovely an' all.'

'I'm glad, but something's puzzling me.'

'What?' Suddenly, she was uneasy again.

'Don't worry, it's nothing awful. You mentioned a cabin earlier. You don't really live in one, do you?'

'Wey aye, me an' three other girls. It's actually a bedroom in the staff quarters of the Hotel Emilia, but we have to call it a "cabin" because it sounds more nautical than "bedroom". The officers have the proper hotel rooms, but even some of them have to share.' As if the question had just occurred to her, she asked, 'Don't you sleep in a cabin?'

'Yes, it just sounded odd. I was thinking of Charlie Chaplin's log cabin in *Gold Rush*.'

'Charlie Chaplin's about right for you.' She smiled nevertheless.

Conveniently, the quartet waited until they'd finished the main course before starting 'Dream a Little Dream.'

He asked, 'Shall we give another demonstration?'

'Why not?' She allowed him to take her hand and lead her on to the floor, which was considerably more crowded than when they'd danced earlier. 'I was going to say,' she said, 'that it beats dancing to a piano in the club at home, but "dancing" isn't quite the word for this.'

'I know. Let's shuffle.'

They did, cheek to cheek, which was much to Ivor's satisfaction, because, as well as the intimacy it created, he could enjoy the fragrance of whatever perfume Grace's cabin-mate had generously donated. Perfumes, like make-up, were in very short supply, and he was grateful for the gesture, even though he'd never met the girl.

Eventually, Grace said, 'I have to go. I need to be back by twenty-three hundred.'

Ivor paid the bill, sent for Grace's coat and declined the offer of a taxi. They weren't particularly plentiful, and they hadn't far to walk to the Emilia, according to Grace.

'Take my arm,' he offered. 'It'll make up for cutting me to the quick earlier.'

'When did I do that?' She took his arm nevertheless.

'When you said I was full of it. You didn't say what I was full of, by the way.'

'It wouldn't have been nice.' Her thoughts seemed to be elsewhere.

'What's on your mind?'

'Oh, just that I'm glad there was nobody in that restaurant from

Western Approaches. There's a party of some kind in the wardroom tonight, and I'm sure that helped.'

He asked a question that had occurred to him earlier. 'Have you never thought of joining them in the wardroom, Grace. I mean, you're a bright girl with a good School Certificate.'

'Me an officer? Absolutely not. I'd never remember the names of all the cocktails.'

'There's more to being an officer than cocktail parties.'

'Not for some of them.' She gripped his arm, as if to make sure he was listening. 'Do you remember the three-oh who left her bag loafing in the passage?'

'Yes.'

'She was at the signals school with me when we were both OD Wrens.'

'Where was that?'

'*HMS Cabbala*, in Gloucestershire. Anyway, everybody knew what she was after. She called all the instructors "Chiefy darling", whether they were chiefs or PO's, and she couldn't wait to persuade a naval officer to give her a leg-up with the Interview Board. She had a pregnancy scare at one stage in her bid for success, but that's another story.'

He nodded sagely, as if the situation were all too common. 'You don't surprise me.'

'About what?'

'I knew she was careless.'

'How could you possibly know that?'

'It was the way she left her bag loafing. A girl who can do that is quite capable of casting caution to the four winds and finding herself in an interesting condition. Anyway, keep walking. You don't want to be adrift.'

'That's another thing,' she said. 'Sailors can't stop laughing when we say things like "adrift" and "ashore", but if we speak to them in plain English, they think that's funny as well.'

'Put it down to stunted intellect,' he advised her.

'I already have.'

The sign of the Hotel Emilia came in sight. 'Don't come right to the door,' she said, 'in case somebody sees you.'

'Another time, I'll disguise myself as a Wren.'

'Don't be silly. I'm going in now, so thank you for a lovely evening, and I mean that.'

'Thank you, Grace. I've enjoyed your company, and I'll write to you as soon as I'm back in Liverpool.'

'Will you?'

'Yes, I mean it.'

'Be careful, Ivor.' It was a serious plea.

He leaned towards her and kissed her cheek. 'I'll be careful,' he promised. 'You do the same, and keep an eye out for loafing handbags.'

'You look out for U-boats.'

'I'll be doing plenty of that,' he assured her. 'Goodnight, Grace.'

'Goodnight, Ivor.'

He waited until she was safely inside the hotel, before turning and walking back to the ship.

5

Ivor looked through his night glasses and reported, 'Ship bearing red oh-four-five, sir.'

'Very good.'

'Ship bearing red oh-four-five, sir,' reported the port bridge lookout.

'Wake up,' the Captain told him. 'The First Lieutenant reported it half-an-hour ago.'

'It's an HDML, sir,' said Ivor, smiling at the captain's exaggeration.

'You've got damned good eyesight, Number One.'

'I believe so, sir.' He was proved correct when the vessel drew closer and the letters HDML, standing for 'Harbour Defence Motor Launch', and her number became clearly legible.

'Signalman, be ready with the authentication,' said Ivor.

'Aye, aye, sir.'

As the motor launch approached, its signalman flashed the challenge, and Maynard replied with the single letter of authentication. The ML's crew waved as they passed.

'Very good,' said the Captain. 'I think we'll continue on this course for another ten miles before we start playing games. We can't practise firing torpedoes or depth-charges, simply because we can't afford to waste them, although I have to say I'm not all that worried about depth-charge attacks.'

'I don't suppose we'll have all that much use for them, sir,' said Ivor. 'Without asdic, we'd have no idea what we were depth-charging, anyway.'

'The thinking,' explained Newell, 'is that we would use them in the event of a U-boat surfacing and then thinking better of it.

We'd go to a point ahead of where the U-boat dived and hope for the best.'

'That makes a kind of sense, sir.'

'Except that it mustn't come to that. If a U-boat escapes, our secret will be out.'

'Exactly, sir.'

'In the event of an attack with torpedoes, however, the target would have to be too close to miss.' Turning to Ivor, he said pointedly, 'That leaves the guns.'

'And the rest, sir, the changing of ensigns and the lowering of the screens. We must drill them until they can do it in a split second and in their sleep.'

After two hours' gunnery practice, the Captain spoke to everyone on the upper deck.

'We're now going to find out how quickly we can make the ship ready for action. This will begin with the call to Action Stations. The next command will be "Let Go!" On that command, the ensigns will be changed, red for white, and the screens will fall to reveal the guns and torpedo tubes made ready to fire. As soon as the red ensign is flying from our masthead, we'll begin.' He waited for the Royal Navy's white ensign to be lowered and the red ensign of the Merchant Navy to be hoisted. Then, with a quick smile to Ivor, he spoke into the Tannoy. 'For exercise, for exercise, Action Stations!' Then he pressed the Action Stations button to sound the klaxon before starting his stopwatch.

From almost every direction came the sounds of running footsteps. Newell peered from forrard to aft and saw that the gun and torpedo crews were in position.

'That took far too long,' he commented, stopping his watch. 'They'll have to cut that time by half.' Speaking into the Tannoy again, he ordered, 'For exercise, for exercise, Let Go!'

Ivor watched in painful silence as the plywood screens that concealed the guns and torpedo tubes were released. After two minutes, 'Y' Gun's crew were still struggling with theirs.

'If you'll excuse me, sir, I'll pay "Y" Gun a visit,' he said.

'I think you should, Number One.'

Ivor made his way aft to where the embarrassed gun crew had finally managed to collapse their screens. Leading Seaman Dwyer saluted and said simply, 'Dodgy workmanship, sir.'

Ivor examined the poorly-made frames and associated ironmongery. 'I'm inclined to agree, Dwyer,' he said. 'I'll report it to the Captain.'

'Thank you, sir. We can do without a black mark against us already.'

Ivor made the return trip to the bridge to report. 'It's a case of shoddy workmanship by the Dockyard, sir, one of those things we were unable to test before taking over the ship.'

'Bloody marvellous.'

'In the absence of a chippy, sir, I'll speak to the Chief ERA. I've no doubt one of his chaps will help us out.' He smiled at the thought. The Chief Engine Room Artificer was an excellent man, who took pride in his ability, and he would be ready enough to prove his adaptability.

'Thank you, Number One.' Speaking to the ship's company once more, he said, 'The hitch with "Y" Gun's screens was not the gun crew's fault. The problem will be rectified. Otherwise, however, the exercise took far too long. A U-boat would have had no difficulty in blowing us out of the water. We shall exercise again when repairs have been made. Secure from Action Stations. That is all.'

For the next three weeks, the ship's company exercised repeatedly until each man became a seamless part in the operation. Ivor's gunners also developed skills they had never previously known, and the pride he'd mentioned in his first meeting with the Captain was now immediately apparent when they went about their duties.

'They're proud, and I'm proud of what they've achieved, Number One,' said the Captain, pouring two gins, 'and you've been responsible for much of it.' He opened his cigarette case and offered it to Ivor.

'No, thank you, sir. I've given up smoking, but thank you for the compliment.' He smiled as he spoke, recalling as he did the effort he'd put into training his men, although he was momentarily distracted by the size of the drink that the Captain handed to him.

'And you did it well.' Picking up a message from Flag Officer Western Approaches, he said, 'Seventy-two hours' Christmas leave has been granted to most of the ship's company. There'll be a skeleton crew left on board, and two officers will also remain on board. I shall be one of them, of course. Thereafter, we shall be "in all respects ready for sea and for war".'

'Is there any point in your being on board, sir. I'll be here, and one subby can keep me company.'

'I was about to offer you the opportunity of Christmas leave, Number One. It's going to be a special time for everyone, and I thought you'd like to share in it.'

'That's kind of you, sir,' said Ivor awkwardly, 'but I've no home to go to, so I may as well be one of the caretakers, as it were.' As an afterthought, he asked, 'What makes this Christmas so special, sir?'

Newell grinned broadly. 'Another signal, this time to the whole fleet. I shall speak to the ship's company in a minute or so, but I'll tell you now, that on the morning of the seventh, Japanese forces attacked the American Pacific Fleet in Pearl Harbour, Hawaii, inflicting heavy damage. Consequently, the USA is now in the war.' He held up his glass. 'Here's to final victory!'

Ivor joined him in the toast, adding, 'I'm still happy for you to take the seventy-two hours, sir. What with the Russians and the Americans, this war is getting a little crowded, and I'd just as soon be in familiar surroundings.'

'You're a sportsman, Number One. Thank you. You do realise you'll have to go through all the rigmarole on Christmas Day, don't you?'

Ivor was puzzled. 'Do I have to dress up as Santa Claus, sir?'

'Only if that kind of thing appeals to you. I was actually referring to lunch on Christmas Day. That's when the officers are expected to wait on the Lower Deck.'

'Oh, I'll manage that, sir. I haven't lost the common touch.'

When the Captain had given the ship's company the news and the excitement of drawing lots for leave had died down, Ivor wrote a note to Grace.

10th. December, 1941.

Dear Grace,

I hope you're well, happy, and keeping well out of the way of loafing handbags.

When you get this note, we'll be tied up alongside, so if you're still happy for us to meet again, just pop a note into the internal mail c/o the ship, giving me details of your watches, and then we can make arrangements.

He wondered for a moment about the best way to sign off, and then wrote:

Love,

Ivor X X

P.S. I'm looking forward to seeing you again.

On the second day in Salthouse Dock, he was delighted to receive a note in the internal mail. It was addressed in a neat, girlish hand to: *Lt. I. R. Loveday, R.N.V.R., First Lieutenant, H.M.S. Maynard, Salthouse Dock.* She'd even remembered his middle initial. He took out the letter to read it.

Dear Ivor,

Thank you for your letter. It's lovely to hear from you, and I'm glad you're safe and all right. You are all right, aren't you?

Of course I want to see you again. I have managed, so far, to dodge lurking hazards.

My next evening off will be on Wednesday, 15th. I hope this coincides with your off-watch time.

It's a funny old world. My brother Jack is being made an officer in the Royal Engineers. Knowing that he was a draughtsman, the army put him in the Catering Corps to begin with. He says they do that kind of thing all the time, but it wasn't long before they found out that he doesn't know a soup ladle from a rolling pin. Anyway, with so many officers in my life, I'll have to be permanently on my best behaviour.

I've been given 72 hours for Christmas, starting on Christmas Eve, and it's as much use as a concrete football. Considering the way the trains are running, I'd no sooner be home than I'd have to leave again.

Take care and let me know if you can make the 15th.

Love,

Grace XX.

P.S. As you might expect, this letter will be read by a third party and possibly censored. Stand by for fun and games.

Ivor couldn't see what the fuss was about. Wrens weren't subject to the Naval Discipline Act, they could go ashore in civilian clothing, so why shouldn't they go ashore with officers? It made no sense.

Even as Ivor folded the letter and placed it in his bedside drawer, Grace was summoned to 2nd Officer Barlow's office. She knew the reason even before she knocked on the door.

'Come in.' 2nd Officer Barlow was a dark and slender woman of thirty or so, with the reputation of being strict but usually more sensible than most of her juniors. Grace had cause to be optimistic.

'Wren Headley,' said Miss Barlow, returning her salute, 'as you know, all mail leaving military establishments must be read by a supervising officer. Third Officer Treadwell tells me she read a letter from you to the First Lieutenant of *HMS Maynard*.'

It seemed to Grace that some kind of response was expected of her, so she said, 'Yes, ma'am, I wrote to Lieutenant Loveday.' It was a heavy touch of irony that 'Ever Ready' Treadwell should have made the report, but Grace had to keep quiet about that.

'I gather from Third Officer Treadwell that the two of you are making plans to meet.'

'Yes, ma'am.'

'But not for the first time?'

'No, ma'am.'

'You are aware, are you not, that Wrens are actively discouraged from consorting with naval officers?'

'Yes, ma'am.' She had to answer carefully. 'I know that, but I understand it's a matter of unwritten guidance rather than an actual rule, ma'am.'

'So you see it as being for the obedience of fools and the guidance of wise Wrens. Is that the case?'

Grace was aware that Miss Barlow had been a barrister in civilian life, and that she was said to be capable of extracting a confession from a saint. Even so, there had been no breach of King's regulations or Admiralty Instructions. 'No, ma'am, that's not the way I see it at all.'

'Then I'm waiting for your explanation.'

'Of course, ma'am. The fact is that Lieutenant Loveday and I are distantly related.'

'Really?'

'Yes, ma'am.' It was true. She was a Geordie and he was an adopted one. 'We've known each other for some time, ma'am.' That was also true, several weeks having passed since their meeting on board *HMS Maynard*.

'Oh.' For the first time, 2nd Officer Barlow seemed unsure.

'Everything's perfectly above board, ma'am. Lieutenant Loveday is a gentleman. He treats me with complete respect and, whatever anyone else may imagine, I have my standards too.' It was a swipe at Ever Ready Treadwell, but she hoped Miss Barlow wouldn't see it as such.

'Of course you have, Wren Headley. I think what you've told me puts a rather different complexion on this matter. I'm going to put it down to exceptional circumstances.' Almost as if she were asking a favour, she said, 'You will be discreet, won't you?'

'Of course, ma'am. Thank you, ma'am.' Grace waited to be dismissed, but it became apparent that 2nd Officer Barlow hadn't quite finished with her.

'Wren Headley, you're an intelligent, educated young woman. I haven't got your details here at the moment, so maybe you'll refresh my memory. What School Certificate did you get?'

'I matriculated with four distinctions and five credits, ma'am.'

'I suspected as much. Have you ever considered applying for a commission?'

'Never, ma'am.'

'Why ever not?' It seemed that Miss Barlow regarded it as a Wren's most obvious course of action, and that was something Grace had never understood.

She had to express herself carefully. 'I don't think I have what it takes, ma'am.'

'You do surprise me, Wren Headley. Why are you so unsure?'

'Officers I've met, ma'am, have demonstrated particular qualities in order to reach the Admiralty Interview Board, and I really can't see myself equalling their standards.'

'Well, I suppose you know yourself better than anyone, but it's an awful shame.'

'I'm not unhappy about it, ma'am.'

'Oh, well, that's the main thing, I suppose. Thank you, Wren Headley. That will be all.'

6

It was a rush, but Grace was able to grab a sandwich and change in time to meet Ivor outside the Hotel Emilia and arrive at the Regal Cinema in time for first house.

'I've booked a table for supper,' he told her.

'You've heard my tummy rumbling, haven't you?'

'Yes, it's quite entertaining. Can you make it do that again?'

Grace wasn't listening, being taken more by the photographs that lined the staircase to the balcony. 'Anton Wallbrook is really handsome,' she said. 'Don't you think so?'

'He's all right if you like that kind of thing.'

'I suppose you're more interested in Sally Gray.'

'Oddly enough, I am.'

They took their seats just in time for the main picture, which was *Dangerous Moonlight,* a romance between a Polish concert pianist and an American journalist. Grace was spellbound from the start, where the hero was in hospital and knocking seven bells out of a Bechstein, having lost his memory. For Ivor, it was sufficient to be sitting in the darkened auditorium with Grace, who had often occupied his thoughts at sea whenever his attention was not required elsewhere. He reached for her hand, and she responded by slipping her other hand beneath his, making it a willing captive.

When the lights came up at the end, she said, 'Oh, that was lovely. It was smashin' to hear not just the *Warsaw Concerto,* but other music as well. I'd like to have heard more of Beethoven's "Emperor" *Concerto.* It's always been one of my favourites.'

'You like music, obviously.'

'I used to enjoy listenin' to it at school,' she said as they took the stairs down to the foyer. 'Concerts were out of my reach.'

'They're not so expensive, surely?'

'Expensive enough, and anyway, who was I going to go with? None of my family was keen on music.' She gripped his arm again in a way that was becoming familiar. 'If I'd mentioned Beethoven at home, me dad would have belted us for swearin'. That's how much he knows about music.'

'I'll take you to a concert, Grace.'

'Will you?'

'Wey aye, pet. You cannot come to Liverpool without hearin' the Philharmonic.'

She punched him playfully. 'You know, if you live in Newcastle another ten years, you might just begin to sound like a Geordie.' By loose association, the memory of her conversation with 2nd Officer Barlow returned to her and she said, 'I got hauled over the coals because of you.'

'Because of me?'

'Well, not reprimanded exactly, but called to account for my actions. Do you remember Three-Oh Treadwell, the blockhead who left her bag loafing in the corridor?'

'Oh yes, the one who looks as if she's left her brain at home but can't remember where she lives?'

Grace considered the description. 'I suppose she does, a bit. Anyway, she was going through the correspondence and she read my letter to you and reported me to Two-Oh Barlow for consorting with a naval officer.'

'Didn't you tell her I'm not a real naval officer, just pretending to be one until the war's over?'

'No, I said we were distantly related and that we've known each other for a while.' Realising that he was peering at her very obviously, she asked, 'What's the matter?'

'You should have grown a long nose by this time.'

'Aye well, you have to be a bit inventive on occasions. At all events, she let me off.'

'I should think so.'

'Aye, but it won't have gone down well with "Ever Ready" Treadwell, the wardroom bike of *HMS Cabbala*. By the way, are we nearly there yet?'

'Yes, it's not far. Is your tummy rumbling again?'

'Can't you hear it?'

He bent and put his ear to her middle. 'Oh yes,' he confirmed. Just round this corner.'

'Hey,' said Grace as they turned into the next street and she saw the restaurant, 'this is where we came last time.'

'Yes, I thought I'd keep it familiar.'

'You're very thoughtful, Ivor.'

'I do my best.' He opened the door of the restaurant and held it for her.

'I could get used to this,' she said.

'Good evening, sir. Good evening, miss.' The waiter who had served them before took their coats and welcomed them to the restaurant.

'Your table is this way, sir.' He picked up two menus and led them to a table in a secluded corner.

'This is very private,' said Grace when the waiter had gone.

'I asked for privacy.'

'Oh, what have you got in mind?'

'I thought we could play a game. I can pretend to be an RN officer at *Cabbala*, and you can be Ever Ready Treadwell, ready to sacrifice everything in the name of ambition.'

'You do talk bunions sometimes.' She looked at the menu and said, 'I wonder if they've got any of that pate.'

'Let's look first at what we're having as the main course.' He opened the menu and said, 'Look, they've got smoked haddock.'

'Why is it smoked?'

'To give it a particular flavour.'

'That might be worth a try.' Reading the page of first courses, she asked, 'What are *vol au vents*? It sounds as if they have something to do with wind.'

'No, it's your rumbling tummy you can hear. They're puff pastry parcels filled, in this case, with creamed mushrooms and shrimps.'

'Oh, I like shrimps. Let's have that.'

He closed the menu and said, 'I bet Ever Ready Treadwell isn't as easy to please.'

She looked at him suspiciously. 'You're very interested in her all of a sudden.'

'Not really. She's a waste of time. I suspect she reported you because I told her to pick up her bag before someone else tripped over it. I could tell she resented it at the time.'

'I wouldn't be surprised. She's a spoilt brat.' She nodded, as if confirming her judgement, and then changed the subject by asking, 'What do you think about the Americans coming into the war?'

'It's just what we need. With Custer and the Seventh Cavalry on our side, Jerry doesn't stand a chance, and just let him try his tricks with Tom Mix of the Wild West.'

'You really do talk bunions, don't you?'

'Bunions?'

'My dad never uses language when me mam and me are around, so where some men might use a swear-word, he says, "bunions". Likewise, when he's really vexed, he says, "Fun and hi-jinks" or "blood and sand".'

The waiter arrived to take their order, so Ivor had time to think about Grace's latest revelation. When he'd ordered a bottle of Chablis and the first course, he said, 'I admire your dad.'

'Because he doesn't swear?'

'Not just that, but basically, because he lives by certain standards, and that's a measure of civilisation and how he sees it.'

She studied him and shook her head. 'I never know whether to take you seriously or not.'

'I mean it. I'll tell him that to his face one day.'

'He'll probably tell you you're talkin' bunions.'

'Well, he'll know best.'

Grace smiled as a thought came to her. 'You should meet my Uncle Trevor,' she said. 'He swears like a trooper. He's as bad as the sailors at work. Mind you, some of the girls can do their share an' all.'

'I don't believe it, Grace. Young ladies have never behaved like that in my experience.'

'There's nothin' ladylike about the ones I'm talkin' about, believe me.'

The band began to play 'Change Partners.' Ivor asked, 'Would you like to dance?'

'Aye, I would. I love this song.'

'So do I.' He led her on to the floor.

'I didn't like to ask my friend again for her perfume, so I don't smell nice tonight.'

'Yes, you do. You just don't smell of Chanel.'

'Worth.'

'I knew it was one of those French firms. Anyway, you smell of... let me think. I know, it's Lux toilet soap.'

'You're uncanny. In any case, though, it's a let-down.'

'Let me tell you, Grace, that nothing about you is a let-down.'

'Do you mean it?'

'You can depend on it.'

They danced to the end of the number and returned to their table.

'I think I'm getting the hang of recognising when you're being serious,' she said.

'Good. It saves me having to wave a green flag every time.'

'You give the impression that you don't take anything seriously, but just sometimes, you do.'

'First impressions can be deceptive.'

'Yes, they can, but I've rumbled you.'

The waiter brought the wine, and Ivor gave it his approval. When he'd gone, he said, 'Do you want to know what I like so much about you?'

'Tell me. I'm dying to know.'

'Give me your hand.'

'Oh, that again.' She let him take her hand.

'It's that you're completely genuine. There's nothing posed or pretentious about you.'

'Is that all?'

'No, but I'm going to tell you the other things one by one, in instalments. It could take some time.'

She gave him a down-to-earth look and said, 'There's no point in being anything but genuine. My Uncle Trevor, the one who swears a lot, says, "If you cannot be yoursel', divven't try to be any bugger else, because you'll find it even harder.'

'Wisely put.' He stroked her hand. 'Grace?'

'Yes?'

'Aren't you going home for Christmas?'

'No, I'm not. As I said, with only seventy-two hours, there's no point. I'd get home very late on Christmas Eve if I was lucky, and I'd have to set off back ridiculously early on Boxing Day morning.'

'I'm going to be here as well. I have to be on hand to take Divisions and serve lunch to the Lower Deck on Christmas Day, and I have to share watches with one of the subs, but we can sort something out. There's no point in us both being miserable.'

She looked at him with new interest. 'You know,' she said, 'it's not going to be such a lousy Christmas after all. In fact, there's just me birthday to worry about now, and worryin's not going to do any good, so that's okay.'

'When's your birthday?'

'The second of February.'

He nodded.

'What does that mean?'

'I'm just making a mental note to take you somewhere that's right for a special celebration.'

She let the waiter bring the first course, and then said, 'Do you reckon we're still going to be going out together in February?'

'I hope so. I haven't upset you yet, have I?'

'No, but there's time for me to upset you.' She tried some of the shrimp *vol au vent*, and her features became a study in ecstasy. Eventually, she said, 'This is lovely. It's been a string of new experiences so far, going out with you. I don't know what you're going to spring on me next.' She studied his face and said, 'The lads I work with would have jumped in there and said something rude. I'm sorry, I know you're not like that.'

'You didn't know me when I was on the Lower Deck. "Leading Lecher Loveday, licentious, lascivious and lewd," they called me.'

She gave him a dismissive look. 'I don't believe you were ever anything but the gentleman you are now.'

'You're very generous with your compliments, Grace.'

'I told Second Officer Barlow you were a gentleman and completely honourable.'

'Thank you. Did she used to drop her nether garment for a leg-up the promotion ladder as well?'

'I doubt it. I can't see her misbehaving. She was a lawyer before the war, a barrister.'

He nodded sagely. 'I imagine she talked her way into her commission,' he said.

'She can talk all right. I had to be very careful what I said to her.'

'What's her job?'

'She's in the Plot Room. You'll have seen Wrens in bell-bottomed trousers around Western Approaches HQ. Well, they all work in the Plot Room.'

'She likes dressing up, then, Second Officer Barlow? First a wig and gown, and then, I imagine, officers' trousers.'

She smacked his wrist playfully. 'She doesn't wear trousers. The girls do. It's because they have to go up ladders.'

He looked puzzled.

'The first time a Wren went up a ladder in a skirt,' she explained, 'the men in the Plot Room forgot all about the war, such was the scale of the distraction.'

'I see.'

She favoured him with a smile that was almost maternal, and said, 'You really are innocent, aren't you?'

'No.'

'No?' Her surprise was genuine.

'Remember what I said about first appearances.'

'All right, you've warned me.'

The time came eventually for them to leave. As they stepped outside the restaurant, Grace gasped. 'By heck, it's suddenly turned cold.'

'I thought of ordering a taxi, but we could have waited a long time for it.'

'Don't worry, I'll survive.' She took his arm and snuggled closer.

As they approached the Hotel Emilia, Ivor spotted a passageway between two buildings, one of them damaged, no doubt in the Blitz. 'Come in here,' he said, unbuttoning his greatcoat.

'What for?' Alarm showed in her features.

'Nothing naughty, I promise.'

She joined him hesitantly.

Holding his greatcoat open, he said, 'Come into my tent and let me warm you.'

She evidently thought his offer was innocent enough, because she said, 'All right,' and put her arms round his waist. After a couple of seconds, she realised the benefit. 'You're as warm as toast,' she said, 'lovely and warm. I wish I could take you into the Emilia.'

'Do you think anyone would notice?'

'Of course they would. The girls in my cabin don't miss a thing.'

He lowered his head to where her curls tumbled out from beneath the brim of her hat, and inhaled deeply. He asked, 'What kind of shampoo do you use?'

'Lux. At least, that's when I can get it. Why?'

'It smells divine.' He scented it again, and then, because it felt so natural, he kissed her gently on her cheek, relishing the soft smoothness of her skin.

She looked up to say, 'I keep wondering what the catch is with you, but I haven't found a one yet.'

'I have lots of dark secrets.'

'Go on, I'll believe you.'

He lowered his head again to tease her parted lips for the moment before ending the suspense with a long, searching kiss.

Eventually, she said plaintively, 'I hate to do this, especially now, but I have to report in.'

'Goodnight. I'll be in touch.'

'Goodnight, Ivor. Thanks for a lovely time.' She said it with much feeling.

As was his way, he waited outside until she was safely inside the building.

7

Ivor had never visited a pawnbroker, so he was quite fascinated by some of the wares in the window, and he was delighted when he found just the kind of thing he wanted. It was sad that people were obliged to part with their treasures, but maybe the original owner would have been pleased to know that the brooch was going to someone who would appreciate it. He asked the man to find a box so that he'd be able to wrap it properly and make it look like a present.

He arrived back at the ship with thirty minutes to spare before the Captain was due to go on leave.

'I've left you a list in the wardroom, Number One. Also, you have my home telephone number.'

'I shan't need that, sir,' Ivor assured him, 'but thank you. Just enjoy your leave.'

'Thank you, Number One.' He picked up his valise and gloves. 'Have a happy Christmas if you can.'

'I shall, sir. A happy Christmas to you, too.'

The Captain was gone only a short time, when the quartermaster's messenger came to the wardroom.

'There's a visitor for you, sir, a Pilot Officer Loveday.'

'Thank you, I'll be along.' Huw's arrival was not unexpected; Ivor had received a letter from him a month earlier, telling him about his posting to RAF Hooton Park in Cheshire. His brother had never been a ready correspondent, and one letter per month represented an effort on his part. That was unless he was short of money, and then he never hesitated to call on Ivor.

Ivor found him at the gangway, and the two shook hands warmly.

'Book Pilot Officer Loveday in as my guest, Quartermaster,' said Ivor.

'Aye, aye, sir.'

Huw looked bemused. 'Am I supposed to salute the quarterdeck or something?'

'No, only naval personnel are expected to do that. The Junior Service is exempt.'

Had the quartermaster not been aware of Huw's surname, he might easily have suspected he was related to Ivor, because the two were extraordinarily alike and separated by just three years.

'Come down to the wardroom and have a drink,' invited Ivor, leading the way down the ladder and pulling the wardroom curtain aside.

Leading Steward Denison appeared in the doorway, ready as ever to receive orders.

'Relax, Denison,' Ivor told him. 'We'll help ourselves. I know you've drawn the short straw, quite literally, but it's Christmas Eve, so take it easy.'

'Aye, aye, sir, and thank you, sir.'

Denison left, and Ivor showed Huw to a seat. 'What'll it be?'

'Beer, if you have one, please.'

'Coming up.' Ivor opened a bottle of Bass and poured it into a tumbler.

'I'm actually on my way to spend Christmas with a chap in my squadron and his family,' said Huw.

'Good for you.' As it was the first Christmas since the loss of their parents, he'd been concerned about Huw. Eric and his wife would be all right in Belfast, and he probably wouldn't spare too much thought for his younger brothers. He seldom did.

Huw asked, 'How are you? I mean, after the sinking. Are you really all right?'

'I was cold and wet for two days and nights, but men have fared worse. Far too many did.'

'I'm glad.' He added hastily, 'That you're all right, I mean.' It was a genuine comment, and having satisfied himself of his brother's wellbeing, Huw looked unnecessarily around him and said, 'Bit of a change, this? We used to be in the same business, you and I, hunting U-boats, but you seem to have diversified.'

'Oceanography,' confirmed Ivor, 'that's right.' Reluctant to discuss his work more than he had to, he wondered when Huw would get around to asking a favour. He was quite transparent.

'What will you be doing over Christmas? I mean, ship-minding, of course, but what else?'

'I'll be donning my dog collar in the morning. That's my first job.'

'What?'

'Not really, but I'll be taking church parade. Then the sub and I have to wait on the Lower Deck at lunchtime. After that, I have a visitor, and then on Boxing Day, who knows what might happen?'

'Good. I'm glad you won't be too bored.' Huw looked as he always did when he was about to make a request. Eventually, he said, 'Actually, I hate to ask you this, but Christmas has left me a bit short.'

'And you thought you'd come over and tap me for a sub?'

'Not exactly. Well, in a sense, I suppose, basically, yes. It's not the reason for my visit, of course....'

'Trot it out.'

Almost relieved, Huw asked, 'Could you lend me a fiver?'

'Seeing as it's Christmas, I think so.' Ivor took five one-pound notes from his wallet and gave them to his brother.

'Thanks, Ivor. That's really decent of you. I'll settle up with you next month.'

Ivor knew from long experience that 'next month' was a movable feast, but he made no comment, because it was clear that Huw had something else on his mind.

'I've taken over a rented cottage on the Wirral. It happens a lot on air stations. Chaps are posted and they hand things on, so to speak, when they leave.'

'So you've got a love nest near the station? No wonder you're strapped for cash.' He was teasing, but Huw had left himself wide open.

'It's not a problem. The rent is only twenty-two-and-six a week. Actually, you could use the place as a bolt hole when I'm not there. Other chaps use it from time to time, but you'd be first in line.'

'But I spend most of my time at sea, Huw.'

'I suppose you do.'

'You could call it an occupational hazard.'

'I'm afraid so, but the offer's there all the same.'

With the main business out of the way, Huw took his leave of Ivor and left for the railway station.

In the morning, after a particularly good breakfast, Ivor switched on the Tannoy to make the pipe, 'D' you hear there? D' you hear there? This is the First Lieutenant wishing everyone a happy Christmas. All hands muster in the forrard seamen's mess at oh nine hundred for Church Parade. Thank you. That is all.'

At oh eight fifty-five, he went to the mess to see that most of the remaining ship's company were present. When he was sure they were all mustered, he said, 'We'll begin with a reading. Any volunteers?' He imagined he would have to do it himself. Incredibly, however, one of the ordinary seamen raised his hand and said, 'I'll do it, sir.'

'Good man, Richardson. It's St Luke, Chapter Two, verses one to seven.' He handed him the Bible bookmarked at the appropriate place.

Richardson took the Bible, found his place and began reading confidently.' "And it came to pass in those days, that there went out a decree from Caesar Augustus, that all the world should be taxed...." '

It was evident from the start that the right man had volunteered, because Richardson was reading fluently and sensitively. He continued to the end.' "...And she brought forth her firstborn son, and wrapped him in swaddling clothes, and laid him in a manger; because there was no room for them at the inn." '

'Well done, Richardson. Let's say together The Lord's Prayer.'

The ship's company joined Ivor in saying the prayer, after which, he said, 'I think it's appropriate, considering where we are and what we're about to take part in, that we say the Naval Prayer. It's on page forty-two.' He led them in the prayer that sailors with any service behind them knew by heart.

' "O eternal Lord God, who alone spreadest out the heavens and rulest the raging of the sea; who hast compassed the waters with bounds until day and night come to an end: be pleased to receive into thy almighty and most gracious protection the persons of us thy servants and the Fleet in which we serve. Preserve us from the dangers of the sea and from the violence of the enemy; that we may be a safeguard unto our most gracious Sovereign Lord, King George and his Dominions and a security for such as pass on the seas upon their lawful occasions…." ' It seemed to Ivor that there was not one man present who did not find those words especially poignant at that time.

'Finally, turn to hymn number sixteen, "O Come, All Ye Faithful". Now, Leading Seaman Rogers, are you in good voice?' Rogers was known for his rich baritone voice.

'I hope so, sir.'

'So do we. We're depending on you. Will you lead us in the hymn?'

'Aye, aye, sir. I'll do my best.' Rogers sang the first line, and then everyone joined in and sang to the end. Christmas in *HMS Maynard/ Hosta* had officially begun.

At the pipe 'Hands to Lunch', Ivor dispatched Sub-Lieutenant Cartwright to the Chiefs' and Petty Officers' Mess to discharge his duty as temporary steward. He made himself responsible for the junior ratings, who were mustered again in the forrard mess.

There was a cheer as PO Barnes and his assistant bore in the turkey and everything that went with it.

'Would you like me to carve, sir?' PO Barnes picked up his carving knife and fork in readiness, because he knew what the answer would be.

'I've been rather hoping you would, PO. Yes, please.' Some operations called for expert training.

With that task delegated and accomplished, Ivor helped the portions on to the plates and passed them round. There was much good-humoured banter between him and the men, everyone knowing that normal discipline would be in force the next day, and the occasion was as merry as those necessarily left behind at Christmas could make it. Eventually, Ivor was free to join Sub-Lieutenant Cartwright in the wardroom for an extremely well-earned lunch.

As they sat down, Cartwright said, 'Actually, Number One, I wondered if I might go ashore this afternoon and, if possible, part of this evening.'

'It sounds like a reasonable request. I take it you have a lady in tow?'

The younger man blushed slightly. 'Yes, sir, a Wren from Western Approaches HQ. I know they're not supposed to socialise with officers, but it's not actually a King's Regulation or an Admiralty Instruction, is it, sir?'

'No, it's not, but the Wren hierarchy tend to get over-excited about that kind of thing. Tell her that if she's questioned by her officers, she's to tell them that you're old family friends from before the war.'

'Thanks, Number One. That sounds like good advice.'

'You're welcome, Brian. Actually, I'd like to stake a claim for tomorrow afternoon.'

'That's fine, sir. My party will be on the oh eight hundred to twenty hundred tomorrow.'

Ivor had to smile. Naval slang always sounded strange coming from a novice. 'I can see that you and I are going to work easily together, Brian.'

'Oh, I hope so, sir.'

'And I hope you and your party will have a splendid time this afternoon.'

Ivor saw his subordinate off the ship and stayed at the gangway. Grace would arrive soon, and he didn't want her made to feel awkward if the quartermaster challenged her. While he waited for her, he chatted with the quartermaster and learned that all three of the armed forces were represented by members of his family.

'They say variety is the spice of life, don't they, sir?'

'They do, and I'm inclined to agree with them.'

The quartermaster narrowed his eyes and looked along the dock. 'There's a lady heading this way, sir.'

'That'll be my guest.'

The quartermaster opened his book in readiness.

Ivor greeted Grace, who was carrying something in a paper carrier bag, and said to the quartermaster, 'Book Miss G. Headley in as my guest.'

'Aye, aye, sir.'

'And then nip down the ladder, if you will, and warn anyone around to keep clear for the next minute or so, as there's a lady coming down.'

'Aye, aye, sir.'

The Quartermaster carried out the order and returned. 'All clear, sir.'

'Thank you.' Ivor waited while Grace negotiated the ladder, and then climbed down after her. 'Happy Christmas,' he said, kissing her on the cheek.

'Happy Christmas. You remembered what I told you, as well, about skirts and ladders.'

'I don't know what I'd do without you, Grace. Before we go to the wardroom, though, I need to look in on the drunks and reprobates. Will you join me?'

'If you think it's safe.' She followed him to the forrard mess, from which the words of the ribald song 'The Harlot of Jerusalem' were emanating.

'Forgive the profanity,' he said. 'They're good lads, really.'

A half-hearted attempt was made to rise to attention, but Ivor waved them down. 'Relax,' he said. 'I'll be in the wardroom. Carry on enjoying yourselves, but don't do anything daft.'

Their look of innocence seemed to protest against the very suggestion; in fact, one man stood up, holding his glass of beer aloft, and said, 'Three cheers for the Jim… for the First Lieutenant and his lady.'

When the cheers had died down, Ivor said, 'Thank you, all of you. Enjoy the rest of the day.'

As they went to the wardroom, Ivor said, 'That must be the first time "three cheers" and "the First Lieutenant" have occupied the same sentence.'

'And "his lady", but it's Christmas, after all.'

He drew back the wardroom curtain for her. 'You look wonderful,' he said.

'Thank you, but it's the same dress that I wore the first time I went ashore with you.'

'You looked wonderful then and you look just as wonderful now. That must be true, because I'm the First Lieutenant, and if I say something, it's official. What would you like to drink?'

'Er, something harmless, please. I had a drink at the Wrens' quarters, so I don't want to overdo it.'

'Is orange blossom cordial acceptable?'

'Perfect.' Looking around her, she said, 'So this is the exclusive wardroom I've heard so much about.'

'It's not the most opulent example, but yes, this is it.'

While he was pouring a drink for her, she took a parcel from her bag. 'This is for you,' she said. 'It's just a little something to say it's Christmas.'

'What a surprise.'

'Don't get excited, Ivor. It's nothing extravagant.' She watched him open the parcel and take out a white towel. As he unfolded it, an embroidered design emerged. It was a skilful representation of a lieutenant's rings, and beneath them it said, *First Lieutenant*. 'I asked one of the officers what they appreciated most on an open bridge in stormy weather – I think you called it a "force ten" – and he suggested a dry towel round his neck.'

'It's wonderful, Grace. You couldn't have given me anything better.' He folded it carefully so that the embroidery lay uppermost. 'Did you embroider it yourself?'

'Of course I did. I haven't got a ship's company to do my bidding.'

'It's wonderful,' he repeated. Then, feeling in his pocket, he took out a tiny parcel and gave it to her.

'What's this?'

'Open it and find out. I hope you like it.'

She unfastened the string and took the box out of its wrapping. Then, when she opened it, she gave a gasp of delight. 'It's lovely,' she said. 'It's silver, isn't it?' She held it against her dress to see the effect. 'It's really lovely.'

'I'm glad you like it.'

'It looks like an officer's cap badge.'

'That's the idea. It's a Royal Navy sweetheart's brooch. You won't be allowed to wear it on your uniform, but it'll look very *chic* when you wear it with civvies.'

She examined it, still fascinated, and said, 'When I'm in uniform, I'm going to wear it on a chain that I've got, and I'll wear it underneath my shirt and everything, so that it's always there. Thank you, Ivor. It's really beautiful.'

He crossed to the curtain, checked that no one was around, and then returned to kiss her.

'Oh, Ivor,' she said when she was able to speak, 'I couldn't believe it when you walked me home after the pictures and you kissed me. I'd never been kissed that way before.'

'How do they usually do it?'

'Silly. I mean you did it properly, as if you meant it.'

'It wasn't difficult. I did mean it.' He kissed her again. 'Just so that I don't forget the procedure,' he explained.

'You do talk bunions.'

'Oh no, I don't.'

'Oh yes, you do.'

He performed a deliberate double-take and said, 'That reminds me. Do you fancy going to a pantomime?'

'Oh, yes. I've only ever been to one, an' that was ever such a long time ago.'

'Good, because I've got tickets for tomorrow's matinee. 'It's *Mother Goose*.'

Her smile widened. 'Oh, Ivor,' she said, 'this is going to be a Christmas to remember.'

8

Ivor looked up idly to the masthead, where the red ensign was now fluttering innocently. Until further notice, HM Ships *Hosta* and *Maynard* had become the *MV Snowdonia*.

'Lookouts,' said the Captain, 'no relaxing. Keep a sharp look out. Remember that the USA is in the war now, so even though we're approaching their territorial waters and we've almost reached our destination, there's always the risk of a U-boat.'

'Aye, aye, sir.'

'Aye, aye, sir.'

Ivor wriggled inside his duffel coat. December and January had brought a cold, wet spell that had a way of striking through the warmest of clothing and that had stayed with them throughout the Atlantic passage. He thought of Grace snuggling inside his greatcoat, and then dismissed the memory so that he could concentrate on his job.

Watching him wriggle, Newell asked, 'What's the story about the towel?' He'd seen Ivor fold it carefully before wrapping it round his neck.

'It was a Christmas present, sir. If it were a little warmer, I'd show you the embroidery. It's rather good.'

'Yes, leave it where it is for now and let it do its work. The lady obviously has your welfare at heart.' A gust of wind made him dash the rain from his eyes. 'It's been an easy trip up to now, Number One. You can't beat a drop of roughers for keeping our sparring partners submerged, but as we're here to do battle with them, the thought seems unworthy.'

'I imagine we'll get our chance soon enough, sir.'

'I wonder, Number One. It wouldn't surprise me if the convoy, unladen though it is, is proving to be an effective if unintentional decoy. The testing time is likely to be when we make the eastbound trip.'

The crossing had been so uneventful that, on the sixth day, the ship's company were allowed, by watches, to celebrate the dawning of 1942. Operational restrictions made it a muted celebration, but the occasion had been observed, and that meant a great deal to the men, particularly the Scots and those from north-east England, for whom the New Year meant so much. Again, Ivor found himself thinking of Grace and wondering if she'd managed to celebrate according to her Geordie tradition.

Following the loss of his parents in March and his own close call in August when *Taunton* was torpedoed, Ivor had lost interest in social occasions of any kind. All he wanted at first was to get back to sea, where he could hunt U-boats, so his meeting with Grace was all the more remarkable for the way it had changed his outlook. He had disguised his troubled state of mind so effectively that hardly anyone could be aware of it. He recalled telling Grace that not everyone was able to recognise the truth behind a first impression, but she'd seen through his casual facade, at least to some extent, and that was remarkable in so short a time.

In a few days, the ship docked in New York, and arrangements were put in hand for refuelling and the replenishment of stores. The Captain organised shore leave carefully, long experience having taught him that a reliable sailor could be a different character ashore. It was a busy time for the officers, however, and Ivor stayed on board to supervise refuelling and replenishment. Eventually, though, he managed to slip ashore, where he found a convenient taxicab.

'Where to, mack?' The driver spoke the words whilst chewing gum assiduously.

'I need a shop where they sell things such as make-up, perfume and that kind of thing.'

'You mean a department store. No sooner said than done.' The driver swung confidently into a stream of traffic, and asked, 'Are you from England?'

'That's right. I just hopped across the pond to do some shopping. Those things I mentioned are all rationed in Britain.'

'You don't say. It's true, then, what they've been saying.'

'What have they been saying?'

'About you having a tough time of it over there.'

'Things have been a shade difficult for more than two years now,' admitted Ivor.

'Oh, not as bad as they say, then.'

'Maybe not.' Ivor wondered if all Americans were strangers to understatement.

'Well, you can relax now the US has gotten itself involved. We'll take care of things from now on.'

'That's quite reassuring.' He watched the huge buildings go by, and wondered a little about the benefit of being a young nation with the facility to make straight roads and erect modern office blocks. There was something cosy and familiar about the old buildings in London, Newcastle and Liverpool, at least, those the Luftwaffe had left standing.

The driver pulled into the side of the road, announcing, 'Bloomingdale's, Third Avenue. You should find what you're looking for here.'

'Thank you.' Ivor paid the driver.

'Thanks, mack. Enjoy your visit to New York City.' Without waiting for a response, he drove off and picked up another fare a hundred yards or so further along the avenue.

On the ground floor of Bloomingdale's, the atmosphere was laden with the scent of cosmetics, and Ivor found an overwhelming array of counters, where perfume and make-up seemed to be the chief merchandise. At the first one he came to, a girl was helping someone choose a perfume. It was very convenient, because, in walking past the customer, he was able to rule out Chanel, although not because he disliked it; it appealed to him strongly, but it simply wasn't the one Grace had worn. He walked on, careless in his naivete, and dismissed two more fragrances. Eventually, however, he found a counter where the assistant was free.

'Good afternoon, sir,' she said. 'How may I help you?'

'Good afternoon. I'm looking for some perfume. Unfortunately, I don't know what it's called. All I know is that it's made by Worth, and I should be able to recognise the aroma.'

'I see, sir.' Her response was one of easy confidence, as if dealing with his kind of idiot presented her with no challenge. 'What do you think of this?' She held out her arm with her wrist turned upward, so that he could enjoy the benefit of her perfume.

'That's very nice indeed,' he said, taken completely by surprise. 'I don't think it's exactly what I'm looking for, but it's very similar.'

'In that case, sir, let's try one that's a little different.' She took a tester from the shelf behind her and transferred a little to a *mouillette*, which she held for a spell before offering it to him.

Ivor scented it and recognised at once the perfume Grace had been wearing. 'How clever you are,' he said. 'That's just the one I've been looking for.'

'Oh, I'm delighted for you, sir. Your lady obviously has immaculate taste. This perfume is called *Dans las Nuit*. That's French for "In the Night".'

'Yes, I thought it might be.'

'There's a range of sizes, sir.' She showed him the relevant boxes and told him the prices. He chose the twenty-five millilitre bottle, which was expensive, but he was to be at sea for a whole month, and was therefore unlikely to spend very much in that time.

'I'd like to buy some bits and pieces of make-up as well,' he said.

'Make-up, like perfume, is a very individual choice, sir. What is the lady's colouring?'

Ivor had been studying the salesgirl as discreetly as he could, and had anticipated the question. 'Her complexion is very similar to yours,' he said, 'and she has the same blue eyes. Her hair is slightly redder than yours. She's a strawberry blonde.'

'She sounds very pretty, sir, and she's obviously a special kind of lady. Let's look out a few items.'

Ivor spent the next ten minutes choosing lipstick, eye make-up and powder, after which he asked, 'Where can I buy stockings and a birthday card?'

'Hosiery is on the next floor up, sir, and gift stationery is at the other end of this floor, by the escalator.'

'I see, well, thank you for your assistance. You've been an invaluable help.'

The assistant waved his gratitude aside, saying, 'It's an honour to serve an officer of the British Mercantile Marine, sir.'

'It probably is,' he agreed, 'but I'm in the Royal Naval Volunteer Reserve.'

Unabashed, the assistant replied, 'You're just as welcome, sir.'

Thus assured, Ivor went in search of a birthday card, gift wrapping paper and the item that was spoken of in awed whispers in Britain: namely, nylon stockings. Silk, and even lisle stockings had become almost impossible to find, and the new American invention of nylon sounded fabulous but so exotic as to be beyond anyone's reach. He eventually left the building with little more than his taxi fare to the docks, but he was very satisfied with his afternoon's work.

On the 16th of January, the convoy left New York, heading out into the Atlantic to form up in accordance with the complex arrangements laid down in the Captains' Conference. *Hosta* was once again flying the red ensign as the *MV Snowdonia*. Ivor learned that several of the merchant vessels in the convoy had been sunk on the way to New York by U-boats, which seemed to bear out Newell's theory regarding *Hosta*'s temporary immunity from attack.

As the convoy progressed further eastward, *Hosta* slipped ever further astern, posing as a 'straggler' unable to keep up with the convoy. Her tactic was rewarded on the eighth day, when the port lookout reported, 'U-boat bearing red oh-four-oh, sir! Range eight hundred yards!'

All eyes moved to the reported bearing, where a submarine was breaking surface. The Captain pushed the Action Stations button, sending each member of the crew to his allotted station. Two seamen stood by the mast, one ready to bend on the white ensign when the other struck the red ensign. Ivor could see the gun and torpedo crews waiting in readiness.

As the German gun crew appeared on the casing, Newell ordered, 'Let Go!' Immediately, the red ensign came hurtling down to be replaced by the white ensign of the Royal Navy, the screens concealing the guns and torpedo tubes fell away, range takers reported the range, and the gunlayers trained their weapons.

Ivor took the handset and ordered, 'All guns, independent rapid fire! The machine gunner abaft the bridge was already raking the U-boat's casing, and the pom-pom crew were firing as well. Several enemy sailors already lay dead or wounded.

'Come on,' urged Ivor, seeing more enemy gunners take over the U-boat's gun.

As if to make up for the earlier hitch, which had not been their fault, the crew of 'Y' Gun were first to fire, their shot falling several yards short of the target. 'A' Gun joined in, and then 'Y' Gun scored a direct hit beneath the conning tower. Another shell struck the U-boat further forrard and it settled in the water, sinking rapidly.

Ivor ordered, 'Cease firing! Check, check, check! His order was unnecessary in the circumstances, as the gun crews, mesmerised by the result, were making no effort to fire, a fact that Newell was quick to point out.

'I realise that, sir,' said Ivor. 'I just hate shoddy workmanship.'

Newell took over the Tannoy handset. 'D' you hear there? This is the Captain speaking. *Hosta* has just destroyed her first U-boat since coming out of retirement. Well done, everyone. We shall celebrate the milestone in the usual way when we reach Liverpool. Stand by to pick up survivors and then secure from Action Stations. That is all.' Turning to Ivor, he said, 'Well done, Number One. You trained them well.'

There was only a handful of survivors, who were taken down to the cells to be given dry clothing and a tot of rum. Ivor spent the remainder of the watch thinking about the rest of the U-boat's crew. For all he'd suffered at the enemy's hands, a sailor was still a human being, regardless of his nationality.

—⧓—

Grace had delivered a pile of encrypted signals to the Wireless Telegraphy room and was making her way back to Coding, when she heard two officers, both of them senior and talking with muted excitement. One said, 'Have you heard? *Hosta*'s got a U-boat!'

Grace already knew that; she'd decrypted *Hosta*'s signal when it came in, but it was the other officer's response that set her wondering.

'Bloody good show,' he said. 'Mind you, it's important that we keep it to ourselves. We don't want hysterical, cheering Wrens lining the dock when she comes in. Whatever else happens, we've got to keep her *in cognito* intact.'

His insulting reference to Wrens was all that Grace had come to expect from some officers and ratings, but the remark about *HMS Hosta* having an *in cognito* puzzled her.

She walked into Coding and saw Beryl from her cabin. She was a telegraphist and she'd just brought some more signals to be decrypted.

'Hello, Grace,' she said. 'Have you got your leave sorted out yet?'

'Yes, I've got from the first of February to the fifth.'

'So you can have your birthday at home after all.'

'Aye, it'll make up for Christmas, although I'm not complainin' about that.' Smiling shyly, she said, 'It was nice enough.'

'That sweetheart brooch he gave you was a lovely present.'

'The whole of Christmas was. Even havin' me Christmas pud served by Ever Ready Treadwell was a treat, but bein' with Ivor was better.'

—⧓—

When the mail came aboard in Liverpool, Ivor didn't have to look far for an envelope addressed in Grace's handwriting, because it was the only letter addressed to him. He opened it with boyish eagerness.

Dear Ivor,

I hope you get home safely. I'm away on leave from the 1st to the 5th of February. As you know, it's my birthday on the 2nd, and my mam and dad will be pleased I can get home for it. They missed me at Christmas. If you get in while I'm away, I'm sorry, but I'll be back on the 5th. Mind you, for all I know, you could be away for months on end.

Take care of yourself, and thank you for a Christmas I'll never forget.

Lots of love,
Grace XXX

It was the second, and she would be back on the fifth. It was three days away, but he might be back at sea before then. He put the letter away and took down his cap. The Captain was about to pipe 'Up Spirits!' Each man would receive a double tot of rum to celebrate the U-boat's sinking, and Ivor would have to supervise that.

9

Ivor retrieved a cardboard box from the husbandry store. It was too bad that the label read *Bluebell Metal Polish*, but boxes were in short supply. It would do the job, anyway. He put the stockings in first, and then the perfume, soap, shampoo and make-up. Before sealing the box, he wrote his birthday greeting in the card and put that inside. Finally, he wrapped it in the paper he'd bought in New York and wrote a label, which he stuck on with Gloy from the Pay Office.

When he arrived at the Hotel Emilia, the armed sentry on the door stood aside to let him in.

The old reception desk had evidently become the office, through which, according to the notice above it, all communications must be made.

A rather plain PO Wren came to attention and saluted.

'Good afternoon. I'm delivering a parcel for Wren Headley.'

'Wren Headley, sir?'

'Nine four eight three six two seven,' he confirmed, pretending to read it from a scribbled note.

'Excuse me, sir.'

The voice came from behind him, and he turned to see a Wren, who must have entered the building immediately after him.

'Did you say, "Wren Headley", sir?'

'Yes.'

'She's in my cabin, sir, but she's away on leave. Would you like me to take it up for her?'

'That would be most kind of you. Thank you very much.'

'It's no trouble, sir. I'm going up there now.' She picked up the parcel. 'Wren Headley will be back on Thursday. I'll see she gets this.'

'Thank you again. Don't try to salute with your hands full.' It was a mistake that very junior Wrens and ratings sometimes made, and he wanted to save her embarrassment.

'No, sir.' She made for the stairs.

Noticing that the PO Wren was eyeing him suspiciously, he said as he turned to leave, 'In case you're wondering, Wren Headley is my second cousin.'

'I see, sir.' Seemingly satisfied, she saluted him.

The sentry on the door also gave him a strange look.

'Your right gaiter is an inch higher than the left,' Ivor told him, pointing to the offending accessory.

'Sorry, sir.' The man crouched to make the adjustment.

On Thursday, the Captain told him that the ship was stood down until the following week. It was good news, and the same Wren who had taken Grace's parcel brought him some more when she reported at the gangway.

'Hello,' he said.

'Good afternoon, sir,' she said, saluting him. 'There's a letter for you.'

'Thank you.' He took the letter, which was addressed, as he had suspected, in Grace's hand. 'Thank you for bringing it.'

'It's no trouble, sir.' She saluted again and made for the dock entrance.

Ivor took the letter down to the wardroom to open it.

Dear Ivor,

I'm sorry I wasn't here. I've just returned from leave, and Beryl offered to deliver this note to you, so please excuse the scribble.

Thank you, thank you, thank you for the most amazing birthday present I've ever had in the whole of my life! I still cannot believe it. I never, never, never imagined I would ever own nylon stockings, not to mention the make-up and perfume and things! You are... I'll tell you what you are when I see you. If you're still going to be here and you can get away, I finish at eighteen hundred tomorrow. Let me know when and where to meet you.

Lots of love,

Grace XXX and one more X

P.S. As it's being delivered by hand, this note is private! XXX!

'Ivor, it's so good to see you again!' She took his arm and made a gesture of defiance by reaching up and kissing his cheek, even though their meeting place was within yards of the Hotel Emilia.

'You're wearing the perfume,' he said. 'Good.'

'Where did you buy it, Ivor? The card came from America. It said so on the back.'

'Everything came from Bloomingdale's in Third Avenue, New York, except that everyone has to say, "New York, New York" over there.'

'Why do they say it twice?'

'Because New York City is in New York State.'

'That's daft,' she said, shaking her head at the apparent nonsense. 'Nobody says, "Durham, Durham." It's either "Durham City" or "County Durham". Anyway, where are we going?'

'Philharmonic Hall. It's not far.'

Gripping his arm in her excitement, she asked, 'Are we going to a concert?'

'Yes, and the guest pianist is Eileen Joyce.'

'Wonderful. She's amazing.' After a while, she asked, 'Ivor?'

'That's me.'

'What were you doing in America?'

'Shopping. With your birthday coming up, I wangled a trip to the Big Apple. That's what they call it over there, although I never saw an apple of any size all the time I was there.'

'You're not going to tell me, are you?'

'No, I'm not.'

'Okay. 'Nough said.' Her curiosity soon returned. 'What did the assistant in the store say when you asked for all that stuff? I bet she was surprised at a fella buying those things.'

'She said you must be "a special kind of lady".'

'What did you say?'

'I said, "Yes, the best kind".'

'Haddaway. Anyway, how did you know which perfume to ask for?'

'I got all the assistants to line up, each wearing a different perfume, and I walked along the line with my nose twitching until I found the right one.'

'I might have known you wouldn't give me a sensible answer.'

'I went to a lot of trouble to find that perfume,' he protested, 'but I had to.'

'Why?' She was gripping his arm again.

'Simply because you're the best kind of special lady.'

'Well, however you did it, I'm very grateful.'

'I know.' He stopped.

'Why have we stopped?'

'Because we're going to cross the road. Philharmonic Hall is just across there.' He pointed to show her.

'I've never been to a concert in my life.'

'Well then, bonny lass, we're about to put that right.'

It was one of a series of concerts arranged to take entertainment to hard-hit areas of the country. Although the Blitz had been over for some time, Liverpool was still struggling to recover after the damage that had been inflicted, and Eileen Joyce was one of those performers throwing themselves enthusiastically into the task.

Grace had never heard Cesar Franck's *Symphonic Variations*, but she was immediately captivated by the work and by Eileen Joyce's sparkling and sensitive performance. Beethoven's *'Egmont' Overture* and Mozart's *'Jupiter' Symphony* also provided a sense of wonder and perpetuity after the horrors of the Blitz.

As they walked back afterwards, Grace said, 'Me tummy's rumblin' again.'

A bus ground past them in the blackout, and Ivor said, 'I know, I just heard it.'

'Silly. Wasn't Eileen Joyce wonderful, though?'

'Yes, it was an excellent concert.'

After a minute or so, she asked, 'Ivor?'

'I'm still here.'

'Do you know a ship called *Hosta*?'

He stiffened momentarily. 'I've heard of her,' he said. 'I can't say I know anyone who's served in her, but you know what they say about the Navy being a large family and a small world.'

'What kind of ship is she?'

'A sloop, I think.'

'They say she sank a U-boat.'

'Yes, I heard something about it.' Changing the subject deliberately, he asked, 'Shall we stop for fish and chips?'

'Again?' They'd stopped at a fish and ship café after the pantomime. 'Treats are coming thick and fast, but I'm game if you are.' Presently, she asked, 'Ivor?'

'That's me.' He hoped she wasn't going to ask him about *Hosta* again.

'You know how you gave me that sweetheart brooch at Christmas?'

'Yes, have you lost it already?'

'No,' she protested, 'it's precious, and I wear it all the time. I just wonder if that's how you think of me.'

'What, careless and losing things?'

'No. You're infuriating sometimes.' She tried again. 'I've been wondering if you think of me that way.' To discourage further silly answers, she prompted, 'I mean, as a sweetheart.'

'Of course I do. I don't go shopping in New York for just anyone, you know. Ask any of my former conquests and they'll tell you the same story. They've all begged me to do it, but without success.'

'You're still joking. Have you ever given anyone else a sweetheart brooch?'

'Of course not.'

'But you must have known lots of girls.'

'Thousands.' He saw that she was becoming increasingly

impatient, so he said, 'But I didn't give any of them a sweetheart brooch, because I wasn't in love with any of them.'

She stopped and gripped his arm. 'Are you saying what I think you're saying?'

'I know I'm not saying it very well, but yes. I can't help it. You see, it's because you're such a special kind of lady.'

'Oh, Ivor.'

A voice from behind them said, 'What do you think yer doin', like? People are wantin' to get past.'

'Sorry. Feel free to play through.'

'What d' yer think this is, like? A golf course?'

'No, you're right. My mistake.'

As the couple walked on, the man said, 'Bloody officers. Just 'cause he's got a bit of gold braid on his shoulders, he thinks he can do what he likes.'

Ivor steered Grace towards the fish-and-chip café where they'd eaten after the pantomime. It was quite full, but people were leaving.

Grace asked, 'Do you think we'll get a table?'

'I'll commandeer one.'

'Don't be daft.'

'I've got gold braid on my shoulders, Grace, and I can do as I please.'

A counter assistant saw them and said to Ivor, 'Give me your order, an' I'll bring it to yer when it's ready, love.'

'Haddock and chips twice, please,' he asked.

'Right yer are, love. Where are yer sittin'?'

Ivor pointed to a recently-vacated table, and the assistant nodded.

He asked Grace, 'Would you like a glass of Tizer?'

'Fish and chips wouldn't be the same without it.'

Ivor went to the counter and returned with two tumblers of Tizer. 'Never say I don't know how to show a special dame a good time,' he said, adding, 'You can tell I've been to America, can't you?'

'Yes, I can, and I'm happy enough.'

'I can see that.'

'Well, it's not every day a girl gets told what every girl wants to hear.'

'I suppose not. Maybe I should have told you earlier.'

'Do you mean you've been holdin' out on me?'

He considered the charge and said, 'Not "holding out", exactly, just waiting for a suitable time.'

'Well, I'm glad you found a one.' She was unable to say more, because the assistant arrived with their order.

'Thank you,' said Ivor.

'You're welcome, love.'

When she'd gone, Ivor said, 'Things have been so hectic, I haven't asked you about your leave.'

'Aye, it was nice to be home again, an' our Jack had leave as well, so we were all together, for once.'

'I shouldn't ask this, but was it your twenty-first birthday, by any chance?' He'd wondered about that when he was choosing her card at Bloomingdale's.

'No, that was last year. I'm an old woman of twenty-two now.'

'You're wearing well.'

'I hope so. How old are you?'

'As of last August, twenty-three. I spent my twenty-third birthday in the middle of the Atlantic.'

'Bad luck.'

'It was,' he agreed. 'I was on a Carley raft with a lot of others.' He didn't know why he was telling her that. The words just seemed to tumble out. 'We were cold and wet, and we weren't inclined to put a huge bet on being picked up, but we were, so everything was all right, at least for some of us.'

'I didn't know.'

'There was no reason why you should.'

'How many survivors were there?'

'Out of a hundred and fifty, twenty-one survived.'

She reached for his hand and squeezed it. 'Ivor,' she said, 'I'd no idea.'

'It's all in the past.' It was what he kept telling himself.

Tactfully, she avoided any further mention of the sinking, and the atmosphere lightened to the extent that, by the time they left the café, they were both in good spirits.

Ivor was experiencing a fair measure of guilt, however, and he raised the subject when they were approaching their usual place fifty yards short of the Emilia.

'I'm sorry I brought up that business of the *Taunton*'s sinking,' he said. 'I never intend to. It just comes out sometimes, like a cuckoo out of a clock.'

'You can talk about it anytime with me,' she assured him. 'It's what I'm here for.'

'Is it?'

'Well, one of the things, anyway.'

He kissed her at some length, partly out of appreciation and partly because he found it difficult not to.

'It's just a shame that we've nowhere where we can be private,' she said.

'Actually, we have.' He'd not given it much thought until then. As he'd told Huw, he spent most of his time at sea, but it might be a possibility.

'Where?'

'My brother rents a cottage on the Wirral. It's only a short train ride from here.'

'How short?'

'Three-quarters of an hour at the most.'

Mentally subtracting an hour-and-a-half from a typical evening, she said, 'It doesn't leave us a lot of time.'

'No, it's all down to chance. If you could get forty-eighters when I'm alongside, we could do it.'

'It's a lot to ask after five days' leave, but I might get a stand-down sometime.'

'That's true.' A night off would be a luxury. 'Let's work on that, then.' Thinking quickly, he said, 'If it turns out to be awful, we can always de-camp and get a couple of rooms in a hotel.'

They kissed again, and then something occurred to Ivor that he thought he should mention. 'According to Huw, the cottage has two bedrooms.'

'Uh-huh?'

'Yes, I thought you'd like to know that.'

'You're a gentleman, Ivor. Give us a kiss before I go inside.'

They kissed again with the urgency that lovers feel when time is short and their next meeting seems an age away.

'Now tell us again, what you said tonight.'

'You're some special kind of lady, Grace, and I love you.' He felt easier now he'd said it.

'You're a lovely fella, Ivor. I love you too.' With exactly one minute to spare, she slipped away to report in, and he watched until she was safely inside.

10

The next convoy arrived in mid-Atlantic, escorted by ships of the Royal Canadian Navy, whose crews greeted their British counterparts before heading back to Nova Scotia.

The mid part of the Atlantic was the most dangerous, as it was beyond the range of land-based anti-submarine aircraft, and aircraft carriers were in short supply, so *Hosta* remained visibly detached from the convoy.

They were actually only four days from home when the starboard lookout raised the alarm, and the Action Stations klaxon sounded.

The Captain gave the order to Let Go, and the ship's company, went about its meticulously rehearsed drill.

Ivor checked quickly that the white ensign was at the masthead before ordering, 'All guns, independent rapid fire!'

The U-boat replied with its machine-guns whilst others rushed to bring the eighty-eight into action.

Taking the handset from Ivor, the Captain ordered, 'Fire one torpedo!'

Sub-Lieutenant Moore's torpedo crew, who had been tracking the U-boat, fired immediately. The range was only about seven hundred yards, and Ivor could see the reaction on the U-boat's casing when they spotted the torpedo's wake heading towards them. The U-boat's captain tried to turn to port, but it was too late. Some of the crew were already in the water, swimming away from the doomed vessel.

The torpedo struck its target beneath the conning tower, and the smoke resulting from the explosion made it impossible to see anything at first. When it cleared, the broken halves of the

U-boat were disappearing beneath the waves. Incredibly, three men could be seen, still swimming towards *Hosta*. Ivor ordered calmly, 'All guns, cease firing. Check, check, check.' As an aside to the Captain, he said, 'With their luck, I'd like them to mark my race card sometime.'

'Stop engine. Away the sea boat's crew and pick up survivors.' The Captain watched 'A' Gun's crew carry a man away from the gun and lay him carefully on the deck. 'There's a casualty, Number One,' he said. 'I can't make out who it is.'

Ivor ordered, 'Stretcher party to 'A' Gun.' Switching off the Tannoy, he said, 'It's Petty Officer Thompson, sir.'

Two men arrived with a stretcher, but a leading seaman was shaking his head with obvious finality. Looking up to the bridge, he said to Ivor, 'He's dead, sir.' The leading sick berth attendant, who had arrived on the deck examined Thompson and confirmed the diagnosis.

When the sea boat returned, a deck party helped the U-boat's survivors aboard. One of them was an officer, and he was visibly angry. A seaman came to the bridge to report to the Captain, 'The officer wants to speak to you, sir. I think he wants to make a complaint.'

'Bring him up here and tell the others to take the rest of the prisoners below.'

'Aye, aye, sir.'

'Chief Petty Officer Danby?'

'Sir?'

'See that the ratings guarding the prisoners are armed,' he said, handing him the key to the firearms cabinet, 'give the prisoners dry clothing and lock them in the cells.'

'Aye, aye, sir.' CPO Danby stood aside as the German officer was brought to the bridge.

'*Herr Kapitän-Leutnant*,' he said, clearly bristling, I am *Oberleutnant Zur See* Bäcker, and I have the strongest possible complaint to make.'

'Have you, by Jove? Oh, CPO Danby?'

'Yes, sir?'

'See that the prisoners get a tot. It'll drive out the cold after their ducking. It's also likely to be their last proper drink until after the war's over.'

'Aye, aye, sir.'

Returning his attention to Bäcker, he said, 'Very well. Let me hear your complaint.'

With unabated anger, Bäcker said, 'You are guilty of an act of piracy, *Herr Kapitän-Leutnant*.'

'Nonsense. It was a legitimate *ruse de guerre*. For what it's worth, I held my fire until the white ensign was flying and your gun crew was in position. What I did was a damned sight more sporting than torpedoing defenceless merchantmen from beneath the waves.' As a sop, he said, 'When I conduct the burial service for the member of my crew who was killed, I shall invite you to honour your dead countrymen.'

'That, *Herr Kapitän-Leutnant*, is the very least you can do.'

Unabashed, Newell said, 'You speak English remarkably well.'

'I attended Oxford University for some years before the war, *Herr Kapitän-Leutnant*.'

'Oh, what subject did you read?'

'International Law, *Herr Kapitän-Leutnant*.'

'Really? You didn't learn much, did you?' Addressing the rating who had brought the officer to the bridge and who was still standing woodenly to attention, he said, 'Take this officer below and hand him over to CPO Danby.'

'Aye, aye, sir.'

'It was a great shame about PO Thompson, Number One.'

'Yes, sir. After the Wrens' tea party episode, I told him he would have to work hard to make me think better of him, and I think he achieved that with his contribution today.'

'Yes, but don't dwell on it, Number One. It doesn't help.'

'Aye, aye, sir.'

Newell switched on the handset. 'D' you hear there? D' you hear there? This is the Captain speaking. In case it's escaped your notice, we've just sunk another U-boat. Well done, everyone, and thank you for your efforts. We shall celebrate properly on our return. Secure from Action Stations. That is all.'

The burial at sea of PO Thompson was a poignant affair, his being the first life to be lost, and Lt Cdr Newell allowed an interval of ten minutes before permitting Bäcker to pay his respects to the dead submariners. It was as well, because Bäcker's ranting performance would not have been out of place in a comic opera. Ivor's German was fairly basic, but he made out the word '*emordet*', meaning 'murdered' no fewer than three times, or nine, if he counted the slavish echoes from the two ratings. They had to be given their opportunity to take their leave of their comrades, however, although it was a relief, on their return to Liverpool, to see them marched away from Salthouse Dock under an armed guard.

Ivor sent his customary note to Grace via the official mail and was delighted to receive her prompt, if guarded, reply.

Dear Ivor,

Welcome back! I've got a stand-down on Friday, the 20th, from 1800. Peg-in on double 2. Let me know about bait and that. Hope you've got the hooks.

Lots of love,

Grace XXX

He had to give her credit for ingenuity. It wasn't the kind of cypher she encountered in her work, but it would probably fool the censor. 'Peg-in on double 2' might not mean a thing to the ambitious third officer, but to him it meant that Grace had to report for duty on Sunday the 22nd. He would find out the time later. 'Bait and that' meant food and anything else she should bring. Getting 'the hooks' had to mean that she hoped he would understand her code.

He replied immediately.

Dear Grace,

It's good to be back. I've got the pegs for winter fishing and the hooks aren't a problem. I'll take care of bait. Just bring the usual equipment.

Lots of love,

Ivor XXX

For maximum security, he dropped it in the mail box at the Hotel Emilia.

11

Grace was on time as usual, and carrying a large, blue, canvas valise, which Ivor took from her. It was surprisingly light compared with the two he was already carrying, but it seemed to him that, whilst women's clothes were more numerous, they were usually lighter than men's.

'I'm glad you understood my gibberish,' she said. 'I didn't want to go into detail about watches in case Ever Ready tried to change things just out of devilment. As things stand, she thinks I'm going fishing. She's not very bright.'

'We are going fishing. I hope you've brought something warm to sit on. The banks of the Mersey can be like an iceberg at this time of the year.'

'Haddaway.' She took his arm and snuggled closer to him as she usually did. 'Will it be all right, like, for me to be in the same train compartment as you?'

'As we're cousins, I should think so.'

'Cousins, eh?'

'That's what I told the PO Wren when I delivered your present.'

'Which one? The one who looks as if nothing nice has ever happened to her?'

'She did look a bit passed-over, now you mention it.'

They arrived at the station, and Ivor studied the departures. 'Platform seven,' he said.

'Ellesmere Port?'

'That's right. Let's find a seat.' To avoid any delay, he'd bought their tickets beforehand.

They walked along the outside of the train until they found a compartment with empty seats, and they climbed in.

'You said not to worry about bait,' she whispered as he put her valise on the rack, 'but what are we doing for food?'

'I've brought it.' He indicated the bag between his feet.

'You're joking.'

'No, I have my sources.'

There was a slamming of doors, the guard blew his whistle, and the train pulled out.

'I'm glad we got seats,' she said. 'It's rare nowadays. I had to stand most of the way to Newcastle.'

'I bet there were men in some of the seats,' he remarked. 'The age of chivalry has passed into history.'

'Yes, there were, and I agree, it has.'

He placed his cap strategically so that he could hold her hand beneath it. After more than a month at sea, it was a welcome feeling.

In just over forty minutes they walked out of the station.

Grace shivered and said, 'It's turned bitter again. Where do we go now, Ivor?'

'Follow me.' With their feet crunching the frost that covered the pavement, he led her past three streets until he stopped beside a row of cottages. 'Number fourteen,' he said, reading his notes by flashlight. 'This is number twenty-two. Okay, twenty... eighteen... sixteen.... Here we are.' He put the bags down and knocked on the door.

Grace asked, 'Will there be somebody at home?'

'I hope so.'

The door opened and Huw welcomed him inside.

Grace followed him into the cottage, drawing the blackout behind her.

'Grace, this is my little brother Huw.'

'Grace,' said Huw with a touch of awe, 'you're even prettier than Ivor told me you were. I have to admit, I didn't believe him, but now I know I was wrong.'

'Haddaway, man.' She shook his hand all the same.

'I've lit the fire, there'll be hot water soon, and you'll find coal in the shed round the back. There's a slot meter for the gas, as I told you. The kitchen's through there.' He pointed to the back of the house, and then, remembering something else, he said, 'Oh, and you'll probably need to air the bedding. Upstairs hasn't been used for a while. Leave it when you go. I'll take it to the station laundry.'

'Thanks, Huw. I think you've covered everything.'

'Good. Must get back to the station before everything gets eaten. Shove the key through the letterbox. I've got a spare. Lovely to meet you, Grace.'

'And you.' She shook his hand again and he left.

As he closed the door, she said, 'What a lovely fella, and he's so organised.'

'He usually organises things so that I pay the bill, but never mind.'

They looked around the room, which was basically furnished with rugs, a moquette-covered sofa and an armchair. The wallpaper was dated, but that didn't concern them. All in all, it seemed to provide all they needed.

Food was the next consideration. 'I brought eggs, bacon, bread and all the basic stuff,' he said, but as far as this evening's concerned, I think we should try that place we passed on the way from the station. It looked all right.'

'Anywhere that sells food will satisfy me for now,' she told him. Then, performing a double-take as she checked the bag of food again, she said, 'There's four weeks' egg rations in here, man. Where on earth did you find 'em?'

'Denison gave me them.'

'Who?'

'Leading Steward Denison. I told you about him.'

'I remember now, but where does he find fresh eggs?'

'When we're at sea, we have powdered eggs, the same as you do, but there's a time when we're in harbour, when he can lay his hands on all kinds of good things. I ask no questions, and he does like to keep his first lieutenant happy.'

'I bet you terrorise the poor man.'

'I have to. It's part of my job.'

She treated him to the look that told him he was talking bunions, and said, 'Howay, pet. Let's go to that café before everybody else does.'

⸻

As they sat together in front of the fire, thawed and glowing after their foray in the bitter cold outside, Grace looked down at her uniform tunic and skirt. 'I suppose I should get out of this uniform,' she said, showing little enthusiasm for leaving the fireside.

'Why not? Make yourself at home.'

She moved away from him, resolved to do the sensible thing. 'Do you mind if I change into me pyjamas?'

'Not in the least.'

She hesitated. 'I haven't got a dressing gown. I usually use my coat.'

'Here.' He opened his valise and took out his dressing gown. 'Use this one.'

'What will you do?'

'I don't need it. I'm a hardy son of the sea, at least until the stumps are drawn and I have to go back to being a reporter.'

'You're a lovely fella. Thank you.' She took the dressing gown and her valise upstairs to change. Ivor, who was feeling the benefit of the fire, removed his jacket, collar and tie. Then, to make things cosier, he put out the gaslight, so that the only illumination came from the flickering glow of the fire.

After a while, Grace came downstairs with a bundle of sheets and blankets. 'Why-yer-bugger, man,' she said, 'it's like a butcher's store room upstairs. There's frost on the insides of the windows. I've brought these things down to air.'

'Good thinking.'

As if noticing for the first time that the light was out, she asked, 'Has the gas run out? I've got two bob in me purse upstairs.'

'No, it's nicer like this. Don't you think so?'

'Well, I can just about see what I'm doing.'

He watched her lower the creel on its pulley and then arrange the bedding on it before hoisting it again to the ceiling and securing the cord on the wall cleat.

'A seaman would have struggled to do that job better than you,' he commented.

'Aye well, if you'd dried washin' as many times as I have, you'd be handy at it an' all.' With that job out of the way, she joined him again on the sofa.

'Mm,' he murmured like a purring cat, 'you feel soft and snuggly.'

'Are you sure you don't want your dressing gown back?'

'Absolutely. If I'm cold, I'll get into it with you.'

'If I'm cold enough, I might let you.' She was quiet for a while, and then she asked, 'Ivor, where are we going to sleep tonight? It's far too cold upstairs.'

'You can stay down here if you like. I'll go upstairs.'

'No, you can't, man. You have no idea what it's like. You'll freeze to death.'

'All right, we'll both sleep down here. The fire's going well and there's plenty coal in the box, so we'll be all right.' He kissed her again. 'You take the sofa, and I'll sleep in the armchair or on the deck. I'm used to roughing it.'

'Are you sure?'

'Positive.'

Evidently satisfied that he wasn't going to suffer too much discomfort on her account, she stopped worrying, relaxed and began to return his attentions.

After a while, he asked, 'Are you warm enough?'

'Aye, this dressing gown of yours is very warm.'

'I'll take your word for it. I never wear it.'

'Why not?'

'When I'm on board ship,' he explained, 'I just fall into my bunk and sleep soundly until I'm shaken. There's no time for niceties like dressing gowns, slippers, nightcaps, nightshirts, bed warmers and smoking jackets.' On a whim, he said, 'You can keep it if you like it.'

She looked surprised for a second and said, 'I couldn't possibly accept it. If I turned up with this, the other girls would be sure I'd been up to no good.' Loosening the cord, she opened it slightly. 'It *is* very warm,' she remarked, 'but thank you, anyway.'

Kissing her, he slipped his hand inside the gown to stroke her through the flannelette of her pyjama jacket.

'Hey,' she said, 'that's me under there.'

'What, here?' Between the buttons of her jacket, he stroked her naked midriff with his fingertips.

'Yes, behave yourself.' It was the mildest of protests, and she made no effort to repeat it, but joined him in a long, searching kiss, during which he unfastened two buttons so that he could explore further.

'Ivor, that's naughty. Anyway, you'll find I'm a disappointment in the bust area, if that's where your mind's leadin' you, an' somethin' tells me it is.'

'Nonsense, they're exquisite.'

Between kisses, she said, 'You can't possibly know that, and they're tiny, so there.'

'I don't believe you.'

'That's up to you, but I've known them all their lives, so I should know.'

Unfastening another button and running his hand round her back to hold her closer, he kissed her repeatedly, at the same time enjoying the satin feel of her skin against the palm of his hand.

'Just what are you doing behind my back?'

'Sorry.' He changed his route, earning an immediate reaction.

'Hey.'

'I told you they were perfect.'

'Ivor, that's naughty. I've never let anybody touch them.'

'Yes, I know I'm honoured, because they are truly wonderful.'

'I'm glad they meet with your approval.' The irony in her tone was evidently playful, because she made no attempt to resist him, but returned his kisses as readily as ever.

After some time, she broke off to say, 'Ivor?'

'I'm still here.'

'I know you are, and especially when you do that. Listen, have you got a one of those things that men carry around so that they won't make a girl pregnant?'

He nodded. 'I've got a boxful of them. I supervised pay parade before I left the ship, and I pocketed some, not with anything in mind, but just to be on the safe side.'

Despite her immediate concern, curiosity made her ask, 'What have they got to do with pay parade?'

Ill-timed though the interruption was, he had to explain. 'When we grant shore leave, we give the liberty men contraceptives with their pay. Some of them are not too discriminating in their choice of female company, and we don't want them coming back in need of medical attention in the trouser area. You see, they're not just to prevent pregnancy, they're a precaution against infection as well.'

'Ugh.'

He had to clarify one thing. 'Look, I don't want you to think I brought you here to have my wicked way with you. It wasn't my intention, but,' he sighed guiltily, 'on mature reflection, I have to admit that it does feel like a good idea.'

'I'll believe you.' Now noticeably more relaxed, she made no demur when he unfastened the rest of her buttons.

'Truly superb,' he repeated, kissing her modest but perfectly-formed breasts. 'You know, Grace,' he said, 'I love everything about you.'

'It's just as well, considerin' you've seen nearly everythin'.' It was a passing observation as his attentions took further effect on her. 'Oh, that's lovely,' she said. 'You're so gentle.' She was clearly happy for him to continue, and was apparently oblivious to anything else until she realised that her trouser cord had come undone, and that he was pursuing a new line of investigation. 'What are you doing?' Her question was born of surprise rather than ignorance.

'I'm checking that everything's where it should be,' he told her soothingly.

'Well,' she gasped, 'I hope it is, 'cause it's too late to swap things 'round.'

'Yes,' he reported, 'everything seems to be in order.'

'That's a relief.' Between gasps, she said, 'I hope you've got those things from the pay parade handy, 'cause there's... no going back... now.'

Leaving her reluctantly for the moment, he took the cushions from the armchair and laid them on the floor. Grace stood up to lift the cushions off the sofa, and her pyjama trousers fell to her ankles. In the urgency of the moment, she showed no sign of embarrassment, but stepped out of them and shrugged off the dressing gown and pyjama jacket, allowing them to form a heap on the floor. She was naked except for her sweetheart's brooch and its chain.

Ivor undressed quickly, throwing his uniform trousers over the armchair, and then joined her in front of the fire. Together, they sank on to the cushions, kissing urgently. Presently, she gave a gasp, and he felt her body arch to receive him.

As she lay in the firelight, Grace's thoughts were making their own journeys. 'I can't imagine you being anchor-faced and shouting at your men,' she said.

'I don't have to. They're so terrified of me, they'd never dream of stepping out of line.'

'Bunions. You weren't like that when you caught us all in the seamen's mess that time.'

'No,' he admitted. 'Finding myself in mixed company, I was more reserved than usual.'

'You were nice,' she insisted, not wishing to be proved wrong. 'You gave us a tin of plum jam.'

'Have you finished it yet?'

'Yes, we had the last of it some time ago.'

'I'll give you another tin.'

'You're lovely, Ivor. That's why I love you.'

'It's as good a reason as any,' he said.

She leaned sideways to kiss him. 'It was wonderful. I'd no idea it would be like that.'

'Mrs Ellison really knows something about making plum jam, doesn't she?'

'I wasn't talking about jam. I meant what we did earlier. Other than odd things girls have told me, I didn't know what to expect.' Perhaps remembering something else she'd been told, she said, 'It didn't hurt at all.'

'Good.'

'I thought it might, you know... the first time.'

'Have you done a lot of bike riding?'

'Lots. I used to ride me bike every day to school and back.'

'That would explain it,' he told her confidently.

'What do you mean?'

He wondered how best to put it. In the end, he said, 'Bike riding has robbed many a virgin of her credibility.'

'I didn't know that. I just know it was lovely.'

'I can't guarantee satisfaction every time.'

'But it was my *first* time, Ivor, and it was smashin'. From what I've gathered, most girls aren't as lucky as I was. I'm even beginning to feel sorry for them.'

'I'm glad.' He added quickly, 'I mean I'm glad you enjoyed it, you understand, not that other girls have been short-changed.'

'I know what you mean, pet.' She snuggled more comfortably against him and asked, 'Why do survey ships have to go to sea in wartime?'

'Search me. I'm only the First Lieutenant. I don't get involved with the technical stuff.'

'I don't believe you.'

'You don't believe me whatever I say, so it doesn't matter.'

'I just wondered, because it's not as if *HMS Maynard* is a proper warship. It just doesn't seem right to expose her to danger.'

'You know, you can be quite wounding,' he told her, kissing her in spite of what she'd said. 'It's just as well she couldn't hear you say that. She'd have sunk at her moorings.'

'It came out all wrong, but you know what I mean.'

'I usually do.'

Her catechism was not yet over, because she asked, 'What was it like when you were shipwrecked?'

'Oh well,' he said, stroking his chin in recollection, 'there I was with my telescope to my eye and my parrot on my shoulder, shouting, "Abandon ship, me hearties! 'Tis all over for the good ship *Hispaniola*. If any of you scurvy swabs can't swim, grab me wooden leg as I float past, and hang on to it. Long John Loveday will tow you to safety." '

'Don't be rotten,' she begged.

'Okay.' There was no avoiding it, so he told her. 'There was a loud explosion,' he said, 'and the ship keeled over when the water rushed in. We got as many as we could over the side, and we loosened the rafts, but there was no time to lower the boats.' He paused in his description, recalling the event in awful detail. 'We counted thirty-one on the rafts, but three died during the first night and four during the second. When you're cold, wet and exhausted, it's easy just to let go.' He paused again, remembering. 'The worst thing was seeing men die, and being unable to help them. That's what keeps coming back to haunt me.'

'I'm sorry,' she said, kissing him as if he were a child waking from a bad dream. 'I asked you to tell me, and it must be horrible for you, talking about it.'

'Talking about it is the easy part. It's living with it that's the real problem.'

She rested herself on one elbow to face him. 'If there was nothing you could do, you've nothing to blame yourself for.'

'Logically, no, but just being helpless can make you feel guilty. Also, just the fact that you survived and others didn't can have the same effect.'

'I wish I could help you.'

'You already have, Grace. I've been much happier since I met you.'

'In that case, I'll try to keep it up.'

12

The next convoy was uneventful for *Hosta*, but not for the others. It seemed that the U-boats had been attracted to the main prize, and the resulting losses were heavy. For the time being at least, the solitary straggler was forgotten.

Once back in Liverpool, Ivor lost no time in sending a note to Grace, who responded promptly, and they met on her next evening off. Largely for the sake of convenience, but partly because the place had already engendered a feeling of nostalgia for them, they went to The Grapevine, where the waiter welcomed them as the regular patrons they were.

They were dancing to 'The Band Played On', a waltz song made popular the previous year by Guy Lombardo and his Royal Canadians, and Grace became suddenly aware that other dancers were looking at them and smiling.

'Is it my imagination,' she asked, 'or is everybody staring at us?'

'If they're looking at you, Grace, their attention is good-natured enough. You have to blame the song lyrics.'

'I don't know them.'

He sang softly in her ear, ' "...He'd ne'er leave the girl with the strawberry curls, and the band played on." '

'Oh, heck.'

Mercifully for Grace, the number reached its end, the dancers applauded the quartet, and Ivor beamed at the others before taking her back to their table.

'It was nice,' he said, trying to reassure her. 'The band was playing a song about a strawberry blonde, and there on the dance floor was a pretty girl with strawberry blonde curls. They just thought it was charming.'

'It felt as if they were undressin' us,' she complained.

'No, they weren't doing that,' he told her confidently. 'Honestly, I'd have noticed. I can spot a naked woman at five hundred yards without a telescope or binoculars.'

'You're not taking it seriously.'

Reaching across the table for her hand, he said, 'Think of something nice.'

'All right.' Suddenly, her face brightened, and she said, 'Guess what? We're getting the flat caps soon.'

Ivor was aware that the new flat caps were as popular with Wrens as the felt, 'pudding basin' hats were resented. Even so, he couldn't resist teasing her. 'That's good news,' he said, 'but it'll be even harder for you to hide those lovely curls.'

'And have everybody starin' at us on the dance floor.'

'For the right reason, Grace, believe me.'

Unconvinced, she said, 'They used to call us "Ginger" at school.'

'They must have been colour-blind,' he told her gently. 'You're strawberry blonde, and I can vouch for the authenticity of your colouring.' He glanced discreetly in the vague direction of her middle region.

Her eyes opened wide, and she whispered, 'That's *rude*.'

He mimed a kiss of apology.

Changing the subject, possibly to pre-empt further embarrassment, she asked, 'What will you do after the war, Ivor?'

'Marry you and live happily ever after.'

'No, seriously.'

'Oh well, if you prefer it, seriously ever after.'

'No, be serious for a moment.'

'All right.' He adopted a thinking pose, and then, gauging the level of her impatience, he said, 'I suppose I'll go back to the paper or maybe try for a job on a bigger paper.'

She nodded, as if she'd expected as much.

'How about you?'

It seemed that Grace had her ambition dusted and ready. 'I was pretty good at French and German when I was at school,' she said. 'I'd like to work on them and maybe do something abroad.' Almost guiltily, she said, 'There's not much call for languages in Newcastle, not unless you count Maltese and the various ones they speak round the docks, and they all seem to get by without an interpreter.'

'There is one thing I'd like to do,' he ventured.

'Is it going to be silly?'

'Some people might think so. I'd really like to write about the war. I don't mean a factual account. I imagine there'll be more than enough of them around.'

Now convinced that he was being serious, she asked, 'What, then?'

'I want to write a novel with real people in it.'

She eyed him uncertainly. 'Do you mean people who really exist?'

'No, I mean fictional people that you can believe in, rather than some of the soulless characters you sometimes read about. You see, doing the job I do, I see people reacting to all kinds of incident and in conditions that don't exist in peacetime, and I feel as if I really know them.' It was clear from her expression that Grace only half-understood what he was trying to tell her, so he seized on an example. 'Take *Maynard*'s three sub-lieutenants. When they came on board, they were like the Three Little Pigs.'

Grace shook her head in disbelief.

'Bear with me.' He topped up her glass and tried again. 'They were innocent, inexperienced and timid. Anderson was the first to come out of his shell, although rather too confidently, I felt. I had to give him a roasting after I discovered you and the other girls on board.'

'What was so awful about us coming on board?' Her question contained a hint of resentment.

'It was a matter of security. You were unauthorised personnel on board a warship.'

'I cannot see the problem. None of us knows a thing about surveying the ocean, so I don't know what secrets we could have found out.'

'Security is like that,' he told her. 'It doesn't always make sense, but the overall scheme dictates that we have to abide by it.' Aware that he'd been side-tracked, He pressed on with his explanation. 'When Moore recovered from chronic seasickness,' he said, 'he showed himself to be a plodder, reliable and unimaginative, but conscientious, whereas Cartwright is different from both of them. At first, he was scared to death of making a mistake, but he tackled the job nevertheless, and now, through determination and concentration, he's become a reliable, trustworthy officer. To summarise, Anderson is the little pig that knew best and built his house of straw, Moore is the unimaginative one who built his house of sticks, and Cartwright is the methodical, resourceful one who built his house of bricks and kept the fire going and water in the pot.'

'All right, Doctor Freud, how does buildin' houses translate into what they have to do at sea?'

Ivor poured the last of the wine and said, 'I have to watch two of them carefully. Anderson is capable of making rash decisions, and Moore might struggle to adapt in an emergency. Of the three, Cartwright is the most dependable.' He saw the waiter heading their way and asked, 'Ice cream again?'

'Wey aye.'

When he'd given the waiter their order, he asked her, 'Would you like to dance?' The quartet was starting 'Bewitched.'

She nodded. 'It's one of my favourites,' she confirmed, joining him on the dance floor, 'an' the best thing is that it's not about girls with blonde hair.'

'It's a lovely number,' he agreed, enjoying her perfume as he always did, and wondering when he might be able to replenish it.

They danced in silence. At the end, he kissed her lightly on the side of her neck before applauding the band.

As they took their seats, she said, 'I wonder when we'll get a chance to go away again.'

'What made you think about that?'

'It was you kissin' me just now, like you did at the cottage. It brought everythin' back, how lovely it was an' everythin'.'

'If we get away again, it'll be a lot easier just to book a hotel somewhere that's not frequented by Admiral Horton's staff.'

Her eyes widened in a way that had become familiar. 'Do you mean as Mr and Mrs, like?'

'Why not?'

'What would I do for a ring?'

He took the signet ring from his little finger. 'Try this on.'

She slipped the ring on to the appropriate finger. 'It's a bit loose,' she said, 'but it would pass muster if I turned it round.' She turned the top half inward to demonstrate.

'I think that's convincing enough.'

'I wonder what sort of Little Pigs that would make us,' she said.

'I don't know about you,' said Ivor, 'but I rather see myself as the Big Bad Wolf.'

They stopped at their usual parting place, and Grace remarked, 'It's not as cold as it's been, but I'd still like to come inside your coat for a minute.'

'I think that might be arranged.' He unfastened his buttons and drew her inside.

'I suppose we're lucky,' she said. 'We see each other about once a month, but some fellas are away for months an' sometimes years.'

'Very lucky,' he agreed.

'When are you leaving?' As soon as the question left her lips, she winced at her mistake. 'I'm sorry,' she said, 'I shouldn't ask you that question.'

'You're allowed to ask, but I shan't tell you.'

They kissed, but it was clear that Grace had something on her mind, because she said, 'As close as we are, things still come between us.'

'What things are they?' Their physical proximity had led Ivor's thoughts naturally along a different route, and he had to concentrate afresh on her latest observation.

'I'm saying that, as close as we are, some things still have to be kept secret.'

'I'm afraid so,' he confirmed, conscious that the fact caused her a degree of resentment.

'I suppose it's just one of the differences between us.'

'How do you work that out? I have to keep quiet about things to do with the ship and operations, but you have to be just as tight-lipped about your work.'

'No,' she said, 'my work doesn't come between us.' Then, changing the subject quite deliberately, possibly because the argument was going nowhere, she said, 'You know how, when we were at the cottage, you used those things that sailors take ashore with 'em? They came out of a box with an anchor on it.'

Ivor was aware that anything that was supplied by the service usually bore an anchor as its label, but he imagined he knew what she meant. 'Contraceptives?'

'Yes, well, I've learned that there's something better, that doesn't get in the way, like. It's something I have to put... inside me.'

'Inside you?' He wondered what she was saying.

'Aye.'

'Do you mean you have to swallow it?'

'No, of course not. I have to put it inside my....' She whispered in his ear.

He was incredulous. 'Is that what you call it? Your *pansy*?'

'Aye, well, I have to call it something, an' I don't like the names the sailors call it.' She looked around nervously and said, 'An' keep your voice down.'

'Sorry.'

'All right. Anyway, there's a clinic in Liverpool, where I can go to get a one. It'll be a lot better.'

'You'll have to talk to a doctor, I suppose, about your... pansy.'

'Aye, well, doctors are different, an' stop makin' fun of us.'

'I'm sorry.' He kissed her to make it a proper apology, telling her for good measure. 'I love you.'

'It's just as well. I love you too, even when you laugh at me.'

'I wasn't laughing. I was just surprised.' A glance at his watch told him that only a minute remained, so he kissed her again and watched her as far as the entrance.

Ivor had only just returned and entered the wardroom, when the Captain looked in.

'Hello, Number One. Did you have a pleasant evening?'

'Most enjoyable, thank you, sir. Can I get you a drink?'

The Captain looked agreeably surprised. 'Yes, please, Number One. I'd like a pink gin if we have the bitters.'

'I think we have everything, sir.' Ivor prepared two pink gins and handed one to the Captain.

'Thank you, Number One. I received some good news today. We're going round to the Cammell Laird shipyard in Birkenhead on Tuesday, to have two depth-charge throwers fitted, one on each side. I suppose they had to avoid the Easter holiday as they're dealing with civilians.'

'I imagine so, sir, but it's good news, as you say. If we have to attack a diving U-boat, I'd rather do it that way than have to steam into position and roll them off the stern.'

'Quite.' Newell sipped his drink and nodded his approval. 'There is also the matter of leave. Everyone will be given seventy-two hours, and that includes us.'

'Excellent, sir.'

'The question is, Number One, what will you do? You stayed with the ship at Christmas, but that's not an option this time.'

'Don't worry about me, sir. I'll stay in Liverpool. I have plenty to occupy my time here.' It was true. Leave was a bonus, especially if Grace could get away.

13

Incredibly, Grace was allowed a stand-down from the end of Wednesday until 1800 on Thursday. Ivor booked a double room at the Royal Estuary Hotel, and he was there to meet her when she arrived.

He took her to their room and asked her, 'Do you want to change before dinner?'

'I'd better, just in case we bump into a Wren officer. It won't take long.' Looking around her, she said, 'Ye gods. It's even got its own bathroom.'

'Never let it be said that I don't know how to treat a girl.'

'I wouldn't dream of it.' Hurriedly, she doffed her uniform shoes, jacket and skirt, and then sat down to remove her stockings. Looking across at Ivor, she said, 'Hey, you. Watchin' me undress, are you?'

'Of course. That's the whole point of bringing you here. You're a sight to behold in black stockings and knickers.' Eyeing her critically, he said, 'I imagined your knickers would have elastic round the bottoms as well, if you know what I mean.'

'I know what you mean all right. I've got a pair of them that I keep for kit inspections. If you like, I'll wear them next time instead of these an' you can have a real treat.'

'Please don't. I prefer the ones you're wearing.'

'Ah well, they're coming off, anyway.' She stood up and divested herself of them, replacing them with a pair of white cotton French knickers, asking him, 'Do these meet with your approval?'

'They're truly magnificent.'

'That's all right, then.' Carefully, she donned a pair of the nylon stockings he'd bought for her in New York, and then stepped into the sage green dress that she'd worn on their first date. 'Will you hook me up at the back, pet?'

'Wey aye, man.' He ran the zipper up and fastened the hook and eye. 'Perfection,' he pronounced.

'I haven't finished yet.' Taking her make-up bag from her valise, she went to the mirror. 'Don't watch me while I'm doin' this,' she said, 'or I'll get nervous.'

'I'll look the other way,' he promised, turning to the window and watching the traffic. Because of wartime daylight saving, it wasn't yet time for the black-out.

'It was a stroke of luck, wasn't it, you getting seventy-two hours?'

'It certainly was.'

'One of the girls walked down by the dock this morning and she said your ship wasn't there. She had me worried. I thought you might have gone somewhere in a hurry.'

'We took her round to the shipyard this morning.' He thought it was safe to tell her that.

'Oh, is she havin' some repairs done, or is it a secret?'

'Just a few repairs,' he confirmed.

'Right.' She zipped up her make-up bag and left it on the shelf behind the wash basin. 'I'm ready.'

He lent her his arm, and they went down to the restaurant.

'This is nice,' said Grace, admiring the ornate plasterwork and gilding.

The head waiter greeted them. 'Good evening, sir. Good evening, madam.' His practised eye had taken in the signet ring on Grace's finger.

'Good evening,' said Ivor. 'Loveday, room two-hundred-and-ten.'

'Please come this way.' He led them to a table not far away. 'I'm afraid the veal is no longer available, sir,' he said as he handed them the menu.

Ivor narrowed his eyes at Grace. The veal was always off. He asked, 'What's not on the menu?'

The waiter looked around discreetly. 'Ragout of game, sir.'

'I see. You like game, don't you, darling?'

Grace was slow to respond, possibly wondering who Ivor was addressing. 'Er, yes, I love it.'

'Shall we have the ragout of game?'

'Mm.'

He asked the waiter, 'What do you recommend as a first course?'

'There are the fried lamb sweetbreads, sir.'

Ivor shook his head. 'I don't think so.'

'There is a chicken liver pate that's not on the menu, sir. I should have mentioned it earlier. I do apologise.'

'There's absolutely no need to apologise.' Ivor was picking up signs of enthusiasm from Grace, so he said, 'Shall we have the chicken liver pate and the game ragout?'

The waiter made a note and asked, 'Would you like me to send the wine waiter, sir?'

'Please.'

As the waiter withdrew, Grace asked, 'What's a ragout?'

'Meat cooked with vegetables. In this case, it'll be like game pie without the crust.'

'Smashin'.'

The wine waiter came, and Ivor ordered a bottle of red Burgundy, which turned out to be quite expensive. He learned that the war and its resultant shortages were to blame. 'It's more like someone's doing well out of the war,' he said when they were alone.

Grace's attention was elsewhere, because the band was playing 'Deep Purple'. 'I love this,' she said.

'Would you like to dance?'

'Oh, yes.'

He led her on to the floor, and it was clear from the start that 'Deep Purple' was one of her top favourite songs. They danced in silence to the end. When they returned to their table, Ivor said, 'So "Deep Purple" is special. What else do you like?'

'Oh, lots. One that I'd really like to hear again is "Love Walked In". It's by George Gershwin.'

'And Ira. Let's not forget him.'

The wine arrived, and Ivor tasted it. 'Excellent,' he said, so the wine waiter poured some for them.

'It's quite remarkable when you dance to a number you really like,' said Ivor.

'What's remarkable about it?'

'You're so involved, it's as if you're a part of the music. It's a wonderful thing.'

'Haddaway, man. I just like dancin'.'

'You know,' he said, 'you really must learn to accept compliments gracefully, otherwise I'm wasting my breath, saying nice things to you.'

'Aye, aye, sir.'

'Good girl.'

'They're playing "Two Sleepy People".'

'There's no rest for the talented and good-looking, I suppose.' He stood up and offered her his hand.

As they danced, she said, 'You're like a purring cat. Do you feel like one?'

'Yes, but not with potatoes as well, and I think I'll skip the first course.'

She pulled a face at him. 'You need to learn how to take kind remarks seriously,' she said, 'otherwise there's no point in me makin' them.'

'*Touché*.'

'At least I know when you're just bein' daft.' She hesitated. 'At least, I think I do.'

The evening passed with no further disagreement; in fact, there was an unexpected highlight, at least for Grace, when the bandleader announced Ivor's request for 'Love Walked In'. Once more, Grace demonstrated her remarkable capacity for being at one with the music, and that dance alone made the evening special for them both.

Eventually, they made their way upstairs. Closing the door, he took her in his arms and reached for the hook and eye.

'Just a minute,' she cautioned. 'I need to go to the bathroom.'

'Of course.'

'Not just that. There's me "do-fer" to see to.' She took a floppy-looking object from her handbag and disappeared with it into the bathroom.

Ivor took off his uniform and hung it up in the wardrobe. He was down to his underwear when Grace emerged from the bathroom.

'This time I caught you in your knickers,' she said.

'Drawers, cellular, officers', actually,' he told her archly.

'Doesn't the Navy know just how to keep every bugger in their place? They even issue special knickers to officers.'

'Actually,' he said, unhooking her dress and pulling the zipper down, 'there's no difference between these and the ones I had when I was a seaman.' He kissed the three points of the naked triangle revealed by the parted zipper. 'On the other hand, I have my own first lieutenant's towel to keep my neck dry in foul weather, and that's more special than anything pusser can supply.'

'So is this.' She turned and held up her sweetheart's brooch.

'I'm glad.' He kissed her and then left her to finish undressing.

Presently, she stood naked before him. 'I can't believe I'm doing this,' she said. 'I used to be really shy about me body. I was even shy when I joined the Wrens an' I had to share a cabin with other girls.'

'Your body's too lovely to be hidden away,' he said, opening his arms. 'Bring it here.' He held her, delighting as ever in her perfume, and luxuriating in her smooth softness. 'I have an idea, now,' he said, 'of how those Arab sheikhs must feel when they say, "Have this one washed and brought to my tent." '

'You horror. I suppose you'd like to carry me off on your camel, like Rudolph Valentino.'

'Who needs a camel?' Placing one arm behind her knees, he lifted her and carried her to the bed, joining her seconds later before breaking the spell by asking, 'Is that thing you told me about really safe?'

'They say it's safer than what we used last time, and it makes it a lot nicer, although I have to say in my innocence, I didn't have a lot to complain about.'

'Just checking.'

She narrowed her eyes speculatively and asked, 'What would you do if I got pregnant?'

'I've already told you that. I'd marry you and we'd live seriously ever after.'

'Oh aye?' It sounded like a challenge.

'You can depend on it.' Partly to circumvent argument, but mainly because nature demanded it, he silenced her lips with his, eventually breaking off to say softly, 'I'm potty about you, Grace, and to prove it, I'm going to kiss every square inch of your body.' He reconsidered the scale of the task and said, 'Well, quite a lot of it, anyway.' He carried out a quick survey and reduced his estimate again. 'At least, as much as I can manage.'

Before long, however, he was distracted from his self-imposed marathon by something that never failed to eclipse all other known activity.

'I've been called two things tonight for the first time.'

'Who's been calling you names, Grace?'

'The waiter called me "madam", and you called me "darling". I must say, I've been called "hinny", "pet", "bonny lass", an' a few other names I'd rather forget, but tonight was special.'

Ivor was tracing the line of her backbone lazily with his middle finger. He broke off to say, ' "Madam" was honorary, although the waiter wasn't to know that, but you're "darling" because you *are* special. I've never had a darling before now,' he mused. 'If it comes to that, until I met you, I had no idea who was going to be the mother of my children, and the two tend to go hand in hand as a general rule.'

Suddenly serious, she asked, 'Do you honestly think it would work, Ivor? We're poles apart, you an' me.'

'We're closer than you think. We have a lot in common.'

'We're close all right, even though secrets come between us, but the fact remains that I'm the daughter of a shipyard fitter from North Shields, and you're the son of the Dole Office Manager.'

'That didn't make him the Lord of the Manor, Grace, and I'll never inherit the title, but I'm not going to argue with you – we'd only fall out, and I don't want that – instead, I'm going to wear you down, little by little.'

'Oh, aye?'

'Aye,' he said, bestowing a kiss after each name, 'bonny lass... hinny... pet... darling....'

Feeling beneath the sheet, she said, 'Are you getting ideas again?'

'What do you think?'

'Somebody is. What do you call him?'

'What?'

She adopted a patient tone. 'You had a good laugh about my pansy. Now it's my turn. What do you call him?'

'Herbert.' It was the first name that came to mind.

'You're jokin'.'

'I'm not, and don't laugh. You'll upset him.'

She looked uncertain. 'What does he do when he's upset?'

'Nothing. He goes limp and refuses to co-operate.'

'Oh, Herbert.' She lifted the bedclothes to facilitate communication. 'Herbert,' she cajoled, 'don't go on strike just because I made a daft remark. It's a lovely name, really, an' you don't have to take everything I say seriously.'

'I have a sneaking feeling he's forgiven you,' said Ivor, sensing a reaction.

'Phew.' She wiped imaginary sweat off her brow. 'I can't cope with upsetting both of you in the same night.'

14

HMS *Hosta* was equipped with dummy depth-charges for training purposes. After each practice attack, they had to be recovered from the sea and stored, ready for the next training session, a time-consuming procedure that Ivor found irksome, although that was by no means his chief concern.

He'd been watching the depth-charge crews carefully and he'd noticed a degree of laxity in their drill. It was particularly apparent as it contrasted strongly with the eager confidence of the gun and torpedo crews. He voiced his concern to the Captain after the latest practice attack.

'It's coming from Anderson, sir. It's almost as if he's playing at the job, and the men seem to be following his example. They've already nicknamed him "Easy".'

'After Midshipman Easy? I suppose he does rather posture,' agreed Newell.

'Or maybe it's because he's so easy-going.' The possibility had already suggested itself to Ivor.

'Fortunately, we've never had to rely on him to drop or fire a depth-charge in anger.'

'What do you suggest, sir?'

Newell made a quick decision. 'I'll speak to him again and see if I can talk some sense into him. I may even threaten him with disciplinary action. We'll see if that has any effect.'

Anderson was subdued, but only until the next morning, when

the signs were that he was back to his familiar, smug self. He was on the bridge at 0755, when the Captain relieved Ivor. Anderson greeted him immediately.

'Good morning, sir.'

'Anderson,' said the Captain quietly so that the lookouts were unable to hear him, 'the correct procedure is to salute me. When I have returned your salute, I shall initiate the greetings. Didn't they tell you that at *King Alfred*?'

'No, sir. I think they were concerned with more important matters.'

'Protocol and courtesy are important, Anderson. Without them, discipline falls apart.'

'Yes, sir.' His response was less than humble.

'If you have a growing feeling that you're in my bad books, all you have to do is to stop behaving like an ass.'

'Aye, aye, sir.' Anderson moved towards the bridge ladder, but Newell hadn't finished with him.

'There will be an exchange of roles today, Anderson. It's most important that officers are able to take over the duties of others in the event of casualties being sustained. You will be gunnery officer, and the First Lieutenant will take over the depth-charge throwers. You will report back to me.'

'Aye, aye, sir.' Anderson stopped at the ladder to say familiarly, 'Go easy on my team, Number One. They're used to my gentle touch.'

'Anderson,' the Captain snarled as quietly as he could.

'Yes, sir?'

'Try to take your duties seriously for once. Men's lives may depend on it.'

'Aye, aye, sir.'

Ivor watched him go. 'There must be something in King's Regulations about bumptiousness, sir,' he said.

'If you can turn up the requisite paragraph, Number One, you'll find a willing reader in me, but have breakfast first.'

'Aye, aye, sir.' Ivor went below to eat.

The Captain waited until Ivor had finished breakfast before making the pipe, 'For exercise, for exercise, Action Stations!'

Ivor made immediately for the waist, where the depth-charge throwers were situated.

With the Tannoy microphone in his hand, Newell announced, 'For exercise, U-boat bearing green oh nine oh. Let Go!' He followed his order half a minute later with, 'Guns, what are you waiting for?'

Ivor smiled to himself. 'Make ready,' he told the depth-charge crew.

One rating placed his hand on the firing button.

Ivor asked, 'Haven't you forgotten something?'

'Sir?'

'The depth-charges haven't been primed!'

'Aye, aye, sir.' Flustered, the rating whose job it was to prime the depth-charges bent hurriedly to his task.

The Tannoy crackled again. 'The U-boat is diving. Fire two depth-charges.'

As soon as the priming was complete, Ivor pressed the firing button, and two practice depth-charges shot into the air, describing a wide parabola and hitting the surface on the starboard beam.

Through the Tannoy, the Captain announced, 'Engagement unsuccessful. Secure from Action Stations.'

Ivor re-joined the Captain on the bridge.

'When Cartwright relieves me, Number One, I'd like to see you and Anderson in my cabin.'

'Aye, aye, sir.'

Cartwright appeared, as punctilious as usual, at 1155, and Ivor followed Newell below. Anderson was waiting for them.

The Captain went inside and sat down to speak to him.

'The guns were conspicuously silent, Anderson. What's your explanation?'

'I was waiting for the gun crews to report "Ready", sir. For some reason, they didn't see fit to do that.'

'In all the exercises and actions you've experienced aboard this ship, how many times have you heard the gun crews report "Ready"?'

Anderson appeared unruffled. 'It's hard to say, sir.'

'No, it's not. You've never heard them do that. Both crews are clearly visible from the bridge, and it is obvious when they are ready.' Newell was containing his temper with difficulty. 'Had it been a real U-boat, Anderson, its captain would have realised during your leisurely recess, that we were a Q-ship, and he would have dived immediately with the intention of transmitting at his earliest convenience the news that a Q-ship was patrolling this part of the Irish Sea.'

'And before you make some clever remark about the depth-charge attack,' said Ivor, 'let me tell you that the delay was due to the fact that one of your crew had forgotten to carry out the priming.'

The Captain sighed in disgust. 'You're a disgrace, Anderson,' he said finally. 'I don't know why the Lower Deck call you "Easy", because I find you damned difficult, not to say arrogant, selfish and condescending. You're going to drill the depth-charge crews until you and they can perform the task to my satisfaction, and you're going to do it under the First Lieutenant's scrutiny. Meanwhile, get out of my sight!'

When he was gone, the Captain said, 'I'm sorry to add to your workload, Number One, but I can't allow the shambles to continue any longer.'

'Of course not, sir, and it is one of my functions, after all.'

At 1330, the Captain piped, 'D' you hear there? D' you hear there? For exercise, for exercise, depth-charge crews close up at the rush!'

The crews were at their stations within less than a minute. Ivor counted them and checked that they were all present. The only man missing was Sub-Lieutenant Anderson. After another minute had gone by, Ivor reported the fact to the Captain, who made another pipe.

'D' you hear there? D' you hear there? Sub-Lieutenant Anderson is also invited to take part in the exercise.'

Ivor managed not to smile at the Captain's patient sarcasm.

He could only imagine his next conversation with Anderson. He waited for the miscreant to appear, and was rewarded after another minute.

'Honestly, Number One,' said the latecomer, 'anyone would think I had a target pinned to my back.'

'Maybe that's not such a bad idea, Anderson. We could use the small-arms practice. Now get started with the starboard crew, the whole drill from beginning to end.'

He watched and listened until the crew were ready to fire, and then he had to stop them. 'What have you forgotten, Anderson?'

'I really wasn't aware that I'd forgotten anything, Number One.'

'The depth setting. Also, and yet again, the depth-charges have not been primed. The idea is that, when they reach the predetermined depth, they go "bang" and blow a U-boat to buggery. These things wouldn't even thumb their noses at one. Start the drill again, and remember that a unit takes its example from its leader. A sloppy leader means a sloppy crew.'

He kept the starboard crew busy for the next hour, and then moved over to the port crew, addressing them immediately.

'You must all have heard what I told the starboard crew. It's your turn, now, to see if you can do a damned sight better than they did. Carry on, Sub-Lieutenant Anderson.'

'Aye, aye, Number One.'

'Oh, Anderson,' he said quietly.

'Yes, Number One?'

'It's "sir" from now on. "Number One" is a familiar form of address, and that familiarity has to be earned. Start earning it.'

'Aye, aye, Num... sir.' A hint of resentment was beginning to show through Anderson's usual façade of airy condescension, and that, too, needed to be watched.

The port crew performed much better than their opposite numbers, a fact that Ivor put before both crews at the end of the exercise. 'That's not the end of the matter,' he told them. 'There's time, now, for the starboard crew to become top dogs. It's up to them to make it happen, and the port crew to see that is doesn't. Keep reciting your drill and make it second nature. That way, we shan't have a recurrence of the shameful and embarrassing episode that occurred this morning.' Turning to the somewhat-chastened Anderson, he said, 'Carry on, sub, and remember what I've told you.'

The Captain relieved Ivor again at the start of the First Dogwatch. He told him quietly, 'Anderson made a complaint about you earlier. He told me that your depth-charge drill has seriously undermined his standing with the men.'

'I'm surprised he hasn't simply laughed it off, sir.'

'This time, he couldn't. I told him he had no standing with them to begin with, so there was clearly no harm done.'

Ivor laughed. 'Thank you, sir. You know, I read something once about characters like Anderson.'

'Oh?'

'Yes, sir. I'm not a headshrinker, as you know, but I think he has a superiority complex.'

Newell stared at him. 'What on earth has he to feel superior about?'

'That's just it, sir. Such people apparently develop a mask of superiority in order to hide feelings of inferiority. They say the mask becomes more impenetrable the longer it goes on.'

Newell considered the information and asked, 'Who propounded this theory?'

'A chap called Adler, sir.'

'It sounds odd to me. Maybe he should have stuck to making typewriters.'

Ivor smiled at the thought. He said, 'I think the Adler company makes bicycles and motor cars as well, sir.'

'He's evidently a jack of all trades, Number One, and therefore not to be taken seriously.' After staring out to sea for a while, he said, 'I think we'll exercise guns and torpedo tubes tomorrow. They're our real teeth, after all.'

The day's exercise went extremely well, and the Captain decided to give the depth-charge crews an opportunity to redeem themselves, which, following Ivor's rigorous drills, they did, both performing particularly well.

'Well done, everyone,' said the Captain. 'Now we can sail confidently with the next convoy. Secure from action stations.' Switching off the microphone, he said to Ivor, 'It'll be interesting to see how Anderson reacts to the sudden turn around.'

'For my money, sir, he'll try to bag the credit.'

'I don't care as long as he continues to do the job properly.'

That evening, leaving Sub-Lieutenant Moore on watch, the officers sat down to dinner. As *Hosta* was a small ship, the Captain usually ate with the other officers in the wardroom, and on this occasion, he was keen to observe Anderson's behaviour.

Before long, Anderson brought up the subject of the day's exercise.

'Pretty good show all round, I thought,' he said.

'Ivor asked, 'What was?'

'Today's frolic, of course, Number One. Depth-charges, guns and torpedoes all came up with the goods.'

'The activity in which you took part, Anderson,' said the Captain, 'was an exercise, not a "frolic", and the much-improved performance by the depth-charge crews was the result of the First Lieutenant taking you by the scruff of your neck yesterday and drilling you and your men.'

'Yes, sir.'

'And, as far as you're concerned, Anderson,' said Ivor, 'I am still "sir". Do you understand?'

'Oh, yes... sir.' His face bore a tolerant smile, as if he were humouring his foolish senior officers, but Ivor didn't need to be Alfred Adler to know that old habits took a long time to fade.

15

May

Grace knew about *HMS Hosta*'s latest U-boat. She'd been off watch when the signal came in, but whispered remarks at odd times had put her in the picture, at least to some extent.

She'd already dismissed the subject from her thoughts when she was accosted by a rushed and agitated Wren, who was pushing the officers' tea trolley.

'Be a sport,' said the girl, 'and take Two-Oh Curwen's tea in for her.' She pointed to the appropriate cup and saucer.

'Okay.' Grace picked up the tea and took it to the Second Officer's door. Miss Curwen had recently arrived as a replacement for Second Officer Barlow, and the signs were that she was going to be all right. Officers might come and go, but they could instil calm or wreak havoc during their stay, so it was as well to know which kind they were.

When Grace knocked on the glass panel of the door and heard the invitation to enter, she pushed the door open and saw that the second officer was in conversation with a lieutenant commander. She heard him say, 'Newell's terribly modest, you know. He says it's all down to his Number One, an RNVR chap called Lovelace, Lovelock, or something like that. Apparently, he's an excellent gunnery officer, would you believe? Anyway, good old *Hosta*, I say.'

Miss Curwen was making signs to him to stop talking, but he seemed impervious to them. As he reached the door, he said, ' "Loveday". That was his name. I knew it would come to me. Anyway, I'll see you in the wardroom, Roberta. Cheerio.'

Grace put the tea down on Miss Curwen's desk and was about to leave, when her officer spoke to her.

'Thank you, Wren Headley. Don't go yet. I'd like a word with you.' She indicated a chair on the other side of the desk. 'I have it in mind to speak to someone on the Flag Officer's staff about the loose talk in this establishment,' she said, adding quickly, 'but I'm not accusing you of anything, so relax.'

Grace waited patiently. She imagined it could only be another attempt to persuade her to accept promotion.

'Wren Headley, I understand you're seeing Lieutenant Loveday.'

'Yes, ma'am, but—'

'It's all right. It's been explained to me.' She seemed to be having some difficulty in finding the words she needed. Eventually, however, she said, 'When you came in just now, you heard something you shouldn't. It was a reference to Lieutenant Loveday.'

'Yes, ma'am.' Grace wondered for a moment what on earth could have happened to Ivor. The conversation she'd overheard seemed to be about something he'd done well. None of it made sense.

'Wren Headley,' said Miss Curwen, 'I'm tempted to tell you to forget what you heard, but that would make no sense at all. Being personally involved with Lieutenant Loveday, you couldn't possibly forget it. In any case, forgetting isn't something you do consciously.'

It was too much for Grace. 'I don't understand, ma'am,' she said. 'Lieutenant Loveday is First Lieutenant of *HMS Maynard*, but the officer who was in here just now was talking about *HMS Hosta*.'

'That's right. Now, you're bound by the Official Secrets Act, so you know that you mustn't breathe a word to a living soul about what I'm going to tell you, and that includes your friends, fellow-Wrens and your family. Also, you mustn't discuss it with Lieutenant Loveday. It's better that he doesn't know that you know. It's as sensitive as that.'

It was the strangest thing Grace had ever heard, but she had to comply. 'I shan't say a word, ma'am.'

'Good. I'm not going to tell you the whole story, because you don't need to know it. All I'm going to tell you is that *HMS Maynard* and *HMS Hosta* are the same ship.'

It came as a huge surprise and it explained a great deal, but it left much unexplained. Still, Miss Curwen had told her as much as she could. 'Thank you for telling me, ma'am,' she said. 'The secret's safe with me.'

'Good girl. I know I can rely on you. All I have to do now is persuade someone to put an end to careless chatter in this place. Carry on, Wren Headley.'

'Aye, aye, ma'am.' Grace left the office wiser but less wise, satisfied in some way, but otherwise dissatisfied. Questions occurred to her that she couldn't possibly answer. Why must a ship have two names? How could an unarmed survey ship sink U-boats? The most important question of all, though, from her point of view, was simply, why had Ivor lied to her so glibly about *HMS Hosta*?

The last question continued to trouble her in the days and nights that followed. All right, she knew why he couldn't tell her the truth. As he'd pointed out, keeping quiet about operations was only like her having to be reticent about her work in the Coding office, but she knew it wasn't as simple as that. She'd asked him about *HMS Hosta*, and he'd fobbed her off in a careless, off-hand way, saying that he'd heard of her and that he thought she might be a sloop, whatever that was. And then he'd gone on to tell her he loved her. She didn't resent the fact that he hadn't told her about *Hosta* – that would have been very wrong – it was the way he'd done it, as if she were some prying newspaper reporter trying to get a story, and not the girl he loved and who was in love with him. They were close, but they weren't. It made no sense at all and it continued to nag at her. She was turning it over in her mind for possibly the hundredth time when Beryl came back to the cabin with an envelope in her hand.

'A handsome naval officer left this at the desk for you, Grace. Go on, read it,' she urged. 'You never know, it might put you in a better mood.'

'Thanks, Beryl.' She opened the letter.

Dear Grace,

I'm back again. I couldn't keep away any longer. Tell me when you can get away, and life will once more be worth living.
Yours alone, with oceans of love,
Ivor XXXXX

With a sense of misgiving, she replied.

Dear Ivor,
I'm glad you're back and safe. I'm off at 1800 on Tuesday, the 19th.
Lots of love,
Grace XX.

It was honest enough to say, 'Lots of love', because she did love him. She just felt awkward about it, and she couldn't put that into words.

Ivor felt the familiar upsurge of his spirits when he saw her leave the Emilia and walk towards him. He kissed her and gave her his arm as he always did. They exchanged the usual greetings and walked towards the Grapevine. She was quiet, so he asked, 'Are you all right?'

'Aye, I'm fine. Just a bit out of sorts.'

'Nothing awful, I hope.'

'No, it's a monthly thing. Sometimes it's not too bad and sometimes it's not so good.'

'Shouldn't you see someone about it?'

'Ivor,' she said patiently, 'I said "monthly".'

'Oh, right. I'm sorry. I see what you mean.'

'Honestly,' she said, 'fellas.' She left the rest unsaid.

The waiter at the Grapevine welcomed them as warmly as ever and showed them to their usual table. 'I'm afraid the veal isn't available, sir,' he said.

'It's elusive, isn't it? Don't worry,' Ivor told him, 'I can't remember the last time I had veal, and we haven't decided yet what we're eating, but will you bring us a bottle of red Bordeaux?'

'Of course, sir.'

'Thank you. It'll be most welcome.'

Grace looked carefully at him and said, 'You're looking tired. Have you had a rough time?'

'Fairly rough, but it's over now.' He laid a comforting hand over hers and squeezed it. 'Listen, Grace, if you're feeling unwell, we don't have to stay long.'

'It's nothin'. Don't worry about me.'

'I care about you. I can't stop doing that.'

'In that case, pet, you're going to wear yourself out.'

The band began to play 'April in Paris'. It was an old number, but one that was worth keeping alive. Ivor asked, 'Can you... I mean, would you like to dance?'

She smiled at his awkwardness. 'I walked here, didn't I? Of course I can, and I would.' She let him lead her on to the floor.

'I've been looking forward to this,' he said. 'I think about you often when I'm away.'

'Haddaway, man. I'm sure you have other things to occupy your mind.'

'I have, but I think about you often.' He turned his head to look at her and she seemed a little sad, almost as if he'd said something she didn't want to hear.

Once more at their table, she said, 'If you don't mind, I don't want a lot to eat tonight.'

'That's all right. We can just have a main course, if you like.'

'Aye, that'll be nice.'

The waiter appeared with a bottle of red Bordeaux. He showed it to Ivor, who confirmed his choice.

'Would you like to taste the wine, sir?'

'All right.' He tasted the sample poured for him. 'That's good,' he said. 'What's not on the menu tonight?'

'Hare, sir, in a cream and mushroom sauce.'

Grace said, 'I've never eaten hare. What's it like?'

'Gamier than rabbit,' Ivor told her, 'and there's usually more of it.'

'Okay, I'd like to try that.'

'That's the hare for both of us,' said Ivor. 'We won't have a first course tonight.'

'Very good, sir.' The waiter retreated.

Ivor asked, 'What's been happening while I've been away? Anything dramatic?'

'No, just the usual. I get on with me work. Sometimes I get bored an' I go and have a bit crack, a chat, with Second Officer Curwen. You know how it is.'

'Just to keep yourself informed, I suppose.'

'Aye, you'd be surprised at some of the things she tells me. We're like two gossiping neighbours.'

Ivor couldn't remember hearing the second officer's name, but he had to check, if only to appear interested in Grace's workaday life. 'Is she the officer who took you to task for going ashore with me?'

'No, she went a few weeks ago. Two-Oh Curwen is her replacement.'

He nodded. Also out of politeness, he asked, 'What about the wardroom bicycle? Is she still around.'

'As of this week, no.' For the first time, Grace smiled properly. 'She had to rush to the heads a couple of mornings, an' she's the kind of person who can't be sick without letting everybody hear what she's doin'. You know what some people are like. It's not been made official yet, but she did leave in a hurry.'

'Poor girl.'

'Well, it's taken a while, but it caught up with her in the end.'

The hare arrived, bringing the saga of Third Officer Treadwell to an end. Ivor was still inclined to be sympathetic, but he conceded that Grace knew her better than he did.

Grace tried the hare and said without obvious enthusiasm, 'This is quite nice.'

'I'm glad you like it.' It seemed to Ivor that, with the exception of the story about the pregnant officer, conversation was somewhat laboured. He knew vaguely that Grace's monthly impediment affected women in various ways, and he was sympathetic to that. It was unfortunate, however, that *Hosta* was on a tight turn-around, and that it was unlikely they would see each other again before the next convoy sailed.

Watching her toy disinterestedly with the hare, he asked, 'Are you over-faced?'

'What does that mean?'

'Have you no appetite?'

'Not really. I'm sorry.' She laid down her knife and fork.

'You're not at your best. Would you like me to take you back to the Wrens' quarters?'

'If you don't mind.'

'Not in the least. You should be in your hammock.'

An element of confusion crossed her face. 'I don't sleep in a.... Oh, I see what you mean.'

Ivor signalled to the waiter for the bill, and, having paid it, left the restaurant assuring him that the hare was excellent, but that the lady had no appetite.

As they walked back to the Emilia, Grace seemed very preoccupied. Eventually, she said, 'Ivor, I've been meaning to tell you something.'

'Oh, you're not... as well. No, you can't be.' Her monthly condition ruled that out.

'No, it's not that.' Suddenly, the words came tumbling out, as if she'd been suppressing them for some time. 'I've been meaning to say that this relationship's not going anywhere. There's no future for us, and there's no point in going on with it.'

It was as if a lead weight had hit the bottom of his stomach. All he could say was, 'I thought it was going so well.'

'It was, but there's too much come between us, things that keep us apart.'

'Not to that extent, surely.'

'Listen, Ivor, 'cause my mind's made up. For one thing, you're an officer and I'm just a Wren.'

'But that doesn't—'

'Let me finish, Ivor. There's also the fact that your family and mine have absolutely nothing in common, and, as if that wasn't enough, there's that dividing wall that's your secret life.'

He didn't understand. 'Can't you just accept that there are things in wartime that have to be kept secret?'

'Yes, I can, and I do. I don't expect you to tell me your bloody secret. What I can't accept is the casual way you brush off any reference to your work, as if my feelings don't matter.'

He stopped walking to say, 'Now you really have lost me.'

'You're just so glib about it. There's no hint of "I'm sorry, Grace. I realise it's rotten for you, but I really can't say a word." Instead, it's, "Oh, yes, I've heard of *Hosta*. I think she may be a sloop. Let's stop for fish and chips." It's as if it's all a joke that can be laughed off, as if you're laughin' at me.'

'What do you know about *Hosta*?'

'Nothin' at all. They don't tell mere Wrens about things like that. They just let naval officers joke about them.'

'You really have got hold of the wrong end of the stick. Grace, I wouldn't knowingly do or say anything that I thought would hurt you or make you feel less than the most important person in my life. It's something you've completely misread. As for the other things, what you said about our families, they're meaningless.'

'To you, perhaps, but not to me.' They'd reached the place where they'd met and parted so many times, and now, it seemed, for the last time. 'Ivor,' she said, 'it's been lovely, but it can't go on.'

'Okay, if that's how you feel.' Good manners had to be observed, so he leaned forward to kiss her cheek. 'Goodbye, Grace. I hope you find the right man.'

'Goodbye, Ivor. I'm not very interested in men just now.' She turned and walked to the hotel entrance. Ivor watched until he knew she was safe.

Grace opened the door to the room she shared with three other girls. Two of them were already asleep. Only Beryl was missing, and she would be on watch. Miserably, she undressed and got into her pyjamas.

She'd used her period as an excuse – it wasn't due for another week – it was just a way of explaining her distant behaviour until the right time presented itself. Unfortunately, it hadn't, and she'd been obliged to tell him on the way home. Common sense told her that the hurt would have been the same whenever she'd given him the news, but she wasn't currently interested in logic or common sense.

She climbed into her bunk and wrapped herself into a cocoon of bedclothes, shielding herself from the unpleasantness of the outside world, but it wasn't enough, and she began to sob silently and wretchedly into her pillow.

16

As usual, the excitement for *Hosta* occurred on the eastbound leg. She was less than three days from docking in Liverpool when the port lookout sighted a U-boat. Ivor was almost relieved when it happened. For most of the voyage, he'd found ample time to relive his last evening with Grace, and each time he thought of it, the hurt was the same. Now, however, he had something else to occupy his thoughts, and his concentration returned immediately.

Smoothly and swiftly, the white ensign replaced the red, the screens parted and the gunlayers elevated and traversed the guns.

'All guns,' ordered Ivor, 'independent rapid fire!' He could see the U-boat's gun crew taking their places at the 88, and two more raced to the machine guns. They were well drilled; the machine guns opened up, aiming first at the four-inch gun crews, and then, failing to penetrate the gun shields, aimed higher.

As the gunlayers were finding the range, there was a loud cry from the seaman on the Vickers machine guns, and he fell across the machine-gun platform, his head hanging over the edge, lifeless.

The Captain turned, and, seeing Anderson in the waist of the ship, shouted, 'Anderson, take over the Vickers!'

Anderson made uncertainly for the ladder to the Vickers mounting.

'Get the machine gunners, Anderson, quick!'

Anderson was still hesitating on the ladder when Ivor felt a hammer blow against his left thigh.

The Captain heard him gasp and turned towards him. Grasping the Tannoy handset, he ordered, 'Stretcher party to the bridge!' Then, seeing no one on the Vickers, he shouted, 'Anderson, where are you?'

'Y' Gun had found the U-boat's range and scored a direct hit abaft the conning tower. A moment later, 'A' Gun put another shell through the hull. The machine-gun crew had been caught in the blast of the first shell and they lay dead on the weather deck of the sinking U-boat.

The leading sick berth attendant was cutting Ivor's trousers away to get a dressing on his wounds before allowing the stretcher party to take him below.

'Hold on, Number One,' said the Captain. 'The U-boat's sinking. Your chaps have done it again.' Switching on the Tannoy, he ordered, 'Anderson, get the survivors on board.'

Before losing consciousness, Ivor caught sight of Anderson. He was still gripping the ladder and shaking uncontrollably.

Grace arrived at her cabin, having come off the 'all-night-on' at 0800, and undressed. As if to increase her misery, she had decrypted a signal from *HMS Hosta*.

U-341 engaged and sunk at 0725. Have sustained casualties. Will advise.

Now, on top of everything else, members of *HMS Hosta*'s crew had been killed or wounded. She thought of the open bridge that had led her to embroider Ivor's towel. Those flimsy steel plates would afford no protection. After all that had happened, she couldn't bear the thought of Ivor being hurt. It was bad enough that she'd hurt him.

She was now convinced that her accusation had been unfounded and ridiculous. Of course his denial that he knew anything about *Hosta* had sounded like a joke. That was how Ivor was, and it was only because things between them had become so intense, that she'd forgotten that, if only for a while. If she'd been a little more grown-up about the whole thing, she would simply have accepted his response for what it was, and not expected a silly, mollycoddling expression of regret at being unable to divulge the nation's secrets, even to his beloved.

She continued to fret with self-recrimination until tiredness took pity on her and she fell asleep.

As Ivor regained consciousness, he became aware of the lancing pain in his thigh.

A voice said, 'Take it easy, sir. I'd like to give you more morphine, but it's not a good idea. You wouldn't want to become dependent on it, and it happens easily enough.'

Ivor recognised the leading sick berth attendant. 'Thank you, Durford,' he said. 'You know best, and I'm in your hands. Who else is hurt? I know Stubbs was hit.'

'Stubbs is dead, sir. He was on the Vickers. One of the torpedomen was winged as well, sir. He'll be okay. Oh, and one of the Jerry survivors was wounded.' Durford looked up when he heard footsteps on the ladder, and said, 'The Captain's here, sir.'

Ivor heard Newell ask, 'How's the patient, Durford?'

'The First Lieutenant's in considerable pain, sir. I've stopped the bleeding and splinted his leg in case there's damage to the femur. I've no way of knowing that for sure without an X-ray, sir.'

'I see. Have you given him morphia?'

'Yes, sir, but we have to be careful that he doesn't get too much. It's tricky stuff, sir.'

'Thank you, Durford. Give me a minute with the First Lieutenant, will you?'

'Aye, aye, sir.' Durford went into the dispensary and closed the door.

'Take it easy, old chap,' said the Captain. 'We're nearly home.' He looked rueful. 'I've had to put Anderson under open arrest. I'm undecided whether to charge him with cowardice or just refusal to obey an order. The latter may be kinder, as he's obviously suffering something akin to battle fatigue. Either way, his brief naval career will be over.'

'It's not good for him, but better for everyone else, sir.'

'Yes.' The Captain stood up to leave. 'I don't suppose you have any alternative, but take it easy, Number One. You'll go into hospital when we reach Liverpool, of course. I'll be sorry to lose you, because you've been an excellent first lieutenant.' He gave Ivor a quick smile and said, 'Maybe you'll see more of that girl you have in tow.'

'I'm afraid not, sir. She slipped her tow last time we were in harbour.'

'Bad luck, old man.'

The posters in the Coding Room seemed to taunt Grace. *Be Like Dad And Keep Mum, Keep Our Secrets Secret, Don't Brag About Your Job,* and *Walls Have Ears.* They all seemed to be speaking to her. She wondered how many ways there were of saying, 'I'm sorry. Don't take this personally, but I'm not allowed to talk about it.'

Her silly objection was childish and selfish, and just because she'd resented his easy evasiveness. She winced as a muscle cramp seized her lower abdomen, but it was no worse than she deserved. She'd lied to Ivor about her period, taking its name in vain, and now it was exacting its penalty, not that it really mattered. If only *Maynard, Hosta,* or whatever it was called, would dock, just so that she knew he was safe.

A woman's voice interrupted her mental flagellation.

'Here, Grace. We're in business again.' It was one of the girls from the W/T Room with a handful of signals.

'Thanks, Esther.' She took one and put the others in the 'IN' basket.

Five minutes later, she knew that the convoy was home. Typically, and for whatever reason, *Maynard* would follow one day later.

The pain of being manhandled up the ladder to the upper deck was intense, but Ivor kept himself from crying out by the expedient of clenching his teeth. Eventually, he was on deck, waiting for the ambulance, which arrived ten minutes later.

The Captain came to see him off. 'All the best, Number One,' he said, shaking his hand, 'and thank you for all your efforts, which have been considerable.'

'You're welcome, sir. Thank you for the apprenticeship.'

'You'd served that before you joined the ship.' He stood back and saluted as the ambulance men loaded Ivor and the stretcher into the vehicle. It was the same gesture of respect that Ivor had paid to the ship eight months earlier, and he appreciated it.

He asked the man in the ambulance, 'Where are you taking me?'

'Sefton General Hospital, sir, Smithdown Road,' was the practised reply.

'I wonder what the chances are of my getting back to the same ship.'

The attendant pursed his lips in thought. 'I'm a sporting man, sir, but I wouldn't be inclined to put a bet on it. Not with what you've got.'

Ivor wondered what the man knew about his injury, but it wasn't worth pursuing, so he closed his eyes and braced himself for the journey to Smithdown Road.

Grace had come off the all-night-on, but instead of going back to her cabin for a hard-earned sleep, she walked down to Salthouse Dock. She'd written a note for Ivor, which she intended to hand to the quartermaster on the gangway, and she took it from her pocket as she turned the corner into the Dock.

As she did so, however, she stopped suddenly, because the only ship in the dock was a merchantman of some kind. *HMS Maynard* was nowhere in sight.

Worried and perplexed, she walked back to the Emilia and her waiting bunk.

Ivor clenched his teeth again as he was manoeuvred into position for an X-ray. It seemed that those whose responsibility it was to alleviate suffering had a boundless repertoire of ways to inflict it.

Eventually, he was wheeled into a long ward and moved from the trolley into a bed from which he could see that almost all the other beds were occupied. The war was evidently going less well than the public were led to believe.

He exchanged a few words with the man in the next bed, who seemed to be in a similarly painful condition. As if by unspoken mutual consent, they lapsed into silence.

After an hour or so, a doctor came to examine him.

'Good morning,' he said.

'Good morning, Doc.'

'You are Lieutenant Loveday, I presume.'

'You presume correctly.'

The doctor took his stethoscope from the pocket of his white coat and said, 'I'm just going to check your heart and lungs.'

It sounded an odd thing to do to a patient with a bullet wound in the leg, but Ivor kept silent for the time being.

'Hm, excellent,' said the doctor, taking the notes and clipboard from the bottom bedrail. 'I'm just checking your bowel history, which seems to be satisfactory.'

'My leg is the problem,' prompted Ivor. 'The bullet missed my heart, lungs and bowel.'

'Each to his own, Lieutenant,' the doctor chided him. 'The consultant will see you when he's had a look at your X-ray.'

'There's always something cheery on the horizon, isn't there, Doc?'

'Be thankful that you have something to look forward to,' advised the earnest physician, making a note on a clipboard, which he hung on the end of the bed.

His leg having been left alone for an hour, Ivor lapsed into sleep. When he awoke, his bed was surrounded, apparently by doctors and nurses. A serious man in half-moon spectacles said, 'Good afternoon, Lieutenant Loveday.'

'Good afternoon, Doc. Good afternoon to you all. I'd offer you all a drink, but you've caught me at something of a disadvantage.'

The serious man managed a half-smile and said, 'Your X-ray shows that the bullet fractured your femur before making a very untidy exit. I have to say that the medical orderly on your ship made an excellent job of patching you up, no doubt in less than ideal conditions, but your leg now requires surgical attention.'

'You're not going to amputate it, are you, Doc?' He thought it was as well to check.

'Certainly not. I should like to fix a metal rod to your femur to support it. Then we shall repair the damaged soft tissue. Before we can do that, however, we need your consent.'

It all sounded very complex, but Ivor imagined the man knew what he was doing. 'If that's your recommendation, Doc, I wouldn't dream of arguing with you. You naturally have my consent.'

'Thank you, Lieutenant. When did you last eat?'

'Approximately oh six hundred this morning.'

'In that case, I shall operate tomorrow morning.' Turning to the severe-looking woman beside him, he said, 'See that Lieutenant Loveday signs a consent form, Sister.'

'Very good, sir.'

'Good day to you, Lieutenant.'

'Goodbye, Doc.'

The sister returned later with a form, a fountain pen and an admonishing look. 'The consultant is Mr Halsey,' she said. 'Surgeons are called "Mr", not "Doctor".'

'How confusing. Still, I imagine that the next time he sees me, I'll be unconscious and therefore incapable of giving offence.'

'That will be a welcome state of affairs, Lieutenant.'

Involved as she was in her dilemma, Grace hadn't realised how noticeable her preoccupied state had become, until Beryl asked her during one change-over, 'What's bothering you, Grace?'

'It's Ivor. I don't know what's happened.' Now that she was talking about it, tears seemed to come from nowhere. 'I went down to Salthouse Dock on Monday,' she said, 'and there was no sign of *HMS Maynard*. I don't know if she's been sunk or what's happened to her.'

Beryl thought. 'One of the girls on my watch has been seeing a subby from *Maynard*, a nice lad called Brian, although that's of no interest to you, is it? I'll be seeing her in a minute or so, and I'll ask her if you like.'

'Oh, will you, please?'

'Leave it to me.'

Grace retired to her bunk, satisfied at least that she would soon know something. Sheer tiredness meant that she slept almost until supper.

She went down to the W/T Room at the start of her watch, but Beryl wasn't there. One of the telegraphists looked up and saw her.

'I'm looking for Beryl,' she said.

'She went off watch early,' said the girl. 'A call of nature, I shouldn't wonder.'

Frustrated, Grace returned to the Coding Room, where she found a note on her desk, addressed simply to 'Grace'. Avoiding the eye of authority, she opened it hurriedly and read it.

Stop worrying, Grace. You looked in the wrong place. HMS Maynard is in Canning Dock, not Salthouse Dock. She's been there since Monday.

Chin up,

Beryl.

I was almost a relief to know that *Maynard* was still functioning and in one piece, even though she'd changed homes for whatever reason. All Grace needed now was the time to go down to Canning Dock and see if she could leave her note for Ivor.

17

Mr Halsey peered at the X-ray through his half-moon glasses. 'Hm,' he said in his non-committal way, and then showed it to the man next to him, who said, 'Hm,' in a slightly different way, and Ivor began to wonder if a humming chorus might be imminent. It seemed not, however, because Mr Halsey then spoke to him.

'Your condition is improving nicely, Lieutenant Loveday,' he said. 'Another week, and you should be ready to leave us.'

'That's good news, Mr Halsey. Just out of interest, when I leave this hospital, where will I go?'

'To a convalescent home for officers, of course. Where else?'

It was obviously a silly question, but Ivor had asked it simply because he still had no home to go to, and Mr Halsey had probably never considered that possibility.

It was frustrating beyond belief that Grace was unable to go to the docks in daytime for the next four days. When the watch bill allowed her to make the visit, she felt like a spring that had been under tension far too long.

She had to find her way to Canning Dock, which wasn't difficult, as it was next door to Salthouse Dock, and her spirits rose tentatively when she saw HMS Maynard. From the end of the dock, however, she could see that damage had been inflicted on her. Holes had appeared and there were broken scuttles. Most ominously, the bridge was riddled with what she could only imagine were bullet holes, although she couldn't see why ships should shoot at one another with little guns when they had much bigger ones and torpedoes as well.

While she was staring, an officer, a lieutenant commander, came down the gangway, so she saluted, hoping he wouldn't object to her being there. When he drew closer, however, he spoke to her in a friendly way.

'Hello,' he said. 'Are you looking for someone?'

'Not really, sir. I was just wondering if somebody could tell me if Lieutenant Loveday's all right.'

'Lieutenant Loveday, eh? You must be the girl he was seeing.'

She lowered her eyelashes. The officer's use of the past tense meant that Ivor must have told him about them breaking up. Either that, or the unthinkable had happened. 'Yes, sir. We had a disagreement, but when I heard that there'd been some casualties, I wondered if, I mean....' Suddenly, she found it impossible to explain.

'Listen, my dear. I don't know how you heard that or what you know. All I can tell you is that Lieutenant Loveday was wounded in action. He was taken to hospital last Monday when we docked.'

'Is he badly hurt, sir?

'His leg was badly damaged. The last I heard, they'd operated on it, and he's going to be fine, so there's nothing to worry about.' He looked at his watch and said, 'I must go. I'm expected at a meeting. Try not to worry too much, because he'll be all right and he's in safe hands.'

'Thank you, sir.' She saluted again. He returned her salute and hurried away. When he'd gone, she realised she'd forgotten to ask which hospital Ivor was in. She imagined it would be one of the main ones in Liverpool.

'We have to move you, Lieutenant Loveday.' Sister Oswald delivered the information in her customary scolding way, and Ivor was beginning to wonder how he could have been such a nuisance without being fully aware of it at the time.

'We need the bed you're occupying,' she told him.

'What are you going to do with me, Sister? Stand me up in a corner? This plaster cast should keep me upright, I suppose.'

'Of course not,' she snorted. 'As soon as a bed is found for you elsewhere, you'll be transferred there.'

It sounded pointless to Ivor. 'Why don't you send the person who wants this bed to wherever you're thinking of sending me? Wouldn't that be simpler?' He intended it as a helpful suggestion, but Sister Oswald evidently thought otherwise.

'We do know what we're doing, Lieutenant. The fact is that the patient who needs your bed is also in urgent need of Mr Halsey's attention.'

'Well, in that case, I can hardly object, can I? Go on, then. If your conscience will stand it, you'd better go ahead and throw me out into the harsh, inhospitable world.'

'We'll let you know as soon as we've located a hospital with a spare bed,' she assured him.

It was all the same to Ivor, who couldn't have cared less where he was going. His verbal joust with Sister Oswald was simply one of a series of deliberate distractions from his main preoccupation. When he'd been at sea, there had been plenty to occupy his thoughts, but now he had too much time for thought.

Girlfriends had come and gone in the last few years. He'd rarely initiated the parting; so many of them had objected to his apparent lack of commitment, that he'd never had the need, and he'd developed a thick skin in the process. The difference was that Grace had found her way into his deepest and previously-untapped susceptibilities. He'd become hopelessly in love with her, and that was going to take some shrugging off.

He lay in the disputed bed, working his way through his brooding list, which naturally included German machine-gunners and heartless nursing sisters. First place, however, went to the ultimate oxymoron – female logic, the kind that had persuaded Grace that their relationship was doomed to failure.

Later that afternoon, when he was writing a note to Huw, he learned that he was to be moved to a hospital on the outskirts of Manchester. He really didn't care.

Grace had spent time and money she could ill afford in trying to trace Ivor's whereabouts. The main hospitals had no record of a Lieutenant Ivor Loveday, and she was told that he could have been taken anywhere, such was the demand for hospital beds. Someone at Sefton Park Hospital told her that they were busy enough answering enquiries from patients' families. Friends would have to wait.

As soon as she could, she made another trip to Canning Dock to find someone who might be able to tell her more, but on entering the dock, she found that *HMS Maynard* was gone. She made enquiries of various dock workers, and eventually learned that *Maynard* had been taken elsewhere for repairs, and 'elsewhere', like Ivor's whereabouts, could be anywhere.

The ambulance attendant who travelled with Ivor was friendly, cheerful and inquisitive. She wore her dark hair caught back in a comb, which gave her a professional, business-like air that was at odds with her easy-going manner.

Her first question was, 'Who did this to you?'

'Oddly enough, I didn't catch his name. All I know is that he was German, and if he was aiming at my left thigh, about three inches above the knee, he was a bloody good shot. Other than that, there's not much I can tell you about him.' On reflection, he added, 'In any case, it wouldn't be right, considering what happened to him.'

'What happened to him?' Her question seemed to be born of no more than idle curiosity.

'He was killed.'

'Poor chap. I suppose he was only doing his job. They're like everybody else, really. People forget that.'

'So was I, Doris. That's all I was doing, just doing my job and minding my own business, and look what happened to me.'

'I'm not unsympathetic, Lieutenant, but my name's Jane.'

'Glad to meet you, Jane. I'm Ivor.' He gasped when the ambulance hit a pothole in the road and pain shot through his leg.

'Is it bad?'

'Only when I'm thrown around in an ambulance,' he assured her.

'Just a minute,' said Jane. Opening the communicating hatch to speak to the driver, she said, 'Take it easy, Gladys. There's no hurry, and this poor lad's in pain.'

Ivor heard Gladys say something, but it was difficult to make out. He asked, 'What did she say, Jane?'

'She says she's in a hurry because she's driving with her legs crossed.'

'She could get a job in a circus,' he said.

'How's that?'

'Driving with her legs crossed? If she could do it in tights and bareback on a horse, she'd be a sensation.'

'In tights?' Jane shook her head confidently. 'You haven't seen Gladys. She'd be a sensation all right, but not the kind you mean.'

Five minutes later, the ambulance slowed down and came to an abrupt halt. Ivor heard a door slam, and asked, 'Have we arrived?'

Jane opened one of the rear doors to investigate, and said, 'No, Gladys has gone behind a bush.'

'She must have been desperate.'

'Well, there is a war on.'

'Of course,' he said, 'I keep forgetting.'

The stationary ambulance lurched to one side as Gladys resumed her seat and slammed the door again. There was a grinding of gears, and the ambulance resumed its journey at a more leisurely pace. Ivor could almost feel the relief radiating from the driving seat.

Jane asked, 'What do you do with yourself when you're not laid up with a broken leg, Ivor?'

'I'm first lieutenant of a warship, believe it or not.'

Jane looked at him, as if for the first time, and shook her head. 'Who'd have thought it, just looking at you?'

'I don't wear pyjamas and a plaster cast when I'm on watch,' he explained. 'It's an easy mistake to make.'

'Fair enough. Are you married?'

'No. Are you?'

'No.' As if to show willing, she said, 'I've been a bridesmaid a few times.'

'It's good practice, they tell me, although I've been a best man twice, now, and I don't see that as preparation for occupying the crease.' To counteract possible ambiguity, he added, 'So to speak.'

'No, I suppose not. Have you got a girlfriend?'

'No. Are you volunteering?'

'I might. You seem nice enough.'

'It wouldn't be fair to keep you hanging on, Jane. I've just been jettisoned after a passionate relationship, and I'm damaged goods.'

'As if you hadn't enough on your plate with your broken leg.' She gave him a sympathetic smile and said, 'You never know. Things might change, and you can always find me at the ambulance depot. There's only one Jane there.'

'I'll bear you in mind, Jane.' It was all he could offer her.

After a while, the ambulance slowed down again to take a right turn and then proceeded slowly, finally coming to rest.

'We've arrived,' said Jane.

'Just when we were getting to know each other.'

'It always happens,' she told him sadly.

Ivor wondered if serial disappointment really featured on such a scale in Jane's working week.

'This isn't part of the service, and we're not supposed to fraternise with patients, but....' She leaned over him and favoured him with a gentle kiss on his cheek. 'Take care of yourself, Ivor,' she said wistfully, opening the rear doors.

It seemed to him that things had a way of happening at absolutely the wrong time.

Grace's efforts to locate Ivor were completely fruitless. Having drawn several blanks, she tried Sefton Park General Hospital again and spoke to a rather more sympathetic person than before, who told her that a Lieutenant Loveday had been a patient there, but that he had been moved to another hospital. Her spirits were dashed when her informant told her that she was unable to divulge his destination to anyone but his family.

18

Blackthorn Hall Convalescent Home for Officers, Sussex

July

With the plaster removed, Ivor was more mobile, but nevertheless restricted to walking with crutches. A resident physiotherapist saw him each Monday, to put him, as she said, through his paces. For his part, he was thankful that her clumsiness was restricted to her turn of phrase.

Ivor had just completed a physio session and was relaxing again on the extensive lawn that seemed to be home to almost every known activity. Such things were exhausting to watch, so he turned his eyes towards the house, where one of the nurses appeared to be giving directions to a naval officer; in fact, she was pointing to Ivor, who was surprised as he wasn't expecting a visitor.

As the officer, a commander, RN, came closer, Ivor recognised his late captain and greeted him as he approached. 'Commander Newell,' he said, reaching for his crutches.

'Don't get up, Loveday, whatever you do.' Newell offered his hand. 'How are you?'

'I'm well enough, thank you, sir. Just bored by inactivity.' Eyeing the three gold rings on his visitor's sleeve and the ribbon of the Distinguished Service Cross on his chest, he said, 'Congratulations on your promotion and your DSC. If I may say so, they're both richly deserved.'

'Thank you, Loveday. You'll be surprised and gratified to know that there's a DSC on its way for you.'

'For me, sir? What have I done?'

'A damned good job. Four U-boats destroyed, for one thing.'

'I'm stunned, sir.'

A nurse interrupted their conversation when she arrived with tea for them both. They thanked her, and Newell poured the tea. It was a novel experience for Ivor, who covered his awkwardness by asking, 'How's the ship, sir?'

'*Hosta* is no more, I'm afraid,' said Newell, handing him a cup of tea. 'I'm currently on survivors' leave.'

'Oh?'

'We came to the attention of a *Hipper* class cruiser. We think it was the *Holtzendorff.* At all events, she battered us almost to oblivion, and then, quite unaccountably, ceased firing and continued eastward. I can only imagine her captain was exasperated by his inability to sink us and, at the same time, keen to overhaul the convoy. The story I heard was that he was successful in the latter, but found to his dismay that the convoy was escorted by an "R" class battleship, which rather upset his calculations, because he then had to beat a frantic retreat with fifteen-inch shells bursting around his ears.'

'How soon were you picked up?'

'After three days. The *Iceni* picked us up. I set demolition charges and gave *Hosta* a Viking funeral. It was imperative that she didn't fall into enemy hands.'

Ivor nodded. 'God bless her.'

'You were very fond of her, I remember.'

'I was, sir.'

'I'm afraid the age of the Q-ship is past, Loveday.'

'Really, sir?' Ivor was nonplussed. *Hosta*'s successes should surely have reinforced the argument in favour of the decoy.

'The Admiralty is deploying new tactics against the U-boat. That much I can tell you, although the rest is shrouded, as ever, in secrecy. So, *Hosta*'s secret has not accompanied her entirely to the grave, as we need no longer remain as reticent about her remarkable record.

'What casualties were there, sir?'

'Rather a lot, Loveday. Leading Steward Denison was among them.'

'Oh, no.' It was too bad that the gentle, dedicated wardroom steward had gone. 'Who else, sir?'

'Sub-lieutenant Cartwright. There were others, too many to name.'

'Poor old Brian. He was seeing a girl from Western Approaches, I believe.' Not surprisingly, he remembered that.

'Yes, a telegraphist, poor girl.' Something else occurred to Newell, and he said, 'A few days after we docked in Liverpool, after you were wounded, a Wren came to Canning Dock, asking about you, a pretty girl with reddish-blonde hair.'

'Grace?'

'Was that her name? She was relieved that you were still alive, but upset when I told her you'd been wounded. She said you'd had a disagreement, but when she heard there'd been casualties, she feared for your life, and came down to the dock to enquire about you.'

'I haven't heard from her.'

'It's possible she doesn't know where to find you. I honestly can't remember whether or not I told her which hospital they'd taken you to. I had a great deal on my mind at the time.' After a moment's thought, he said, 'I suppose you could drop her a line at WAHQ or the Wrens' quarters, perhaps.'

'I shall, sir, and thank you for telling me about that.'

'Not at all.' Changing the subject, he asked, 'So what happens now? A medical board, I imagine?'

'Yes, sir. I realise I'm not fully fit as yet, but I hope to return to the fleet at some stage.'

'Let's hope so, Loveday. They've given me a *Hunt* Class destroyer, by the way, which is good news for an old fossil like me. I'm only sorry I shan't have you as my number one.'

'I rather regret that, too, sir, and thank you for the compliment.'

'It's well deserved.' Newell placed his cup and saucer on the tray and stood up. 'Well, Loveday,' he said, 'I have a train to catch. I've enjoyed seeing you again. Take it easy.'

'Thank you for coming, sir. Your visit was just what I needed.'

They shook hands and Ivor watched him return to the house, still sorry that the appointment of First Lieutenant must go to someone else. He had other things to do, though, and he lost no time in taking out his pen and writing paper.

Blackthorn Hall Convalescent Home,
Brighton,
Sussex.
Dear Grace,
I hope everything is well with you.
I have just seen my old captain, who told me about your visit to Canning Dock when you heard there had been casualties. I just want to thank you for your concern.
I'm still laid up with a broken leg that's healing slowly but surely, so please don't worry about me.

He wondered quite how to end it. After some thought, he opted for the truth and wrote:

Yours with very best wishes,
Lots of love,
Ivor.

Grace was both surprised and wary when she was ordered to report to Second Officer Curwen. She couldn't think of anything she'd done that might have attracted wrath from above, but such things were always possible. Such was her state of mind when she knocked on the door marked *2/O R. A. Curwen, W.R.N.S.*

'Come in.'

Grace pushed open the door and stepped in.

'Ah, Wren Headley. Come in and take a seat.'

Grace took the chair on the other side of the desk and waited nervously.

'You're not yourself, Wren Headley. I'm not the only one who's noticed. Tell me, has it anything to do with the officer you've been seeing?'

It was the last thing Grace wanted to talk about, but an officer could not be denied, so she said quietly, 'Yes, ma'am. He was wounded in action and taken to hospital. I've tried to find out where he is, but I still haven't a clue. The awful thing is that we had a disagreement the last time we met, and I told him I didn't want to see him again.'

'Oh, dear. Have you changed your mind since then?'

'Yes, ma'am, but there's no way I can let him know.' She was horrified to feel tears forming in her eyelids. It was the last thing she'd wanted.

'Have you got a hanky?'

'Yes, thank you, ma'am.' She took a handkerchief from her pocket and dabbed her eyes.

Miss Curwen opened a box on her desk and asked, 'Would you like a cigarette?'

'No, thank you, ma'am. I don't smoke.'

'Very wise. Maybe you'd like some tea. It's due about now, anyway, but I'll see if I can hurry it up.' She went to the door and called for tea to be brought to her office. 'Now,' she said, taking her seat again, 'you don't know where he is. Do you know his home address?'

'No, ma'am, he has no home. It was bombed in the Blitz, and he lost both his parents.' She told the story of them living within ten miles of each other on the same river that had endured savage bombing during the Blitz.

'Poor man. That's awful.' There was a knock on the door. 'Ah, the tea's arrived. Yes, bring it in, please.'

A Wren placed the tray on the desk, giving Grace an embarrassed look, and left the office.

'How do you like your tea, Wren Headley?'

'Just milk but no sugar, please, ma'am.' Grace couldn't believe an officer was giving her tea. She asked, 'Do you want me to pour it, ma'am?'

'No, just relax.' She poured tea and milk into both cups and handed one to Grace.

'Thank you, ma'am.'

'Now, Wren Headley, I really do think you need a change of scenery and a distraction.'

Grace couldn't imagine what she had in mind, but she waited in silence to find out.

'I'm arranging seven day's leave for you, starting tomorrow, and then afterwards, you'll go to *HMS Cabbala*, where you'll join the Leading Wren Course.'

'In Gloucestershire, ma'am?'

'No, that one's closed. The new *HMS Cabbala* is not far from here, in Leigh, near Warrington. It's where they train coders now, and where you'll be given your leading Wren's training. After that, you'll be sent to *HMS St Christopher*.'

It was like being led through a maze. 'Where's that, ma'am?'

'It's the coastal forces training base in Fort William, a beautiful town in Inverness-shire.'

'I've heard of it, ma'am. That'll be lovely.'

'I'm glad you feel like that about it, Wren Headley. Now, don't let your tea get cold.'

Ivor addressed the note to Grace at the Hotel Emilia and dropped it in the Outgoing Mail Box. He could only hope. Meanwhile, he had to concentrate on the exercises set for him by the dour and unbending physiotherapist Miss Turner.

A distraction occurred several days later, when Ivor and two other naval officers were called to the part of the house reserved for important visitors. It seemed that a vice-admiral, whose name meant nothing to any of them, wished to see them.

At the appointed time, the admiral was ushered into the room earmarked for the meeting. He was attended by an officer wearing the aiguilettes of a flag lieutenant and carrying several cases that could only contain medals.

The other two officers were senior to Ivor, so they received their decorations first and then watched politely when Ivor's turn came.

'When you read the citation, you will find that this is for exceptional achievement whilst carrying out duties of a special and hazardous nature,' said the vice-admiral. 'Congratulations, Lieutenant Loveday.'

'Thank you, sir.' Ivor took the flag officer's hand.

The DSC called for a letter to Huw in Cheshire, because there was no one else Ivor could tell. It was a shame, because the occasion called for celebration.

Two days later, the PO Wren on the desk at the Hotel Emilia handed a sheaf of incoming mail to the new Wren who had become her assistant. She, in turn, began posting the envelopes into a series of pigeon holes, each labelled with the name of a Wren billeted in the hotel.

'There's one here that must have the wrong address on it, PO,' she said. 'There's no pigeon hole for Wren G. L. Headley.'

PO Wren Davis was busy organising the laundry. She said, 'Say again?'

'There's a letter for a Wren who's not on our establishment.'

'Oh, leave it for now. I'll look into it later.' PO Wren Davis had more important matters to attend to than misdirected mail.

'Yes, PO.' The Wren put Grace's letter on the Petty Officer's desk and continued with her work.

Later that morning, PO Wren Davis cast an unenthusiastic eye over the paperwork on her desk. Some of it was waiting to be filed, and that was the new Wren's job. PO Davis had forgotten her name already, but that wasn't important. She picked up the filing and deposited it on the Wren's desk. In doing so, she failed to notice that the letter to the mysterious Wren had slipped off the bottom of the pile and fallen into the bin marked *Unclassified Waste*.

19

SEPTEMBER

The course had been a timely distraction, but Grace's week at home with her parents had been even more welcome.

True to form, her mother had seen almost immediately that all was not as it should be, and she'd lost no time in persuading Grace to tell her story. For Grace, it was a tearful yet comforting experience, and one that was well overdue.

Her mother asked, 'And where does he live, this sailor?'

'He's not a sailor, Mam, he's an officer. He lived in Tynemouth until the Blitz. It destroyed his house and killed his mam and dad.'

'Oh poor lad. An officer, you say?'

'Aye, but not what you'd call posh. There's no side to him. He used to be a reporter with the Tynemouth Observer.'

'Well, bless my soul.' It was the nearest her mam ever got to swearing. 'First, our Jack gets made an officer, and then you find a one. He's a canny lad, you say?'

'He's a lovely man, and I lost him through me own stupid fault. He got taken to hospital because he was wounded. The only trouble was, I couldn't find out which hospital it was.'

'How long ago was that?'

'About three months ago. He could be back at sea for all I know, or he might have been discharged. I don't know how bad his injuries were.' Her tears returned.

'Oh, come here, pet lamb.' She held out her arms to her daughter. It was what mothers did best, and it was what Grace needed.

Much later, her father came home from the yard. Grace greeted him, knowing how overjoyed he was to see her, even though he showed it less than his wife did. Presently, Grace told a more down-to-earth version of her story again for his benefit.

Having accepted the fact that not all officers were posh and stand-offish, he gave the problem some thought. 'There's one thing you could try,' he said.

'What's that, Dad?'

'You say he worked for the Tynemouth Observer. You could ask there if any of 'em have heard from him. If he's no family, mevve he'll get in touch with his old marrers from work. You never know.'

It was the first good idea Grace had heard since she'd first learned that Ivor had been wounded, and she set out, the next morning, to make enquiries at the newspaper office.

There was a man of advanced years on the front desk, and Grace imagined he'd been kept on because so many, both male and female, were away in the forces.

He asked, 'What can I do for you, bonny lass?'

'Were you here when Ivor Loveday worked here?'

'Aye, and a long time before that. What's your interest in Ivor?'

'He's a friend of mine, and I'm trying to find out where he is.'

The man's eyes went surreptitiously to her waistline.

'No,' she said hastily, 'it's nothin' like that. He was wounded at sea, and they took him to hospital, but I don't know which one or where he went after that. I just wondered if he'd been in touch with anybody here.'

'I haven't seen him, but I don't know about anybody else. Most of them as worked with him, the younger ones, at any rate, are in the forces. Just give me a minute.' He left his place on the desk and went through a door to an inner office, leaving Grace to look around her. The interior wasn't very imposing, although Ivor had never claimed it was. If anything, he'd played it down the way he played most things down. It was one of his endearing characteristics, so she tried not to think about it. She didn't need to make herself miserable when she could be wretched without trying.

Eventually, the old man returned, and Grace could tell from his face that it was bad news.

'I'm sorry, pet,' he said. 'Nobody's heard a word from him since that leave when he came and found his house flattened. Did you know about that?'

'Yes, he told me about it.'

'It was a terrible business.'

'Aye.' It was, but Grace's worries lay elsewhere.

'I wish I could help you, pet.'

'Thank you for tryin', all the same.'

'You're welcome, pet. Good luck with your enquiries.'

Once again, Grace had drawn a blank, so it was as well that she had her leave, the course and Fort William to take her mind off things.

Ivor expected to be called at any time to attend a medical board, but that seemed to be taking forever. While he waited, he amused himself by playing darts, snooker, bar skittles and bar billiards. Now that he was able to walk with a stick rather than crutches, he could also play croquet. He'd always found card games boring, but he made an effort and joined the others in various games, though with little enthusiasm.

He'd given up waiting for Grace to reply to his note. The likelihood was that she'd found someone else; there would be no shortage of men interested in her, and she was a friendly, sociable girl. It was almost a certainty. He'd considered getting in touch with Jane, the ambulance girl. She obviously liked him, and she was quite attractive, although he knew very little about her, other than her career as a serial bridesmaid. Unfortunately, inertia had become a way of life, and Jane remained no more than a cosy memory.

A pleasing distraction came in the form of a visit from his brother Huw, now a flying officer but still stationed on the Wirral. He arrived unannounced, as he usually did, but that made him no less welcome.

'Congratulations on the gong,' said Huw. 'I got your letter, but it was easier to come down than to write.'

'You surprise me, Huw. I'd have put a wartime train journey ahead of posting a letter in terms of difficulty.'

'It was no trouble at all,' Huw assured him.

'Where are you staying?'

'At the local hostelry. I've got a seventy-two hour pass, so it made sense.'

It didn't sound like the kind of thing Huw would usually arrange for himself. 'I don't suppose you had company on the way down, did you?'

'Well, sort of, in a sense, that is....'

'Female company?'

'We're not encouraged to strike up relationships with WAAFs on our own station, but honestly, Ivor, it was impossible to avoid.'

So, Huw had a girl waiting for him at the local pub. 'You don't have to justify yourself to me, Huw.'

'I was just practising for the real thing, when the queen WAAF kicks up a rumpus. Gloria's an assistant section officer – that's the WAAF equivalent of a prune, a pilot officer, that is – and she's truly lovely, and our paths kept crossing, even when I wasn't trying. It would have been churlish of me not to take her under my wing, so to speak.'

'It would have been downright discourteous,' agreed Ivor, 'not to say a missed opportunity.'

'Quite.' Huw was eyeing him speculatively.

'What's on your mind, Huw?'

Huw looked embarrassed. 'The thing is, Ivor, this trip to Brighton and everything has strained the finances somewhat....'

'How much?'

'I wouldn't ask, except....'

'How much do you need?'

Huw steeled himself. 'Could you lend me a fiver, just until I get turned round?'

'It might be arranged.'

'It would be a great help, and I'll let you have it just as soon as I can.'

'Of course you will, but you'll have to stand on your own two feet eventually, you know.'

'The situation's improving all the time.'

'I'm pleased to hear it.' Ivor opened his wallet and took out a five-pound note.

'I appreciate this, Ivor.'

'Enjoy your seventy-two, Huw, both of you, although I'm sure you don't need encouragement from me.'

Grace arrived in Fort William on a glorious day, when everything was bathed in sunshine and the sea reflected the blue of a cloudless sky. It was just as Second Officer Curwen had described it, and she almost dared to believe that it was going to help her get over the loss of Ivor.

The first thing she noticed about *HMS St Christopher* was that the volume of signal traffic was much lower than at Western Approaches. It was less than surprising, of course, but no less pleasing. Things at WAHQ could be hectic at times. It seemed that the girls in the Coding Room had never known pressure, however, and Grace sometimes had to jolly them on when they complained about the workload. It was one of the functions expected of her now that she was a leading Wren, and she was surprised to find that it came to her quite naturally.

The girls in Signal Distribution and the telegraphists were a nice lot, too. Each watch came under either a PO telegraphist or a PO Wren telegraphist, and the PO tel. assigned to Grace's watch seemed okay, although there was a few times she'd caught him looking at her. She didn't mind. He was allowed to look, but that was all.

The liveliest characters were the officers under instruction. They were mainly newly-commissioned sub-lieutenants, and they were all very young, most of them younger than she was. One of them, returning from a training session at sea, stopped on his way to the wardroom to speak to her. She was about to go into the Coding Room.

'Hello,' he said. 'You're new, aren't you?' He was fair-haired and very boyish-looking.

'I'm new here, but I'm not new to the job, sir.'

'Where are you from?'

'Newcastle, sir.' She imagined her accent would tell him which Newcastle she meant.

'Lovely people in the north,' he said, having guessed correctly. 'So friendly.'

She reckoned somebody must have told him that. It wasn't the kind of thing twenty-one-year-old lads usually said or even knew. 'You should try Newcastle Docks at closing time on a Saturday night, sir, and you'll find out how friendly they are.'

'I'm fascinated. Look, when do you come off watch?'

'At eighteen hundred, sir, but before you ask me, we're not supposed to go ashore with officers.' She remembered telling Ivor the same thing, and suspected the result might be much the same.

'Things are very relaxed here. If you like, I'll pick you up at the Wrens' quarters at eighteen-thirty, and we can go for a drink.'

Grace considered his invitation. It wasn't what she'd had in mind when she arrived in Fort William, but it was only a drink and nothing more. 'Okay, sir,' she said. 'I'll stretch a point for you.'

'Terrific. My name's Oliver, by the way. Everyone calls me "Ovie". It's a sort of play on my initials "O. V". What's yours?'

'Grace, sir.'

'Splendid. I'll see you later, Grace.'

Ovie was waiting for her when she got to the door of the hotel that had become the Wrens' quarters. He looked even younger than she remembered.

'Gosh, Grace,' he said, 'you're a sight for sore eyes.'

She was wearing the same green dress that she'd worn on her first date with Ivor. 'Hardly that, but thank you, all the same.' She took his arm, and he led her to a tiny pub behind the hotel. It was half-hidden by cottages.

'It's a quiet place,' Ovie told her. 'Most of the chaps prefer The Fisherman, so it gets quite rowdy, not the kind of thing I'd inflict on a nice girl.'

'That's very thoughtful of you, Ovie.'

'What would you like to drink?'

'Just lemonade, please.'

'Are you sure?'

She nodded confidently. 'I'm on the early watch tomorrow, and I'll need a clear head.'

He asked the barmaid for a lemonade and a pink gin. Grace suspected that he'd only recently discovered the naval officers' staple drink, and that he was working hard at living up to the image. Still, as she'd told herself earlier, they had only come out for a drink.

They found a settle in a secluded corner.

'I suppose I need a clear head too,' said Ovie. 'We're practising torpedo attacks tomorrow.' It was clear that he meant to impress her.

'Ovie, do you think you should be talking about it in a public place?' She was uncomfortably aware that she was pulling up an officer, albeit a very junior one, for loose talk.

'Maybe not.' He nodded earnestly. 'I get carried away.'

'I'll stop you if you do it again. Tell me about yourself instead. What were you doing before you joined the Navy?'

'Not much, I'm afraid. I was at drama school.'

'That's unusual, for me at any rate, because you're the first drama student I've met. Are you going to do actin' for a livin', then?'

'I hope so. It's a chancy business, with so many actors going after so few parts.'

'But just think,' she said, 'in years to come, I might see your name on a theatre bill, and I'll say to whoever's with me at the time, 'I once went for a drink with Ovie in Fort William. You see, I knew him before he was famous.' She looked at him and detected a hint of embarrassment. 'Relax, bonny lad,' she said. 'I'm not makin' fun of you. I hope you will be famous.'

'It's all to be tried for, isn't it?' He didn't sound very confident.

'Just get your head down and work at it, pet.'

Conversation became easier then. He stopped trying to impress her, and she became less careful with him and more protective. He really was very young, and not just in years.

As soon as they left the pub, Grace shivered in the night air.

Ovie said, 'I shan't keep you, because I know you're cold, but will you come out with me again?'

'I will, but let's not do it too often. Wrens can get a name for doing that, and it's not a name I want to be called.'

'Okay, but it's been so nice. Don't you think so?'

'Really nice. Here,' she said, inclining her cheek for a kiss. 'Thank you for a really pleasant evenin'. Let's go home. I've got to get my beauty sleep.'

'You don't need that, Grace. I mean, of course you need to sleep, but... you know what I mean.'

'I do, and thank you for the compliment.'

They parted at the hotel, and Grace went up to bed, having played big sister to an immature boy, who would soon be risking his life in the war at sea. She found it frightening.

20

Grace did go ashore with Ovie again. In spite of what she'd said, his boyish, vulnerable innocence made him difficult to refuse. There was another factor, as well, that neither of them could control, and that was the brevity of the Coastal Forces course. In what seemed like no time at all, Ovie's course reached its end, and his departure was imminent.

On the eve of his final interview with the Base Commander, they went, as usual, to the Spyglass. Ovie was uncharacteristically subdued, and Grace asked him what was troubling him.

'It's having to leave you, Grace. I can face everything else, but you've come to mean a lot to me.'

It was as she'd feared. 'That's very flattering,' she said, 'but we were only ever going to have a drink together. It was no more than that.'

He looked embarrassed, as he often did. 'Oh, I realise we could never be anything... more than we are to each other,' he said. 'For one thing, I believe you said there was someone else in your life.'

'When I can track the bugger down, yes.'

'I hope you do. I mean, I hope you find him.'

'Thanks, Ovie. So, what's bothering you, then?'

He had to think, most likely about how to put his feelings into words. Eventually, he said, 'You've been wonderful for me. I've been able to talk to you about things I wouldn't even hint at with anyone else.' It was true. He'd opened up to her about his private hopes for the future, his frequent doubts about his performance on the course, and that great, looming unknown – how he might acquit himself in action in the North Sea, the English Channel, the Mediterranean, or wherever he was posted.

'I'm glad I've been able to help,' was all she could say, but she meant every word.

'The thing is, Grace, I mean....' He was struggling. 'This is awful, like going away again to school.'

'That's not a world I know anything about, Ovie. You'll have to help me out there.'

'What I'm saying is, will you write to me?'

'Of course I will, bonny lad, an' you can write to me as often as you like, just as long as you don't ever expect it to be more than that.'

'I shan't.' He agreed readily, but he was unable to conceal the regret in his promise.

The evening ended with the customary peck on the cheek, which gave way to a heartfelt hug, and then they parted.

'Good luck, bonny lad.'

'Take care, Grace.'

The DSC was the only evidence Ivor had that the service had not entirely forgotten him, because that had been its only contact with him. Meanwhile, he grew increasingly bored and frustrated, waiting to be summoned to a medical board.

He still walked with a limp despite the frequent physiotherapy, and he found a walking stick helpful for the time being, but he suspected the reason to be nothing more than a minor problem affecting the tendons at the back of his knee. He could see no reason why he shouldn't be fit to return to the fleet. Meanwhile, he joined in the various games and pastimes with other patients, who were as bored as he was.

Another concern for him that had never really gone away was the absence of any reply from Grace to his letter. Even if she'd been drafted elsewhere, they should have redirected her mail. He could only imagine that her concern for him had been a transient feeling of disquiet, now forgotten. There was every likelihood that she'd found someone else, hopefully a rating with the requisite proletarian credentials, who spoke in hushed tones of the need for secrecy, or whose duties were so trivial as to be of no concern to an inquisitive enemy.

He set aside thoughts of Grace several mornings later, however, when one of the staff handed him an official-looking envelope, which he opened to find that he was finally required to attend a medical board. The service had remembered him at last.

Grace finished breakfast and made her way to the Wireless Station and the Coding Room. She was early, and the girl she was relieving was still tidying up, or 'squaring off', to use the quaint service parlance, so she took out the mail she'd picked up on the way over, to find out who'd written to her. There were two letters; one from her mother and one from Jack, whose handwriting was so awful, she could never mistake it for anyone else's. There was also a letter that had been delivered by hand, and she imagined that Ovie must have dropped it off before boarding the transport that would take him away. She opened it and read it.

Dear Grace,
Here is the address I'm going to after a week's leave.

Sub/Lt. O. V. Harris, R.N.V.R.,
HMS Wasp,
Admiralty Pier,
Dover,
Kent.

Thank you for everything.
Love and best wishes,
Ovie X.

As she read it, she felt the now-familiar protective urge that he'd always aroused in her, but now he was gone, and she could only hope and pray that he'd be safe.

PO Telegraphist Squires asked, 'What's that, Grace? A love letter?'

'No, it's from one of the boys on the last course. He's asked me to write to him.'

'Where've they sent him?'

Grace looked again at the note. '*HMS Wasp*, Dover.'

' "Hellfire Corner", eh? Don't worry. He won't keep you busy for long.' He seemed amused.

Suddenly alarmed, she asked, 'Why not?'

'Let's just say that those fellas don't spend much time thinking about their long-term prospects.'

'Why ever not?' She felt naïve even as she asked the question.

'Because their life expectancy is weeks rather than months.'

It was a horrible thought, but now she had to force it from her mind and concentrate on her work.

On boarding the Portsmouth train, Ivor found a seat next to a large, well-fed man, who sat with his feet wide apart, regardless of the inconvenience it might cause his fellow-travellers.

Just as the train began to pull away, the compartment door opened, and a woman obviously in the advanced stages of pregnancy looked in. 'Oh, dear,' she said, finding the compartment full.

Ivor levered himself to his feet and said, 'Please take this one.'

'Oh, but I couldn't. You're....' She was looking at his walking stick.

'Please, madam, I insist. I'm perfectly all right.'

'Thank you. You're very kind.' She lowered herself into the seat he'd vacated, arranging the voluminous skirts of her coat around her.

The large man was viewing him with undisguised interest. He asked, 'Where'd you get that, then?'

'My walking stick? I won it in a snakes and ladders tournament.'

'No, your game leg. Where'd you get wounded?'

'At sea.'

'Ah.' He tapped the side of his nose unnecessarily, 'Not allowed to say, eh?'

'That's right.'

Ivor suffered the man's repeated attempts to start a conversation until the train reached Worthing, which was apparently his stop.

'Well,' said the man, getting up from his seat, 'I'll leave you, then. Don't do anything I wouldn't do.' He turned to the pregnant woman, but Ivor shook his head to indicate the inadvisability of offering her similar advice or even commenting on what she'd already done.

'Disgraceful,' said the woman when he'd left. 'He should have given up his seat for you.'

'Even good manners are rationed these days,' said Ivor, taking the seat the large man had vacated. He was rewarded by nods and smiles of agreement from the other occupants of the compartment.

The pregnant woman asked, 'Are you, by any chance, going to Portsmouth?'

'Yes.'

'So am I. My husband is in Haslar Hospital.'

'I'm so sorry.'

'Oh, he's recovering nicely.' She looked at his stick again and asked, 'Is that where you're going, or shouldn't I ask?'

'There's no secret about that,' he assured her, 'and yes, I'm going for a medical board. Perhaps, when I get a taxi at the station, I can offer you a lift?'

'That's very kind of you. Thank you.'

It was very pleasant, having sociable company on the journey, and particularly, after the convalescent home, someone new to talk to. They chatted easily until the train pulled into Portsmouth, and then they shared a taxi to the Royal Naval Hospital, Haslar, where they eventually parted to follow their destinations, she to the wards, and he to reception.

After what seemed a long time, he was shown to a waiting room, where he sat for almost half-an-hour, before a nurse arrived to take him to an examination room.

'I'll leave you to undress down to your underwear,' she said.

'What, top half as well?'

'Yes, Lieutenant.'

'It was only my leg that was injured.'

She gave him a stern look, so he stripped off down to his vest and drawers, cellular, officers'.

The nurse reappeared after a few minutes, to knock on the door and ask, 'Are you decent, Lieutenant?'

'I try to be.'

Even through the door, he heard her sigh heavily. 'May I come in?'

'Be my guest.'

She entered the room, carrying a robe of some kind. 'Put this gown on,' she said, 'and I'll take you to X-Ray.' She watched him struggle with it. 'It fastens at the back,' she advised.

'I can't tie bows behind my back. It's a skill I never mastered.'

'I'll do it for you.' Beneath her breath, but quite audibly, she sighed, 'Men.' With the tapes fastened, she asked, 'Which is the injured leg?'

'The one with the scar.'

She sighed again. 'In that case,' she said with heavy patience, 'give me your right arm.'

He looked at her in surprise.

'You can use your walking stick if you prefer to, or you can let me help you.'

'It's no contest, Sister.' He gave her his right arm.

'I'm a staff nurse, not a sister. Sister Weatherly would have sorted you out half an hour ago.'

'It seems to be a sister's prerogative,' he observed. 'Take me for a walk, nurse. I'll be good.'

They walked down the corridor, taking two turnings before they came to the X-Ray Department.

Several X-rays later, Ivor waited again in the little room, until the nurse returned.

'Commander Hotchkins will see you now, Lieutenant. I'll take you to his consulting room, and then I'm going off duty.'

'Do you mean I'll never see you again, nurse?'

'Not if I'm very lucky.'

'Well, thank you for your ministrations. You've been truly wonderful.' He offered her his right arm again. As she took it, he kissed the nearest part of her, which was her forehead.

'Lieutenant Loveday,' she chided, 'that's not allowed.'

'All right, I shan't do it again.'

She smiled grudgingly and took him to the consulting room, where she left him.

For the next ten minutes, Surgeon-Commander Hotchkins poked, prodded and questioned him about his general ability to navigate the lawn of the convalescent home. Finally, after looking again at the X-rays, he said, 'The fracture has healed nicely, Lieutenant, but there is permanent damage to the connective tissue.' He tapped on the X-ray that presumably gave him that information. 'The only classification I can give you is "B".'

'So I'm unfit for service with the fleet, sir?'

'I'm afraid so, but your history suggests that you've already done more than your share.'

'If you don't mind my saying so, sir, it doesn't feel like it. I seem to have spent half my lifetime in that convalescent home.'

'Well, now you're going to have a change.'

'Not another convalescent home, sir?'

'No, you're going on leave. Where's your home?'

'I have no home, sir. It was destroyed in the Blitz.' To avoid sounding like a pathetic orphan, he said, 'I may go up to Tynemouth again to look up some of the people I knew.'

21

A visit to the newspaper office confirmed Ivor's suspicions that most of the people he'd known were now serving in the forces. He spent some time with some of the older staff, at least when they could spare the time, but it was Alf, the messenger and the oldest of them all who surprised him by saying, 'There was a bit lass come lookin' for you a while ago. It must have been last month. I was on the front desk when she called.'

'Did she tell you her name, Alf?'

'No, but I'd recognise her again with her lovely blonde hair.' He corrected himself by saying, 'It wasn't blonde, exactly. More sort of reddish.'

'Strawberry blonde?'

'Aye, I reckon you could call it that. She was pretty, too, an' a nice lass, local. Aye, a canny lass, I'd say.'

'What did she tell you, Alf?'

'Only that she was tryin' to find you. She said you'd been wounded, an' she didn't know which hospital they'd taken you to.' He looked Ivor up and down and said, 'I didn't know you'd been wounded. Are you all right now, like?'

'I'm fine now, thanks, Alf. I just need to find the girl. Didn't she leave a name or address?'

'No, an' she looked a bit full up when she left, poor lass. I reckon she was very concerned about you.'

'Thanks, Alf.'

'It's no trouble, marrer. Do you know where she lives?'

'Yes, North Shields. It's a needle in a haystack, an' I don't think her folks'll be in the telephone directory.'

The knowledge that Grace's family lived in North Shields meant nothing to him. As he'd told Alf, they were one family out of thousands. Well, a hell of a lot, anyway, and a look through the Newcastle Telephone Directory confirmed his suspicion.

As he pondered, an idea came to him, and he caught the bus into Newcastle City Centre. It was a sobering journey, as he could see bomb damage all around him, but he tried not to dwell on it, but to concentrate instead on his main purpose.

Thankfully, the Public Library was unscathed, and Ivor managed to find the department that dealt with public records. A librarian asked him how she could help.

'I'd like to look at the electoral roll for North Shields, please.'

She looked at the rings on the epaulettes of his coat and asked, 'Is it an official matter?'

'No, I'm trying to trace a girl I knew in Liverpool, and all I know is that her home is in North Shields.'

'You have her name, then?'

'Yes.' It sounded like a silly question, but he let it go.

'Come this way.' She led him into a room lined with drawers; in fact, he'd never seen so many drawers. The librarian asked, 'Is she likely to have the vote?'

'Yes, she's over twenty-one.'

'What's her name?'

'Grace Headley. That's H-E-A-D-L-E-Y.'

'Are you sure?'

'Positive.'

'I'm asking because "Hedley" spelt without an "A" occurs in the area.'

'No, it's spelt with an "A",' he assured her.

The librarian continued to search, until she said, 'Grace Louise Headley, twenty-nine, Collingwood Terrace, North Shields. That's the only one I can find. There are three other adults at the address.'

'In that case, it must be her. Thank you. I mean, *thank you!*'

Ivor felt like a nervous schoolboy about to meet a girl for the first time in his life. He knew how that felt, because he remembered the occasion vividly. He kept telling himself that it could all come to grief, and that, several months on, Grace might well have found someone else, but he was no less driven by the need to find her, and if it meant visiting her address, then he was partway to his goal.

Maps of any kind had been impossible to find since the invasion threat in the early part of the war, and Ivor navigated the streets of North Shields by the expedient of asking directions of various people he encountered, until he came to Collingwood Terrace, by which time his leg was aching horribly. It was quite a long street, and he'd started at the wrong end, quite unwittingly, but he didn't care.

He limped up to number twenty-nine and knocked nervously on the door. It was starting to rain, so he turned up the collar of his coat to shield his neck.

The door opened, and he stood, staring in surprise. The slightly-built woman who stood in the doorway was smartly dressed, at least as far as he could see beneath her pinafore, but her most striking feature was the same strawberry blonde hair that had first attracted him to Grace. It was beginning to show grey and it was caught back in a comb, but the effect was still uncanny, and there was no doubt as to where Grace's colouring had originated.

'Mrs Headley?'

'Yes?'

'Are you the mother of Wren Grace Headley?' He had to ask, even though her hair alone had convinced him.

Her enquiring expression turned to one of alarm. She asked, 'Has something happened to our Grace?'

'No. At least, not as far as I know. I haven't seen her for at least four months. My name's Ivor Loveday.'

With a look almost of wonder, she said, 'So, you're Ivor.'

'Yes.'

Eyeing the rings on his epaulettes, she asked, 'Is it all right to call you that?'

'Please do.' He huddled into his Burberry and said, 'May I come inside?'

'Of course. Come in before you get soaked to the skin. Let me take your hat and coat and I'll hang them up.' She helped him out of his coat, asking, 'Would you like a cup of tea? You were lucky to catch me on my half-day off.'

'I'd love one. Yes, please.' In his haste to contact Grace's family, he hadn't considered the possibility that her mother might be at work, so he agreed that he'd been lucky to catch her at home.

'Just sit yourself down by the fire an' I'll make a fresh pot.'

Ivor took a seat and looked around him. The first thing he noticed was a photograph of a second lieutenant in the army. Presumably, he was Grace's brother Jack. Further along the wall was a photograph of Grace, self-conscious in her Wren's uniform complete with its 'pudding basin' hat. The Wrens he'd seen in Portsmouth were sporting the new round caps, which were a big improvement. For the moment, however, just seeing her face again was enough for him.

He was still looking at Grace's picture when her mother took the kettle from the hob in front of the fire and scalded the tea.

'You were looking at the photo of our Grace, weren't you? She was only a bit bairn when she had that taken.'

'Even so, she was pretty, as pretty as she is now,' said Ivor.

'You're missing her, then?'

'Yes, I am, Mrs Headley. I wrote to her last month, telling her where I was, but she didn't reply.'

Mrs Headley frowned. 'She never said anything about that, an' she told me everythin' about you.'

Ivor hoped fervently that she hadn't, but he kept that to himself.

'Maybe it arrived after she'd left Liverpool, although you'd think they'd forward any mail, wouldn't you?'

'I didn't know she'd been drafted.'

'Oh, yes, she had a week's leave and then she went on a course, and then she went on to her new draft. She told me lots of things, Ivor. She told me you'd had an argument the last time she saw you.'

'Did she?'

'I held her in my arms here in this room, and she broke her little heart tellin' me about it.'

'Oh, no.' He couldn't bear to think of it.

'She said it was all her fault, as well.'

'How can anyone be completely to blame when something like that happens? There must have been fault on my side as well.'

'Maybe, but you'd know more about that. Do you have sugar in your tea?'

'No, thank you. Just milk.'

Mrs Headley handed him his tea and poured a cup for herself before asking the question Ivor had been half-expecting. 'Do you mind telling me what the argument was about? I never did get our Grace to tell me that.'

'No, I don't mind at all. She kept asking about my ship, and I had to be very evasive. Security reasons, you know. I brushed her questions aside in my usual casual way, and Grace thought I was making fun of her.' He shook his head at the thought. 'I wouldn't say or do anything if I thought it might offend her, Mrs Headley.'

'I don't think you would, either.' She gave him a straight look and said, 'You love her, don't you?'

He was taken aback by her directness, but he said self-consciously, 'Yes, I do. I thought she felt the same way.'

'She does, bonny lad. I think the sooner you get in touch with her, the better it will be for both of you.'

'Will you tell me where I can write to her again?'

'Of course I will.' She got up and went to a brass letter rack on the wall, that bore an engraving of the Tyne Bridge. 'I have her latest letter here.'

'I'm sure it's private. I just need her address.'

'Here y' are, bonny lad. It's written on the back of this envelope.' She put it on the table in front of him.

He read the address and copied it into his diary:

L/Wren G. L. Headley 9483627
HMS St Christopher,
Fort William,
Inverness-shire.

It felt like buried treasure. To cover his euphoria, he said, 'I see she's got her hook.'

'Her what?'

'The killick, the wooden anchor on her sleeve that says she's a leading Wren. Sailors call it a "hook".'

'Aye, she's been promoted. I'd just never heard it called that before.'

'Well, good girl, Grace.'

Again, Ivor caught a shrewd look from Mrs Headley, who said, 'You're more pleased than you're lettin' on, aren't you?'

'An awful lot more,' he admitted. 'I couldn't be more pleased.'

'What I'd like to know,' said Mrs Headley, having extracted his confession, 'is what they do at *HMS St Christopher*.' A moment later, she bit her lip and said, 'It's not a secret, is it?'

'Not really. It's a training base for coastal forces. That's motor torpedo boats, motor gunboats and motor launches.'

'Well, bless my soul.' Suddenly, she looked up at the clock and said, 'Look at the time. My husband will be home soon. You'll stay an' eat with us, won't you, Ivor?'

'It's very kind of you, but I don't want to be a nuisance.'

'You're not a nuisance, an' there's plenty for all of us. I just need to peel some potatoes and carrots.'

'Let me help you, Mrs Headley. I'm a dab hand at spud bashing.'

She gave him a look of near-horror. 'I can't let you do that.'

'Of course you can. You're short of time, so let me help you. I insist.'

With an air of reluctant acceptance, she went to the sink and beckoned to him. 'Men peeling potatoes. I don't know what the world's comin' to. I really don't.'

Ivor removed his jacket and cufflinks, rolled up his sleeves and started peeling.

'Which department do you work in at Binns', Mrs Headley?'

'Oh, you know about that, do you?'

'Grace told me.'

'Of course. I'm in soft furnishin'. That's beddin', towels, table linen and so forth.'

'I used to like to walk through your department when I was a lad,' he told her, pleased that they had something in common, 'just to enjoy the smell of new fabric. It was a hint of luxury. We didn't go very often, but I've always remembered it. I might even have seen you there at some time.'

'You might,' agreed Mrs Headley. 'I've been there since it was Coxon's, before Binns took it over, an' you're right about the luxury, at those prices, at any rate.' It was possibly the mention of his boyhood that made her ask, 'Where do you live, Ivor?'

'I used to live in Tynemouth, but my home was bombed in the Blitz.'

'Oh, I'm sorry, pet.' She grasped his arm with her wet hand in embarrassment. 'I'd forgotten about your home and your family. Our Grace told us. It's awful, what happened.'

'We were only like a lot more,' he assured her.

With her initial embarrassment out of the way, she asked, 'How did you come to live in Tynemouth. You don't sound like a Geordie. Not a proper one, at any rate.'

'No, I was born in North Wales, but we moved to Yorkshire when I was one year old, and then, when I was sixteen, we moved to Tynemouth.' Amused by her comment about his accent, he said, 'Grace told me that Geordies only adopt newcomers if they like us.'

'Well, it's probably the same everywhere.'

'Most likely.'

'I think we have enough potatoes,' she said, looking at the panful. 'My husband can put it away, you know. Mind you, he works hard, so it's not surprisin'.' Then, she said guiltily, 'You said your home was bombed, and I went on about somethin' else when I should have asked you where you're stayin' now.'

'I'm in a small hotel in Tynemouth, just for this leave.'

'In a hotel?' She made it sound like the greatest hardship. 'You can stay with us if you like. There's plenty room for you, now our Jack an' our Grace are away.'

'That's very kind of you, Mrs Headley, but it's my last night here.

I have to report to Postings and Drafts next week. I have to go to them because I've no address for them to write to. Besides, I don't want to put you to any more trouble.'

'It would be no trouble.'

'All my things are at the hotel, so I'm grateful for your offer, but I really do need to go back there.'

'All right. Whatever you're happiest with.' She put the pan of potatoes on the range hob. 'There's just the carrots to do now,' she told him.

They chatted easily for the next half-hour, until they heard the door open and close.

Mrs Headley asked, 'Is that you, Bill?'

A deep voice said, 'Who else would it be, woman? That's unless you've got a fella callin'. If you have, you can tell him to expect a bit fist from me.' Then, in a surprised tone, he asked, 'Who's is this coat an' cap that's hung up here? Are you entertaining the Navy?'

'Of course I am. I always do on my afternoon off, a different sailor every week. Come and meet Ivor.'

There was silence as Mr Headley came into the room, tall and powerfully built, and he saw Ivor. Then he realised who the visitor was. 'So you're the Ivor all the misery an' commotion's been about,' he said.

'I'm afraid so.' Ivor offered his hand. 'I'm glad to meet you, Mr Headley.'

'If findin' you here means that our Grace is going to be happier, I'm glad to see you an' all.' He shook Ivor's hand before lowering himself into his armchair and accepting a cup of tea from his wife.

'Ivor's staying for tea,' she said, adding self-consciously, 'or maybe I should say "dinner".'

'I'm sure it'll taste just as good, whatever you call it, Mrs Headley,' said Ivor, massaging his hand after his host's bone-crunching handshake.

'Ivor helped me peel the potatoes, Bill.'

'Did he now?' With an amused grin, he asked, 'Do they do that a lot where you come from?'

'It's the only way we get to eat,' Ivor told him. 'Peel or starve, shell peas or clam for your bait.'

'There must be a lot of hard women in.... Where are you from?'

'He's from Tynemouth, Bill, and he lost his home and his mam an' dad in the Blitz, so don't get on to him about bein' posh.'

'Haddaway, woman. I only wanted to know, that's all.'

'Aye, well, there's just time for you to wash yourself before we sit down to eat.'

'This is what marriage does to you, Ivor,' he said, going to the sink. 'There's never a minute's peace.'

'Howay an' get washed,' his wife urged him.

As they sat down to eat, Mr Headley asked in his forthright way, 'Just what was it you and our Grace fell out about?'

Ivor explained, as he had to Mrs Headley, their disagreement about the ship's identity.

'Well, I thought that applied to every ship, Isn't that why sailors don't have the ship's name on their caps anymore?'

'It is, but Grace somehow thought I was teasing her. It's just the way I am, I suppose, and she thought it came between us.'

Mr Headley seemed to consider the matter only briefly before saying. 'I can think of a dozen reasons for fallin' out, but none of 'em as daft as that one.'

'That wasn't all.' Ivor had been wondering how to approach the matter without being offensive or patronising, and now he had to do it. 'Grace thought that, because my dad was manager at the labour exchange and he had a job for life, however short that turned out to be, it put her and me on different levels, if you see what I mean.'

'It does, bonny lad, but we're fair-minded folks, and we're not goin' to look down on you, even when you put a pinny on an' peel taters.'

Ivor smiled at Mr Headley's dry humour. It was good that they could treat the whole thing as a joke. 'I wish Grace would look at it that way,' he said.

'She should be able to. We encouraged both our Jack an' her to better themselves so that they wouldn't be caught in the same trap as I was, an' if that's passed her notice, then I don't know what she's thinkin' about. I don't mind tellin' yer, if I had her here, I'd give her a piece of my mind.'

'For half a minute, mevve,' said his wife, clearly unimpressed. 'He's as soft as muck where our Grace is concerned.'

'For goodness' sake, woman, can't a man have some respect in his own house?' His expression was stern, but it was clear that straight-faced, affectionate banter was a way of life in the Headley household. 'Anyway,' said Mr Headley, 'What have they done to you, Ivor? I can only think it's your walking stick that I nearly broke me neck over when I came in.'

'I was hit by a machine-gun bullet,' explained Ivor. 'It broke the thigh bone, so it's taken a while to heal.'

'What are they doin', shooting at each other with machine guns at sea? I thought you had bigger guns than that.'

'We were sinking a U-boat by gunfire,' Ivor told him, 'and the U-boat's crew put up a fight.'

'Aye, well, it's not good to ask too many questions in wartime.'

'You're absolutely right, Mr Headley.' He wished Grace had followed her father's example, but he was happy enough, now he had her address.

22

Grace had never really adjusted to daytime sleeping, so the system at St Christopher came as a welcome surprise.

She had a bath and dressed before going down to the canteen for breakfast. On her way, she checked her pigeon hole for mail. There was only one letter, postmarked *Newcastle-upon-Tyne*, which was odd, because it wasn't addressed in her mother's handwriting. There was no return address on the back, so she opened the envelope and took out the letter, realising with a start whose writing it was.

Dear Grace,

I hope this letter reaches you, as the last one evidently didn't.

Yesterday, I called at your home, where I spent the afternoon and evening with your parents, and I must say it was the most enjoyable day I've had in a long time. I can now see that you inherited your mother's sympathetic and gentle nature, not to mention her beautiful hair colouring, and I can only imagine that your wit and dry humour came from your dad. I have to say that we parted the best of friends.

I'm writing this letter in a hotel room in Tynemouth, because I'm still a resident of 'No Fixed Abode', so I've no address for you to write to until I know where my posting is. I'm no longer fit for service with the fleet, so communication should be easier than before, now that I'm a landlubber. That's if you want to keep in touch, which was the impression your parents gave me. I'll let you know my address as soon as I have one. I've been in a convalescent home in Sussex for what seems like a hundred years, but their Lordships of the Admiralty are now going to find me an honest job.

Take care.

Lots of love,

Ivor X.
P.S. Congratulations on your hook!

'Are you all right, Grace?' The question came from one of the girls on her watch.

'Fine, thanks.'

'I thought I saw tears in your eyes.'

Grace blinked to clear them. 'I've just heard from somebody I haven't seen for a long time,' she said, bursting with happiness, but trying hard to conceal it.

A Wren third officer looked at Ivor's walking stick and asked, 'Is it difficult for you to walk, sir?'

He wanted to say, 'No, I only carry this thing to look like Charlie Chaplin.' Instead, because she was young and quite attractive, he said, 'I'd be grateful for a little help.'

'Of course, sir.' She offered him her arm and helped him up and out of his seat.

'Thank you.'

'Not at all, sir. It must have been an awful injury.'

'I was rather annoyed when it happened,' he admitted, 'but you have to take the rough with the smooth in this game.'

She led him to the office of Commander F. D. Lewis (Postings and Drafts), and pushed open the door to announce, 'Lieutenant Loveday is here, sir.'

'Very good. Bring him in.'

'Aye, aye, sir.' She helped Ivor to a chair opposite Lewis and a lieutenant-commander. The gold rings on their sleeves were interspaced by white ones that showed them to be officers of the Paymaster Branch.

Initially, Lewis didn't impress Ivor. For one thing, he was carrying too much weight for a man on shore station rations, and Ivor suspected that he'd found an additional source of sustenance. He'd been told it could happen in shore establishments, where 'fiddles' were going on all the time. His assistant was less overweight, but certainly well fed, and Ivor was reminded of Julius Caesar and his preference for 'men that are fat'. The Roman emperor would have felt secure in Postings and Drafts, where there was as yet no sign of a 'lean and hungry' man.

'Ah, Lieutenant Loveday,' said Lewis, peering at Ivor through round lenses, as if he'd only just noticed him. 'This is most unusual. Why have you no home address?'

'I lost it, sir.'

Lewis blinked in incomprehension. 'How on earth did you manage that?'

'I left it where the Luftwaffe could find it.' He added, 'They used it for bombing practice.'

'That was most unfortunate.'

His assistant agreed, prompting Lewis somewhat belatedly into an introduction. 'This is Lieutenant Commander Johnson,' he said.

'How do you do, sir?' Ivor raised himself with difficulty to shake his hand.

'Don't get up,' said Johnson when it was too late for Ivor to heed his caution.

'It was most unfortunate,' agreed Ivor, continuing the conversation. 'I remember thinking that same thought when I went home on leave and saw the smoking ruins, sir. In fact, I said as much to the air-raid wardens at the scene, and they felt inclined to agree with me.'

'Quite.' Lewis examined the document in front of him. 'I see your fitness classification is "B",' he observed.

'That's correct, sir.'

'That means you're fit only for duty in a shore establishment,' he explained a little unnecessarily.

'I gather so, sir, but I'm still better placed than the unfortunate Lieutenant Dugger.'

'Oh? Who's he?'

'An officer I knew, sir. He was pronounced unfit even for the most basic duties.'

'Yes, well, these things happen.' Lewis read further and said to Johnson, 'What have we got to offer Lieutenant Loveday, Johnson?' Turning then to Ivor, he said, 'In view of your unfortunate experience, you are allowed a degree of choice in your appointment.'

'I'm grateful for that, sir.'

'There's a desk appointment at *HMS Excellent*,' said Johnson. 'Gunnery is your thing, isn't it?'

'My thing, sir, yes, but I can't imagine that *HMS Excellent* is ready for me.'

'No? There are numerous desk appointments. There always are. For some reason, they're not universally popular in the service.'

Ivor shook his head in negative agreement.

Lewis asked, 'What's the matter with desk appointments, Loveday? I've held this one since nineteen-forty.'

'I'd say you and it are ideally matched, sir, the perfect marriage of bureau and bureaucrat.'

'What? Oh, that's very civil of you. How do you feel about gunnery training?'

Ivor wondered if he'd missed something. 'Are we back at *HMS Excellent*, sir?'

'No, there are other appointments available. You'd have to do some instruction as well as administration.'

'It sounds promising, sir.'

Johnson ran his finger down the list and said, 'You may not be so keen when I tell you where this one is. It has, in fact, been vacant for some considerable time.'

'I'm bracing myself, sir. Where is it?'

'It's at *HMS Wildfire*, Sheerness-on-Sea.'

'Sheer-nasty-ness? No, thank you, sir.'

Johnson looked again. 'There is another. It's in the Scottish Highlands, miles from the nearest city.' Johnson would have been a disaster as a salesman, delivering the news in what he no doubt saw as relatively painless instalments. Clearly, the appointment was an unpopular one, and particularly among the city types. 'It's on the coast of Inverness-shire,' he said, adding unnecessarily, 'Scotland.'

Ivor's heart was singing. His knowledge of Highland geography was less than basic, but he reasoned that wherever it was on that coast it couldn't be all that far from Fort William. 'I'm still interested, sir,' he said.

'It's the coastal forces training base at Fort William, *HMS St Christopher*,' said Johnson.

Lewis, Johnson and the third officer stared at him, waiting for his reaction. Rather than keep them waiting, but keeping his euphoria under control, he said, 'Well, you know, there comes a time when self-interest must take second place to duty. I mean, it's only fair that someone has to accept this kind of appointment.'

They continued to wait.

'I'll take it.'

There was a delay of several seconds, and then Lewis offered his hand. 'Thank you, Lieutenant Loveday,' he said solemnly. 'That's very noble of you. If you'll wait once more in the anteroom, I'll have the necessary documents prepared.'

'Thank you, sir.' Ivor thanked Johnson as well and allowed the third officer to help him up again.

When they were outside the office, she said, 'If you don't mind my asking, sir, who was Lieutenant Dugger? You mentioned him to Commander Lewis.'

'So I did, third officer. I have to paraphrase the original to some extent in the interests of good taste and because I'm addressing a lady, but basically, he was "...the captain of a lugger, who wasn't fit to clean up... the heads, he was such a useless bugger." '

'I thought it must be a joke, sir.'

'More of a messdeck ditty, really. It's been sung in the lowest places imaginable.' Turning to address her face to face, he said, 'Third officer, you've been very kind, but I think I can manage on my own now.' He kissed her lightly on her cheek as a token of his appreciation.

'If you're sure, sir.' She was smiling.

Grace had another letter, this time from her mother.

Dear Grace,

I don't know if you've heard from Ivor yet, but I must tell you that he turned up here on my half-day. He got our address from the electoral register at the library. I'd never have thought of that. Would you? At any rate, he spent most of the afternoon with me and he stayed for tea with your dad and me. The two of them got on like a house on fire, and I thought he was a canny lad as well. He even helped me to peel the potatoes and carrots.

He's very keen on you, Grace, so if you take up with him again, don't go falling out with him over anything silly. I gave him your address so that he could write to you. You know your own mind best, but if things did develop further between you and him, your dad and I wouldn't stand in your way.

I'll write later in the week with the latest gossip, but this was urgent, considering the state you were in when you came home on leave.

It's getting a bit chilly just now, so don't forget to wrap up well when you go outside, and remember you've got your warm, woollen underwear.

Cheerio for now, and lots of love,
Mam XXX.

As she walked to the Wireless Station, she overheard two petty officers talking. One said, 'Have you heard there's a new gunnery officer arriving this week?'

'Bleedin' 'ell. Just what we need, I don't think.'

'They say he's RNVR, but he's got a reputation as a gunnery officer.'

'They've all got a bleedin' reputation, haven't they? Still, we have to work with what they send us. Even Wavy Navy officers.'

Grace didn't care, because her Wavy Navy officer had found her, and she would take her mother's advice not to fall out with him again. As for the woollen underwear, she reckoned she could manage nicely without it.

23

Being a junior officer, Ivor was restricted to travelling Third-Class on a slow train that seemed to stop at almost every station and halt between London and Glasgow. He was fortunate, however, in having secured a seat in a non-smoking compartment, in which the only residual aromas were those of hair cream and the inevitable stale perspiration.

The journey was interminable, as was the delay at Crewe, where a number of American soldiers boarded the train. Ivor's brief shopping trip in New York was no preparation for the mass arrival that was taking place, and, sheltered as he'd been in the convalescent home, his first encounter with Britain's new allies had come when he arrived in London. He found them surprisingly informal and even noisy, but they seemed, on the whole, friendly. He imagined there would be a period of adjustment before the native population became used to their liveliness and high spirits.

A woman in the far corner of Ivor's compartment had succeeded in feeding her baby skilfully and discreetly while Ivor studied the inner pages of *The Times* with equal discretion, and now, having relieved her baby of its wind, she put it down to sleep. The other occupants of the compartment were two women, a boy and a girl. The women had been fascinated by the baby, whilst the children were recovering from their embarrassment at being required to avert their eyes during the feeding process. Meanwhile, the noise from the next compartment was becoming a problem.

'Oh, dear,' said the baby's mother, 'I'll never get her off tae sleep with all that racket gaeing on next door.'

'I'll see what I can do,' said Ivor, putting his newspaper down and going to the corridor, where the noise was even worse.

On hearing their door slide open, one of the Americans looked up and saw him. 'Hey, you guys,' he said, 'Ten-HUT!'

The others leapt to their feet looking surprised and guilty. Two of them even saluted Ivor, although neither he nor they were wearing their caps. That was how naïve and inexperienced they were.

'I'm sorry to spoil your fun,' said Ivor, 'but there's a baby next door, who's propping her eyes open with match stalks, she's so sleepy. Will you keep the noise down for her?'

There was a ragged, *sotto voce* chorus of, 'Yes, sir', 'We're sorry, sir', and 'We didn't know about the baby, sir.'

'I know you didn't. Thank you for your co-operation. Carry on.'

'Yes, *sir*.' Each of them repeated the response with equal alacrity.

'Thank you. Good night.'

He was settling back into his seat, when he heard movement in the corridor. Then, someone chanted on a single note, almost in a whisper, 'Ready you guys?'

In pleasing harmony, the group sang softly, ' "Hush, little baby, don't say a word, Papa's gonna buy you a mocking bird...." '

One of the female passengers looked up angrily, but Ivor raised a cautionary hand. 'This is their apology,' he said.

Incredibly, the soldiers remembered all the words, and when they had returned to their compartment, Ivor could see that the baby's eyes were closed.

'Well, I never,' said the now-pacified woman.

The mother of the baby mouthed her silent thanks to Ivor.

The woman who, Ivor presumed, was the mother of the boy and girl, said to them, 'you two need tae get some sleep as well.'

'I cannae sleep,' said the boy, who might have been about seven years old.

'Neither can I,' said his younger sister, who seemed to follow his lead in most things.

'I'm bringing them back frae their evacuation haem,' their mother told Ivor, as if it explained their inability to sleep.

'It wis awful bad there,' said the boy. 'They treated us like sh—'

'I dinnae want tae hear that word again,' said his mother. 'Such language they learned at that farm where they stayed.'

Ivor nodded sagely.

'Anyway, you two,' said their mother, 'you have tae be quiet for the baby's sake.'

'I'll tell you what,' said Ivor softly. 'Will you be very quiet if I tell you a story?'

'Aye,' said the little girl readily.

The boy eyed the rings on Ivor's sleeves suspiciously. He said, 'You're no a proper sailor, are ye?'

'No,' admitted Ivor, 'I'm just playing at it, really, just until the stumps are drawn.'

'Until what?'

'Sorry, I was forgetting you don't play cricket up your way. I meant, until the war ends.'

'Is that right?'

'Hush,' said the boy's mother. 'The kind gentleman's going tae tell ye a story.'

'Okay, are you both ready?'

'Aye.'

'Aye.'

'Once upon a time,' began Ivor, thinking furiously, 'there was a gigantic forest of Christmas trees. Some were huge, as tall as houses, and some weren't as big, but you'd still call them big if you saw them. Some were small enough to fit into a house, but one was so tiny, you might easily have walked past it and never even noticed it. It was no higher than this.' He held out his hand about three feet above the compartment floor.

'That'd be nae use tae anybody,' said the boy.

'Hush,' said his mother.

The other passengers waited politely for Ivor to continue.

'The little tree felt very much out of things. Everything seemed to be going on over its head. The bigger trees would often sway in the wind, and it looked as if they were laughing at it, so that it felt as if it didn't belong in the forest at all.'

'We didn't belong in that bluidy village,' said the boy, 'or the school, either.'

'I've told ye afore about cussin' an' swearin',' said his mother, aiming a smack that didn't quite connect. It was possible that, having missed her children for so long, she was reluctant to be too hard on them, at least for the time being.

Ivor continued. 'Christmas was coming. Soon, people began to buy Christmas trees. The really huge ones were cut down to go to village greens to be enjoyed by everyone. The eight, nine and ten-foot trees were cut for churches and people with very big houses, and the four, five and six-foot trees were cut down for people who lived in ordinary houses. Still, no one bought the little tree. "Perhaps," thought the little tree, "it's not so bad, being unwanted. At least, they don't bring a chopping axe and cut you off at the roots." But it knew, all the same, that it wasn't at all nice, being the tree that nobody wanted.'

'No,' said the boy, 'it's nae fun at all when naebody wants ye.'

His sister simply shook her head sadly.

'On Christmas Eve, the little tree stood in its lonely clearing, watching the snow come down. Soon, a thick blanket of snow lay on the forest, and the little tree was afraid it might be completely covered.'

The little girl's eyes grew wide as she listened, probably wondering what was going to happen to the little tree. She wasn't alone in that, because Ivor was also wondering. Then an idea came to him, as he'd been hoping one might.

'Just when the little tree had given up hope of being wanted, two children, a girl and a boy, arrived at the forest entrance. The boy was pulling a sledge. The man who owned the forest asked, "What do you want?" The girl said, "We want a Christmas tree for our granny." The man asked, "How big?' The girl said, "Not very big, because it mustn't cost more than sixpence. That's all we've got." "And," said the boy, "We have to be able to carry it on our sledge." The girl said, "It has to have roots as well, so that we can plant it in our granny's garden, so that she'll have it forever." The man said, "You're not going to get much of a tree for sixpence." Then he had a think. He said, "Come with me," and he took them to where the little Christmas tree stood alone and unhappy. "You can have this one for sixpence," he said. "Let me get my spade and I'll dig it up for you." The man dug up the tree, and the children put it on their sledge and took it to their granny's garden, where they planted it. When their granny saw it, she said, "That's the loveliest Christmas present I could ever have hoped for." As you can imagine, the little tree was just as happy as she was, now that it had found a home where it was wanted, and it lived there happily ever after.'

The boy said sleepily, 'Mam, can I have a sledge for Christmas?'

The little girl was already asleep.

One of the passengers said, 'That's the first time I've ever heard that story.'

'I made it up,' admitted Ivor. 'I was a newspaper reporter before the war. You could say that I was paid to make up stories.'

'I suppose reporters find it easy.'

'Politicians find it even easier,' Ivor assured her, picking up his newspaper again. He read about the war taking place in Russia, until he, too, felt his eyes closing.

He awoke when the train jolted and began to pull out of Crewe Station.

'That was a good story about the Christmas tree,' said the children's mother. It was almost as if she'd been waiting for him to wake up so that she could tell him.

'Thank you. It did what was needed. That's the main thing.'

'Were you wounded at sea?' She was looking at his walking stick.

'Yes, but it's much better now.'

'My felly's in the Navy. He's a petty officer stoker. He joined in nineteen-thirty, when there was nae work for him in Glasgae. He's in a destroyer in the Atlantic.'

Ivor nodded. 'So was I.'

'Sunk, was it?'

'Yes.'

Not surprisingly, she was reluctant to pursue the subject, and they travelled in silence until the train stopped at Warrington, and the woman who'd had little to say got out, leaving Ivor, the two children and their mother, and the woman with the baby.

Ivor asked, 'Would either of you like a cup of tea or anything?'

The woman with the baby shook her head and mouthed, 'No, thank you,' obviously reluctant to do anything that might waken the baby.

The children's mother said, 'If it's nae too much trouble, I widnae say no to a cup o' tea. That's milk and two sugars, if you dinnae mind.'

'It's no trouble.' He looked at the sleeping children, and she said, 'No, let them have their sleep.'

Ivor joined the queue at the tea bar and bought two cups of tea just in time to re-board the train before it resumed its journey.

'I thought you were going tae be left behind,' said the woman.

'So did I.' He handed her a cup of tea.

'Thanks. I appreciate ye daeing that.' Presently, she asked, 'Have you ever been torpedoed?'

The question took him by surprise, but he said, 'Yes, once.' He added, 'Once was enough.'

'My felly was torpedoed last year. He was in *HMS Taunton*.'

'So was I. What's his name?'

'PO Stoker Kenny. I'm Mrs Kenny,' she told him unnecessarily.

'I remember him.' Ivor recalled the man from the Carley float he and several others had shared.

'Are ye in the Engine Room Branch, then?'

'No, I remember your husband because we shared a life raft.'

'Is that right?'

'There was only half-a-dozen of us, so I remember him well.'

'He gets in a terrible state when he thinks about it.'

'I'm not surprised, Mrs Kenny.' He thought of the engine room personnel caught below decks when the sea rushed in. Kenny had been lucky to survive.

'What's your name? Just so I can tell him we met.'

'Loveday. I was Sub-Lieutenant Loveday then.'

'I'll tell him I met ye an' how kind ye were tae me an' the bairns.'

'That's kind of you, Mrs Kenny.'

The train rumbled on, stopping at Wigan, Preston and Lancaster.

Mrs Kenny asked, 'Are ye going to Glasgae?'

'Yes, I have to change there.'

'Oh, ye'll be for the west coast, but I'll nae ask.'

Ivor just smiled his appreciation. Being a sailor's wife, she would understand the need for security.

The little girl stirred and muttered something before settling again into a deep sleep.

'They treated my bairns bad at that farm,' said Mrs Kenny. 'That's why I'm taking them haem with me. That an' the bombing seems to have stopped.'

'Yes, let's hope it stays that way.'

'What kind of ship are you joining?' She said hurriedly, 'I'm not asking for its name.'

'I'm unfit for service with the fleet,' he told her. 'I don't think I'll ever go to sea again.'

'Lucky you, I say. I hope you manage tae stay out of it. You're a sound felly.'

'Thank you.'

'Aye, I'll tell Andy what ye did for the bairns an' me. You're sound all right. Are ye wed?'

'No.'

'That's a shame, a man that can tell fairy stories like you.'

It seemed to Ivor that he was involved in a fairy story. Grace was waiting for him in Fort William, and there was a chance of a better story than he could ever invent.

24

Grace received her first letter from Ovie, and she took it out to read when she came off watch. His writing was as boyish as he was, but it was easy enough to read.

Dear Grace,

I hope you're well. I spent an excellent leave with mother, and now I'm getting used to the routine of my new appointment. It's not as bewildering as I feared, although I have to be careful not to forget anything. It feels strange, being a first lieutenant, as if I'm more important than I thought I was. I suppose I'll get used to it. I mustn't write anything about the captain or the crew, but suffice it to say, they're a splendid bunch of chaps. There's actually so much I mustn't say that it doesn't leave me very much to tell you.

I miss you, and I hope you manage to find the chap you lost.

Look after yourself.

Lots of love,

Ovie XXX.

Grace lost no time in replying, now that she had something to tell him. She posted the letter so that it would be collected that same day. Meanwhile, she kept wondering when she might get a letter from Ivor. Fort William was a long way from most places, but Ovie's letter hadn't taken all that long to arrive, and it had come from Dover. She could only wonder and wait, confident, at least, that Ivor was safe.

Almost fifteen hours after leaving London, Ivor walked into the officers' accommodation at *HMS St Christopher*, having reported to the Commanding Officer and been ordered to 'make and mend', which was navalese for catching up on lost sleep.

After soaking in a hot bath, he fell into bed. Sleep claimed him almost immediately, and he slept until 1700.

After dinner in the wardroom, he asked a fellow-officer, 'Where's the Wireless Station from here?'

'The Wireless Station, old man? Why on earth do you want to go there?'

'I know someone who works there.'

'Ah, well, it couldn't be easier. It's actually on the ground floor of this building. Now I think of it, I'm surprised you didn't notice it on your way in.'

'After a train journey of fifteen hours, I could miss anything.' Inclining his head towards the door, he said, 'I'm going to reconnoitre.'

Once on the ground floor, he found the Coding Room easily enough. The door was conveniently open, so he had a look inside. He counted three Wrens, but none of them was Grace. He was about to make enquiries, when a voice behind him asked, 'Can I help you, sir?'

He turned to find that the voice belonged to a Wren third officer of unremarkable appearance. However, she did at least sound helpful. 'I think that's very likely,' he said. 'Can you tell me which watch Leading Wren Headley is in?'

'I can in just a minute, sir.' The third officer consulted a watch list on the wall of the Coding Room, and asked, 'Is there a problem, sir?'

'Not in the least. I arrived here this morning, and, as Leading Wren Headley and I are distantly related, I thought I'd look her up.'

'I see. She's in Able Watch, and they're not on until oh-six-hundred tomorrow.'

'When does that watch end?' Ivor was conscious that the watches kept in shore stations by signals personnel were completely different from the system used at sea.

'At twelve hundred, sir. We don't keep twenty-four hour watches here.'

'How very civilised. Thank you for your help, third officer.'

—•—

Sixteen hours later, Grace looked up at the bulkhead clock. In five minutes, the watch would end, and she would have the afternoon to herself. In such a beautiful location as Fort William, that was a luxury in itself.

Lorna Nevin, her relief, came into the room with a mischievous smile. She was carrying an envelope.

Grace asked, 'What's happening?'

'You tell me. An officer stopped me and asked me to give you this.' She handed over the envelope, which was addressed in block capitals to her simply by name. On the reverse side, it said *NORWICH*.

'Thank you.' Grace squared off her desk and signed out. 'I haven't the foggiest idea who sent this,' she said.

Flora smiled cheekily in reply.

Once outside the Coding Room, Grace slit open the envelope and took out the note, which said:

Grace,

Come to my office (Gunnery Officer) when you come off-watch. Look natural.

Lots of love,

Ivor XXX.

Barely able to breathe in her amazement and excitement, she walked out of the Wireless Station and into the Instruction Block. When she came to the door with a temporary card label that read, *Lt I. R. Loveday, D.S.C., R.N.V.R., Gunnery Officer*, she took a large breath and knocked.

A familiar voice said, 'Come in', so she pushed the door open, still unable to believe that he was there, even though she could see him with her own eyes.

'Close the door, Grace.'

She pushed the door closed. 'Ivor,' she said, 'I don't believe it.'

'You should. This appointment took some wangling.' He held out his arms and folded them round her.

Her voice was muffled partly by the fabric of his jacket and also by her sobs as she said, 'Ivor, I'm sorry for what I said to you. It was bloody silly, and I wish I'd never said it.'

'It's all over and done with,' he told her, offering her the handkerchief from his breast pocket. 'I've an idea how you felt, and I can understand, really, why you were upset.'

'It was so silly,' she insisted, but she was unable to say more, because he kissed her in a way that was so familiar that it seemed to bridge the months that had separated them.

He asked, 'Can we meet after you've eaten, tonight?'

'Yes, there's a little pub that's ever so quiet. It's just behind us, and it's called The Spyglass Inn. The locals use it to get away from us lot at the base.' She stared at him again. 'I'm pinchin' meself. I still can't believe this is happening.' Her eye went to his medal ribbon, and she said, 'And you've got the DSC as well.'

'Oh, well, I think they found that they'd over-ordered, and they had to get rid of some.'

'I don't believe you.'

'You never do. Right, I'll wait for you at The Spyglass Inn after eighteen hundred. Meanwhile,' he said, pointing to the wash basin, 'you'd better get yourself tidied up before people think I've been ill-treating you.'

She washed and dried her face, using the towel she'd embroidered for him the previous Christmas.

'Yes, its seafaring days are over,' he said.

'I'm glad yours are. You're safe now, and that's what matters.' Her eyes came to rest on his walking stick, and she asked, 'Do you have to use that a lot?'

'Only when I can't find a pretty girl to lean on.'

'Haddaway, man. You'll tell me anythin'.' She was about to leave, when she stopped to ask him, 'Why did you write "Norwich" on the envelope?'

'It's just one of those things sailors put on the flap when they write home.' He shrugged. 'It's like "SWALK", "BOLTOP" and "BURMA".'

'I know "Sealed With a Loving Kiss" and "Better on Lips than on Paper", but what does "BURMA" stand for?'

'"Be undressed and ready, my angel". It's used a lot. I'm surprised you haven't come across it.'

'I haven't had all that many sailors writin' to us. Anyway, put me out of me misery and tell us what "NORWICH" stands for.'

'"Knickers Off Ready When I Come Home".' The Lower Deck use it all the time.'

'In that case, they need to learn how to spell "knickers".'

'Spelling must be the last thing on their minds when they write that.'

Ivor was waiting at the pub when Grace arrived. He asked, 'What can I get you?'

'Just lemonade, please. I have to go on watch at oh-six-hundred.'

'Right enough, you don't want a hangover.' He asked the barmaid for a glass of lemonade, which she poured for him, at the same time giving Grace an odd look.

As they took their seats, Grace said, 'She thinks I'm a scarlet woman. I came here once or twice with one of the subbies on the course, just for a drink, mind. Nothin' more than that. He was young and unsure of himself, so I took pity on him.' Watching Ivor out of the corner of her eye, she said, 'He asked me to write to him.'

'Have you written to him?'

'Wey aye. In his last letter, he said he hoped I'd find you again, so I had to tell him the news.' To complete her defence, she said, 'I'm more of a big sister to him than anythin' else. He just likes to tell me things.'

'I've listened to your evidence,' he told her gravely, 'and, not only do I find you not guilty, I commend you for having a heart of pure gold. I love you, Grace.'

'I love you too, even when you tease me.' Turning serious again, she said, 'I'll never forgive myself for saying those things to you in Liverpool. It was just ridiculous.'

'Like it or not, you must forgive yourself. Do you remember what I told you about Love Day?'

'When people forgave each other? Aye.'

'Not only that. They had to forgive themselves as well. It was a fresh start for everyone, you see.'

She eyed him doubtfully. 'You just made that up,' she said.

'No, I didn't. I was a whale on medieval history at school. Ask me anything you like about Robin Hood. Go on.'

'Ivor,' she said, unable to maintain a straight face, 'You do talk bunions.'

'Even so, the slate is clean, and now that *HMS Hosta*, God rest her soul, is on the ocean bed, I can tell you the truth. She was a Q-ship, a mistress of disguise. When she was tied up alongside, she was *HMS Maynard*; at sea, she was the *MV Snowdonia* or any other merchantman of her size and outline, but when a U-boat surfaced with mischievous intent, she flew the white ensign as *HMS Hosta* and revealed her hidden weapons. You see,' he said, 'it was imperative that her secret was known to as few people as possible. There must be countless people in this war engaged in work that's so secret that they're not allowed to tell even their wives and husbands about it.'

'I realise that. It was just that I'd never met anyone like you. It was as if you never took anythin' seriously, and it wasn't the secret as much as a joke that had come between us.'

'Well, it's old coals now. Let's bury it, shall we?'

'Aye, even if it means mixing metaphors.'

'No one's perfect.'

She appeared to study him carefully before saying, 'You're not bad, though.'

He examined her as closely as he could. 'You're not bad either.'

'Ivor?'

'What?'

'I'm changing the subject now, but you must have known an officer called Brian something.'

'Brian Cartwright? He was killed when *Hosta* was sunk.'

'I know. One of the girls in W/T was seein' him. She was heartbroken.'

He nodded. 'He was a nice lad.' Suddenly, a question occurred to him, and he asked, 'How did she know it was *Hosta*? The ship named in the report should have been *Maynard*.'

'She didn't. I did.' She told him about the conversation she'd overheard, and about Second Officer Curwen's explanation. 'That's all she told me, that *Hosta* and *Maynard* were the same ship. That's why I was so upset about it the last time I saw you.'

'But you're not upset now?'

'No, just the opposite.'

'Even so, let me get you a stiff lemonade.' He took her glass to the bar and bought another gin and a glass of lemonade. As the barmaid served him, he glanced at her wedding ring and asked, 'Have you any children?'

'Aye,' she said, openly surprised by the question, 'two boys. Why do ye ask?'

'My friend came here with a frightened boy, a sub-lieutenant, who just needed someone to talk to. He's serving at sea now, and probably in dangerous waters, but he'll feel better for having had someone to confide in.'

'Aye, I can see that now.'

Ivor paid for his drinks and re-joined Grace. 'I've explained to the barmaid that you're not a scarlet woman,' he told her.

'What did she say?'

'Oh, I brought it up, just to clear the air.'

'Thank you, Ivor. I'm not helpless, mind. I can fight me own battles.'

'You don't surprise me.' The look in her eye told him an anecdote was on its way.

'When I passed the scholarship for the grammar school, the uniform an' things were a problem, and I went to school in a skirt, blazer, tie and hat from the hand-me-down stall.' She explained, 'There was one at the start of each term. Girls were always growing out of their clothes, and it made sense to pass them on. There was nothing anonymous about it, though, and one girl in my form called me "Second-Hand Rose". She only called me that the once, mind.'

'What did you do?'

'I belted her. What do you think? I have me pride, you know.'

Ivor thought of the time he'd spent with Grace's parents. 'You've a lot to be proud of,' he said.

'Aye?'

'I told you that I'd never had a close relationship with my parents, didn't I?'

'Aye, an' I can't think why.'

'Well, you know, not everyone's as fortunate as you. It's true that we never knew unemployment or hardship, but neither did we know what it was to be a close family. It was the first thing that struck me when I visited your home and met your mam and dad.'

'They must have made an impression, for you to call 'em that.'

'They made a big impression on me. They're the best kind of people.'

'Aye, an' they think you're a canny lad, an' all.'

It seemed that they were agreed on most things, and they chatted easily until Grace looked at her watch and said, 'Beauty sleep beckons.'

Thinking of the photograph he'd seen at her home, he said, 'I don't think sleep has anything to do with it. I think you broke out of the egg looking just as irresistible as you do now.'

'And I think somebody needs to tell you the grown-up version of how babies are born, but thanks, anyway.' She followed him outside. 'I wonder when we'll be able to go somewhere private,' she said, snuggling against him.

'As soon as we can both get forty-eighters, we can catch the bus to Invergarry or Fort Augustus.'

'I think somebody's been doing his homework with naughtiness in mind.'

'Geography's always fascinated me.' He kissed her to forestall further argument.

'Aye,' she said, determined to have her say, 'an' I know what kind of geography fascinates you most. Kiss me again, bonny lad, an' then let me get off to bed.'

He did, sublimely happy about the way things had developed so far, but conscious that, with one area of disagreement now resolved, her misgivings about social difference still remained. Grace knew her own mind, and would only be persuaded in her own time.

25

A few weeks later, Grace received a letter in a large envelope, postmarked *Haslemere, Surrey.* Knowing no one from that part of the country, she was naturally intrigued. She was due to relieve her opposite number, however, so she was obliged to put the letter away until the end of the watch at 1800, or at least until her stand-easy, halfway through the watch.

As things happened, there was a hitch with one of the systems, and stand-easy never happened. Consequently, she took the letter back to her quarters to read it.

When she slit the envelope open, she was surprised to find an opened envelope inside it. Then, on discovering that the inner envelope was the one she'd written to Ovie, she experienced a cold rush of blood. The accompanying letter was addressed to her. With tears already welling in her eyelids, she made herself read it.

Dear Miss Headley,

You can imagine how sorry I am to inform you that my son Oliver died of wounds received during an encounter with enemy forces in the English Channel on the 29th of September.

Blinking her tears away, Grace looked at the postmark on her letter to Ovie. The date was the 26th. He must have read it only shortly before he was killed.

Your letter to Oliver was among the personal effects that were returned to me. He came home on leave before joining his flotilla at Dover, and he told me about the evenings he'd spent with you in Fort William, and that, although your relationship with him was purely one of innocent friendship, he felt that you and he were close enough that he was able to confide in you about his worries and concerns as well as his plans for the future.

I wish I could adequately express my gratitude to you for your kindness to him, but that, I'm afraid, is a task that is beyond the scope of words alone.

Grace had to stop reading to dry her eyes. Fortunately, there was little more to read.

Oliver's death is the most awful shock and tragedy, and I am still struggling to come to terms with it, although I am no stranger to bereavement, as my husband died only three years ago. Be assured, however, that I shall never forget your kindness to Oliver. I wish you every happiness now and in the future.

Yours most sincerely,
Elizabeth Harris.

After twenty minutes or so, Grace went to the heads to wash her tear-stained face before joining Ivor at the pub. She had no appetite for food, and she was probably too late for supper, anyway.

She found Ivor waiting at the bar. 'I'm sorry,' she said, unable to say more for the moment. Thankfully, he didn't quiz her, but bought her a lemonade and took her to their usual settle, which was conveniently free. In fact, the place was largely empty at that time of the evening, and that was fortunate, too.

'What is it, darling?'

Still not trusting herself to speak, she gave him Mrs Harris's letter. As he read it, she took a series of deep breaths to steady herself.

Ivor reached the end of the letter. 'I really am sorry, darling,' he said, putting his arm around her and squeezing her shoulder. 'The fact that it's happening all the time doesn't make it any easier for you.'

In a voice that was still shuddering, she asked, 'What does "died of wounds" really mean?'

'It means that he didn't die immediately. Someone would dress his wounds and give him a shot of pain relief. He would simply drift into unconsciousness and feel nothing at all.'

She tried to take in what he'd said, but other thoughts were crowding her mind. 'He was no more than a bit bairn,' she said. 'Just two years younger than me, but a bairn all the same. He wasn't fit to be out on his own an' he was killed before he'd got his sea legs.'

'I know.'

'He was worried about how he'd be in... you know, in battle.'

'That's the commonest worry. There's usually so much to do, you just concentrate and get on with it.'

Grace's war had existed so far in places that seemed distant from the conflict, at least, now that the Blitz was over, and Ivor's description was too much for her to imagine. 'He was going to be an actor,' she said. She squeezed her eyelids shut in an attempt to close out the thought of Ovie's suffering, and a tear ran down her cheek. 'They'll have to cast somebody else now.'

'Here.' Ivor gave her his handkerchief.

She was glad he wasn't saying much. She didn't think she could cope with a proper conversation. 'We sat here, on this settle,' she said, 'Ovie an' me.'

'Do you want to move?'

'No.' Distantly conscious of her abruptness, she said, 'I'm afraid I'm not much company tonight.'

'Who cares? You need comfort. If I can give you any, that's all I want to do.'

She squeezed his hand. It was better than talking. Presently, the need to cry abated, at least for the time being. 'He was only a bairn,' she said again. 'What had he done to deserve that?'

'There'll be a mother and a girl somewhere in Germany as well as here in Britain; in fact, there'll be lots of them, all asking the same question. It's something that doesn't seem to occur to politicians.'

Grace didn't want to talk about that. After a while, she murmured, 'One minute he was here in this pub, and the next, he'd gone to Dover and got himself killed. What is there left?'

'For now? Nothing, I'm afraid, but there'll come a time when you'll take something away from it all.'

'Do you think so?'

'I'm sure of it. I've known it happen.' He picked up the empty glasses. 'Will you let me get you a proper drink, just to help you settle?'

'Not a pink gin, thank you.'

'No, it won't be a pink gin,' he assured her.

'All right, then.'

He went to the bar, leaving her to think about what had been said. The trouble was, as her thoughts revolved around Ovie's death, she could make little sense of any of them.

Ivor returned with two drinks, one bigger than the other.

'What's this?' She was looking at the tall glass in front of her. It contained something pink.

'Orange blossom cocktail. Try it.'

She took a tiny sip, screwing up her eyes in concentration. Finally, she said, 'It's nice.' After a little thought, she said, 'I thought you were going to get me a proper drink.'

'It is a proper drink. It's what naval officers used to drink before pink gin was invented.'

'You'll tell me anything.' She didn't pursue that accusation, but went on to say, 'Ovie had a pink gin the first time we came here. I thought at the time, he was working at being a naval officer.'

'They all do, and I was no different. No one's born with maturity and wisdom. We all have to grow into it.'

'You know,' she said, 'this is the first time I've known you be serious for any length of time.'

'I take death very seriously.'

'Of course you do.' As one thought led to another, she said, 'I'm sorry I'm such a wet blanket.'

'Don't be sorry. I've had lots of experience with wet blankets, so be as wet as you like.'

'Okay.' She took another sip from her drink. 'I can taste something,' she said.

'Good.'

'I mean something that's not orange blossom.'

'Maybe it's gin.'

'I've never been much of a drinker,' she told him for some reason, although she couldn't think, for the moment, what that reason was.

'It's overrated.'

She drank some more while she was still finding it pleasant. Sometimes, there was an after-taste that made you wish you hadn't bothered. 'You said somethin' earlier,' she said, 'but I cannot for the life in me remember what it was.'

'Don't worry about it.'

'It was somethin' you were going to tell me.'

'There are lots of things I'd like to tell you, Grace, but now isn't the time.'

'Doesn't it annoy you, though, when that happens?'

'When what happens?'

She took another sip, because it really was pleasant. 'I like this cocktail,' she said.

'I'm glad.'

'I was trying to say, doesn't it annoy you when something's at the back of your mind an' it won't be honest an' come forward an' make itself known?'

'It drives me round the bend,' he said companionably.

'Me an' all.' She added, 'Particularly when it's important.'

'If you can't remember what it was, how do you know it's important?'

'It's just a feeling. It's important, as well, because you're in a serious mood, an' experience tells me that's not guaranteed to last very long.'

'I can switch it on and off. If you remember tomorrow, or whenever it happens, what I was going to tell you, just say the word, and I'll put my maths teacher's face on for you.'

'All right, I may just hold you to that.'

'Good.'

'Ivor?'

'What?'

'What's a maths teacher's face?'

'A face devoid of humour and human understanding, a mask of malign indifference to those who fail to find their loathsome subject fascinating and facile.'

She had to digest that. Eventually, she asked, 'Didn't you get Maths at School Certificate?'

'I did, just. I couldn't have been commissioned without it. Navigation demands it.'

'Can you navigate?' It came out sounding like a challenge, although she hadn't intended it to.

'I found my way here, didn't I?'

'No, you didn't. You got on a train.'

'That calls for a degree of skill. I had to go from Liverpool to Rochdale to Brighton to Portsmouth to Newcastle to London and then to Fort William, the final journey to be with you, I might add.'

'Okay,' she said generously, 'I'll grant you that, even if you did take a roundabout route.'

'Not only that, I silenced the US Army, who were keeping a baby awake, and I entertained two restless children.'

'You're a marvel, Ivor.' She was beginning to feel light-headed. 'How much gin did you put in this drink?'

'Only one.'

'Is that all?'

'It was a double,' he admitted.

She looked at him in alarm. 'Ivor, I haven't eaten anything since lunchtime. I'm going to be blotto.'

'Not on one double, you're not. It was to relax you, and it's done that, hasn't it?'

'It's done that all right. I'll be swingin' from the chandeliers an' singin' rude songs if I'm not careful.'

Ivor looked up at the fixed electric lights. 'There's no fear of that,' he said. 'If the worst happens, I'll carry you back to your quarters.'

'What a prospect.' She pondered the absurdity of it, and realisation began to gather. 'I've just remembered,' she said.

'What have you remembered?'

'What you were going to tell me. It was when you went to the bar. You said I'd take something away, one day, from this awful thing that's happened.'

'I did say that, didn't I?'

'Well, don't keep me in suspense.'

'I was going to say that you'll always know that you did something very important for an insecure, frightened youngster, that probably braced him up in his last hours. For what it's worth, you may as well know, as well....'

'That's two "as wells".'

'I don't care. I got English Language as well, and that makes three "as wells". What you need to know is that I'm so proud of you for what you did for him, that I'd send a signal round the fleet if I could, to tell everyone how proud I am.'

Grace felt her eyes fill with tears again, but this time, the reason was a different one. 'That's a lovely thing to say, Ivor. You're a lovely fella, a canny bloke, an' that's not just gin talkin'.'

'I know it's not. I can see your lips moving. All the same, I think I'd better get you back to your quarters, because, any minute now, you're going to droop.'

26

By and large, the gunnery instructors were a dependable lot, keen to impart what skills they could, whilst accepting that *HMS St Christopher* would never aspire to the standard of gunnery associated with their *alma mater HMS Excellent.* They also had the good sense to dispense with the hectoring, shouting and aggressive delivery that was the daily fare at that establishment.

There were two petty officers, however, who came to Ivor's notice for the wrong reason. Both were experienced gunlayer-armourers, trained before the war at *Excellent*, and both had given commendable service in their respective drafts. Their problem stemmed from their resentment at being drafted to a coastal forces training school, to be nursemaids to hostilities-only ratings and RNVR officers. It was clear that they also objected to being led by an RNVR lieutenant, as Ivor discovered.

He was setting up a single-barrel Mark VIII 2-pounder pom-pom auto cannon for an instructional session, when he realised that the breech block that came with the half-assembled gun belonged to an earlier version of the weapon. He also remembered having the correct part when he stripped the gun down with the morning class. He decided to take a look in the classroom next door, where he knew there was a Mark Two pom-pom.

When he reached the door of Classroom G3, it was slightly ajar, and he could hear voices inside that he had no difficulty in identifying as those of Petty Officers Golding and Bryant.

Bryant was saying, 'What wouldn't I give to be a fly on the bulkhead when he tries to assemble that thing in front of a class of OD's?'

Golding said, 'We'll hear about it soon enough.'

'You're quite right, Golding,' said Ivor, entering the classroom. 'Let me see the breech block that goes with that pom-pom.'

Warily, Golding picked up the part from the collection at his feet, and handed it to Ivor.

'As I suspected, it's from a Mark Eight.'

Grasping at the nearest straw, Golding asked, 'Are you sure, sir?'

'Perfectly sure, Golding. What's more, it says so here.' He indicated the corner where the part number and description had been engraved at the factory.

'I don't know how that can have happened, sir.'

'Oh, don't you? If you intend assembling that piece you've got there, you're going to need the right breech block for it.' From behind his back, he produced the part he'd found in Classroom G2. 'I'll swap you a Mark Two for a Mark Eight. It's only fair exchange, after all, but I'd be very interested to know how these parts came to be changed over in the first place.'

Bryant had been silent until then, but now he lent his voice to the plea of innocence. 'We don't know nothing about that, sir. We just came in here to prepare this one for the sub-lieutenants' class.'

'No doubt planning to give them a hard time into the bargain.'

'That's discipline, sir, and you can't have drill without discipline.'

'I remember hearing that at Whale Island as well, Bryant, but this is Fort William, and the roles are very different.' Weighing the Mark VIII breech block in his hand, he said, 'Bryant, you expressed a wish to be a fly on the bulkhead when someone tried to assemble the Mark Eight in Classroom G2. Who did you imagine that someone might be?'

'I don't know, sir. I don't remember saying anything like that. I don't know where it's come from, or who said it, sir.'

'You're babbling, Bryant, and that's the mark of a cornered liar. Unless there's an accomplished ventriloquist in here, I heard you utter those words shortly before I came in.'

It seemed that Golding realised that the game was up, because he said, 'We didn't mean no harm, sir. It was just a bit of a lark.'

'The purpose being to embarrass an RNVR officer by making him look incompetent. Am I correct?'

Both petty officers remained silent. They were old hands at naval discipline, and their features were expressionless.

'While you're both standing there like a pair of OD's who've been caught smoking in the paint store, I'm going to acquaint you with something you should have realised a long time ago, which is that this country, together with its allies, is at war with Germany, Italy and Japan, and that means that you two, by virtue of your calling, are also at war with those countries. You are not at war with the RNVR, the RNR or the commissioned ranks, but with the enemy. Have you got that?'

'Yes, sir.'

'Yes, sir.'

'By rights, of course, I should get the Master-at-Arms to put you both on a charge. "Conduct prejudicial to good order and discipline" would do for a start. That alone would be enough to get you both reduced to leading hand.' He paused to let them think about the consequences. 'The trouble is, you're both competent and experienced senior ratings, and I need you to help me deliver the course. Do you understand?'

'Yes, sir.' Relieved that they were no longer in danger of punishment, they responded in unison.

'Good. You'll do it without bullying, persecution or any other sadistic practice, and you'll do it under my direction. For my part, I shall be watching you both very closely indeed. Do you understand?'

'Yes, sir.'

'Yes, sir.'

'Very well, carry on,'

'Aye, aye, sir.'

'Aye, aye, sir.'

Grace was becoming used to the sight of newly-commissioned

sub-lieutenants either heading for the moorings or returning from exercises, without the awful memory of reading Mrs Harris's letter. She still winced, from time to time, when she recalled those innocent moments at the Spyglass Inn. The memory of Ovie's boyish features would never leave her, but she was learning to live with it.

She owed much of that adjustment to Ivor and that night at the pub. He was the perfect companion on such an occasion, as she remembered telling him somewhat freely at the time, the double gin having long-since taken effect.

Now that she thought about it, he was the perfect companion at any time. That, and the love she felt for him, made it so much harder for her to decide whether or not they really had a future together.

Having sent the errant petty officers about their business, Ivor was surprised when one of the sub-lieutenants questioned the policy of training officers in the operation and maintenance of the various items of automatic weaponry.

'I mean, sir,' he said, 'surely, our place is on the bridge while the ratings man the guns.'

'I can understand why you might think that,' said Ivor, 'but, if you believe you're going to spend the whole of your time on the ivory tower we call the bridge, you're wrong, and I'll explain why.' Picking up his walking stick to show the class, he said, 'The more observant of you will have noticed that I am less than fully mobile.' He allowed a dutiful chuckle and continued. 'I was serving in a Q-ship, and we were sinking a U-boat by gunfire, although the enemy gunners were putting up a fight. Our lone machine-gunner was killed, and the captain ordered the nearest man, a sub-lieutenant, to take over the Vickers, but he took his time over it, I'm sorry to say.' That Anderson was paralysed by fear was incidental to the story, and there was no need for them to know that. 'Had he dealt with the U-boat's MG 34's a little earlier, I might not have spent half of this year in hospital or in convalescence.' Again, he allowed them a quiet chuckle. 'So, you see, an officer needs to be versatile.' He hung his walking stick once more over his chair and asked, 'Are there any questions?' There were none, so he began the afternoon's session. 'Deflection shooting is about shooting at a moving target. It is the science of aiming at the point the target will have reached by the time the projectile hits it. As I told you only a moment ago, we gunners are versatile people. We can even predict the future.'

The orange blossom cocktail had become Grace's favourite drink, albeit with the gin content somewhat reduced since her initiation.

'I saw two sailors today,' she said, 'petty officers, actually, and I remembered seeing them the week you arrived. They were a lot happier today, I must say.'

'Had you been concerned about them?'

'No, they sounded like trouble makers to me. They were complainin' because they were gettin' a new gunnery officer. I suppose that was you.'

'There is only me, so it would be,' he agreed.

'They didn't like the idea of being under the command of an RNVR officer.'

Ivor smiled.

'What's so funny?'

'Did one of them have a set?'

'Yes, the other one was clean-shaven.'

'And did the clean-shaven one have a face like a full moon?'

'Aye, but it was more like a smacked arse the first time I saw him. He was miserable.' She added, 'I thought I'd better warn you.'

'Thank you, darling, but I dealt with those two on Monday, and they won't put a foot out of line now.'

'Are you sure?'

'Absolutely. They're feeling very humble.'

'Good.' After some thought, she said, 'That's one of the differences between you and me, isn't it?'

Ivor frowned. 'You've lost me.'

'I mean, you evidently gave those two senior ratings a bottle, but I have to keep me head down when a petty officer looks sideways at me.'

' "And little fleas have lesser fleas, and so *ad infinitum*." '

She looked at him impatiently. 'Is that supposed to mean somethin',' she asked, 'or are you just talkin' bunions?'

'It means that, if anyone from a lieutenant commander up to an Admiral of the Fleet looks sideways at me, you'll find me in a bunker much like yours, keeping my head down. Of course,' he added mischievously, 'if I find my way into your bunker, things might not be so bad after all.'

'But you have this power over senior ratings.'

'And you have power over Wrens and OD's.'

'That's nothin'.' She gave him a dismissive look over her cocktail.

'These things are all relative.'

'Exactly, and that's what I'm sayin', that it's one of the differences between you and me.'

'I wish you'd forget about differences and recognise what we have in common.' He stroked her hand in an attempt to appease her. 'We have lots in common.'

'All right, then, who's your man for after the war? Mr Churchill or Mr Attlee? I bet you're a Churchill man.'

He stroked his chin, pretending to consider the question.

'Don't make fun of me, Ivor.'

'As if I would. No, Churchill was a disaster as a peacetime politician, but, two years ago, there was no one else who could have taken on the job he did and braced up the nation.'

'I told you.' She was almost jubilant.

'Wait a minute. Much as I admire Churchill for his leadership, and I do, I think that this country needs a social overhaul on a scale he'd never countenance. To answer your original question, my choice would have to be Attlee.'

'Do you mean that?'

'Cross my heart.'

'Why-yer-bugger, man.' Her face was a study in surprise.

'That's blown your light out, hasn't it?'

'No, I'm pleasantly surprised.'

'Would you like another drink?'

'Yes, please. Just the one.'

He laughed. 'I only bring them one at a time.'

'You know what I mean.'

He went to the bar and bought a gin and an orange blossom cocktail.

'There,' he said, putting her drink in front of her. 'What are we going to argue about now?'

'I'll think of somethin'.'

'I don't doubt it for a minute.' He waited, and when no challenge seemed forthcoming, he said, 'It may just surprise you to know that my maternal grandfather was a village postman in Betws-Y-Coed. That's in North Wales.'

'Haddaway, man. Was he?'

Ivor nodded. 'They called him "Jones the Letters".'

'You're havin' me on.'

'No, I'm not.'

'All right, what about your grandpa on your dad's side?'

'He worked in a Yorkshire woollen mill all his working life.'

'No.'

'Scouts' honour.'

She eyed him suspiciously. 'Were you in the Boy Scouts?'

'No, but I had a girlfriend in the Girl Guides.'

'I don't want to know about that.'

'Girl Guides are pure in thought, word and deed, Grace. She didn't want to know about it either.'

'Ivor,' she demanded, 'are you tellin' me the truth, that your grandpa worked in a woollen mill?'

'I said so, didn't I?'

An element of suspicion remained. 'You're going to tell me he was the manager, aren't you?'

'No, he started as a bobbin boy and he became a weaving overlooker.'

'All right, then. How did your dad come to be in charge of the Dole Office?'

'Exactly the same way as you became a secretary, and your brother became a draughtsman. His parents wanted him to escape the trap they found themselves in, so they encouraged him to be ambitious.' On a mischievous whim, he said, 'Just imagine, as well, the power your brother can wield over NCO's and other ranks, now that he's a second lieutenant.'

'Don't be rotten. Why didn't you tell me any of this before?'

'Because it was me I was trying to sell, not my proletarian pedigree.'

'You're a dark horse.'

'But now you know I'm a working horse, not a thoroughbred.'

'Aye, you've given me somethin' to think about, right enough.' She thought about it while she enjoyed a little more of her cocktail.

'Here's something else to think about.' He waited until he had her full attention.

'Go on, then, don't keep me in suspense.'

'All right. It's about that forty-eighters you've got next week.'

'Have you got some free time?'

'I've got the whole forty-eight.'

'No, really?'

'Paper lads' honour.'

The familiar suspicious look had returned. 'Were you ever a paper lad?'

'Of course I was. It was what sparked off my interest in journalism. Mind you, it was a toil. Up at six o' clock every morning, trudging through snow and ice, carrying a massive bag of newspapers. The bosses' kids had no idea. They didn't have to do anything like that.'

'I'm goin' to hit you in a minute.'

'Don't you want to know where we're going?'

'All right, I'll let you off if you tell me.'

Feigning relief, he said, 'We're going to stay at the Invergarry Hotel. It's about an hour's journey by bus, but it'll be worth it. Invergarry is a beautiful place, I'm told.'

'Who told you that?'

'Only a few people. No more than nine or ten at the most.'

She narrowed her eyes and said, 'You're havin' me on again, aren't you?'

'Yes, it was the receptionist at the hotel who told me when I telephoned to make the booking.'

'How did you know about the hotel?'

For a moment, he was tempted to tease her again, but he settled for the truth. 'I found a brochure in the wardroom,' he told her.

'Well. it sounds all right to me.' She wrinkled her nose and said, 'Mind you, as long as we're together, that's the main thing.'

'You had me wondering once or twice tonight, but I'm inclined to agree.'

27

Eventually, Grace turned her eyes away from the spectacular landscape that lined the bus route, to say, 'This couple of days is going to cost a fortune, isn't it?'

'What else have I got to spend money on? My main outgoings are my negligible wardroom mess bill, your orange blossom cocktails, and Huw's regular subs.'

She favoured him with one of her admonishing looks and said, 'I'll ignore that remark about cocktails, but what was that about Huw's subs?' For the sake of discretion, she was travelling in civilian clothes. Restricted as she was by clothes rationing, she was wearing the sage green dress again. It seemed somehow right for the Highlands.

'He only ever writes to me when he's short of cash, which is quite often. Then, when he does, he calls it a loan. Unfortunately, his understanding of the word differs from the common definition, in which there's usually a reference to repayment.'

Huw's weakness was apparently lost on Grace, whose thoughts were now elsewhere. 'When I was tryin' to find you, I thought about writin' to him at the air station. The trouble was, I didn't know if he was still there or even if he was still a pilot officer. I didn't want to upset him by addressing the letter to "Pilot Officer H. Loveday" if he'd been promoted. These things have to be considered.'

'You'd have been lucky to get a reply from him, anyway. Even Huw would hesitate before touching a Wren for a fiver, and that would be his only reason for writing.'

'I'm sure you're exaggeratin'. He can't be as bad as all that.'

'He's just disorganised. He needs the influence of a steady and reliable woman instead of the kind that usually appeal to him.' An example of Huw's fecklessness sprang to mind. 'When I was at the convalescent home in Sussex,' he said, 'Huw travelled down from Cheshire to visit me.'

'Well, then. There's nothin' much wrong with that.'

'Except that he booked a room in the village so that he could have a high old time with the girl he'd brought from the air station, and he got me to pay for it.'

'And this happens often?'

'Frequently and regularly,' he confirmed.

'It's always you, then. Can't he call on your other brother for help, the one who lives in Ireland?'

'Ah, well, Eric is the one who knows how to say, "No". That's the kind of person he is. Unlike Huw and I, you see, he lives a dull existence in a Belfast suburb, with a dowdy wife who once had her personality removed surgically, and has never regretted the decision for a moment. He runs his finances like the civil servant he is, and he makes a point of avoiding unnecessary contact with his younger brothers in case they want something from him. I never shall, but he doesn't know that.'

Grace was so fascinated by the Loveday family that she forgot the passing landscape altogether, and asked, 'Is that what you meant when you said you weren't a close family?'

'In effect, yes. When Eric was born, my parents had what they wanted, namely a boy to perpetuate the family name and to enter the civil service, as a respectable citizen should. Huw and I were accidents, victims of early closing at Timothy White's.' He leaned towards her and whispered surreptitiously, 'Which reminds me. Have you got your thing with you? Your bowler hat?'

'Of course,' she whispered back. 'I wouldn't leave somethin' like that at home for me mam to find.'

'Well done.'

Nudging him impatiently, she said, 'So the two of you didn't have a very happy childhood, then?'

'It wasn't all that bad. I looked out for Huw, which is probably why I'm still doing it now. I managed to soften a few emotional blows, at least.'

'That's nice. What about you, though? Who was there to take your side when things got tough?'

'You could say that I was adopted, at least during term time.'

Each revelation seemed to sharpen her curiosity. 'How did you manage that?'

'I didn't. My guide and mentor was my English master.'

Ever suspicious, she asked, 'Seriously?'

'Basically, he was the greatest influence on me. It was he, more than anyone, who taught me to take life as it came and not get too het up when the toast landed buttered side down. There was an awful lot going wrong for a good many people at the time, and it was good practice.'

'You're not easily ruffled,' she said, returning her attention for the moment to the scene beyond the window. 'I have to say that.'

'It happens,' he admitted. 'I just don't show it.'

'I know.'

After a while, he said, 'The *Specialité de la Maison* at the hotel is your favourite.'

'Pheasant?' There was new interest in her eyes.

'And partridge and grouse.'

'I've never had grouse,' she said, giving the impression that she would not be averse to trying it.

'Of course,' he remembered, 'I was away during much of the grouse season.'

'You were away far too long.' She underlined her point by taking his hand. He sandwiched hers between his and they continued in silence, because there was no need for either of them to say more.

After dinner, they went up to their room and fell into each other's arms. Privacy had been absent for too long.

As they broke apart, Grace removed Ivor's signet ring from her finger to put it carefully on her bedside table. 'Before it falls off,' she explained, retreating to the bathroom.

Ivor removed his tie, collar and cufflinks, placing them neatly on his bedside table.

When Grace reappeared, she asked him to unhook her dress,

which he did, watching her pull it over her head in the slick way that women had. Her under slip followed, and then she stood in front of the full-length mirror on the wardrobe door and removed her brassiere. 'No,' she said, wistfully pretending to examine her breasts 'they haven't grown at all, an' there I was, thinking that with all the excitement, they might have made an effort.'

'I love them just as they are,' he assured her, kissing them in turn to make his point. 'You have to understand, they're rather like people, in a way.'

'What do you mean, or are you just talking bunions, as usual?'

'Not bunions, but bosoms. You have to love them for what they are, not what you'd like them to be, and you mustn't dismiss them because they're not quite what you had in mind in your ideal configuration.'

She shook her head at his reasoning. 'It still sounds like bunions to me,' she said.

'They're part of you, and that's enough for me. I love you, so I love your bosoms. Similarly, I am what I am. Try to think of me the way I think of them.'

'All right, Ivor. You're a thirty-four "B" bust and I love you. Forget all that stuff about comin' from different backgrounds. You're right – it's what a person is that matters.'

'Hooray.'

'Now, will you take off the rest of your clothes and join the party?'

Obligingly, he stepped out of his drawers, cellular, officers', draping them over a chair with his shirt.

'You didn't wear your elasticated blackouts,' he said, switching off the light. 'Mind you, it's just as well.'

'Don't tell me they'd have got you over-excited.'

'No, but I'd never have found you in the dark.'

'You wouldn't have fancied me in 'em with the light on.'

'Who wouldn't?' He held her close, relishing the smooth softness of her naked body and kissing her slowly and unhurriedly, now that they had time to linger.

Presently, she whispered, 'Do you know if there's anybody in the rooms either side of this one?'

'I don't think so. The hotel's fairly quiet. Don't you like this room?'

'Yes, I'm just worrying about making a noise.'

'They're good, thick walls. The only danger is that, if you get over-excited, some of your high notes might shake the plaster off the ceiling.'

'Okay, don't make me too noisy, then.'

'I'll try not to. I left my plasterer's trowel in the family home in Tynemouth.'

'I bet,' she said, kissing him enthusiastically, 'you wouldn't know how to use a one.'

'You'd be surprised at what I can do with tools. I'm a dab hand with saws and chisels, and I've even been known to wield a big hammer on occasions.'

'I know,' she said fondly. 'I remember those occasions well.'

For the first time since the night in the Liverpool hotel, they had the time and freedom to re-acquaint themselves with each other, and they did so with a sense of long-awaited culmination.

Ivor awoke to a discreet knock on the door. Pulling his dressing gown on, he opened it.

'Your tea, as requested, sir.'

'Thank you.' He took a shilling piece from his bedside table and gave it to the maid, taking the tray from her.

'Thank you, sir.'

'Thank you.' He put the tray down and peeped through the blackout curtains. At Greenwich Mean Time plus one, it was almost light, so he opened them fully. A low moan came from the other side of the bed. Clearly, encouragement was called for.

'Wakey-wakey, rise an' shine, the morning's fine....' he intoned.

'Don't be rotten.'

'Drink your tea and stop complaining.' He took her tea round the bed to her.

She emerged into proper wakefulness. 'Oh, lovely. Tea.'

Ivor removed his dressing gown and joined her again in bed. 'No regrets?'

'No regrets? I thought we ironed that one out when you relieved me of my innocence in Cheshire.'

'I meant about anything you said last night.'

'About what?'

'This is what a night's sleep can do to a woman,' he said, shaking his head sadly.

'It's not the sleep that's made me daft. It was what happened before it.'

It was gratifying news, but he still wanted to know the answer to his question. 'You said last night,' he prompted, 'that it's what a person is that matters.'

'Agreed. No argument there.'

'I'm glad that's out of the way.'

'It is,' she said a little uncertainly, eyeing his cap on the chair, with its officers' cap badge. 'I just keep expecting someone we know to come to the hotel and catch us together.' She said hurriedly, 'I don't mean, you know... *doing things*, I mean just together.'

'I see what you mean. It would be rather embarrassing. It would be different, I suppose, if our intentions were seen to be honourable. If we were engaged, for instance.'

'Well, yes, but....'

Ivor reached into the drawer of his bedside table and took out a jeweller's box. 'This is for you,' he said.

'Oh?' She opened the box and gasped at the sapphire and the tiny diamonds that surrounded it. 'Ivor, it's beautiful!'

'It's the ring I told you about, the one my mother sent in for repair.'

'I remember now. It's too beautiful for words. "Thank you" seems little enough to say.' She slipped it on to the ring finger of her left hand to admire it further.

'In that case, will you let me make an honest woman of you?'

Seemingly unable to speak, she kissed him ecstatically and repeatedly. Eventually, she said, 'Why not? Somebody has to do it, an' there's nobody else here that I fancy, so I reckon you can make an honest woman of me, and one day, I might make a Geordie out of you.' She considered that possibility and said, 'On second thoughts, I'll take you just as you are. It'll save arguments.'

THE END

www.ingramcontent.com/pod-product-compliance
Lightning Source LLC
LaVergne TN
LVHW091052080826
845145LV00002B/723

* 9 7 8 1 6 3 6 8 3 0 1 4 8 *